The Wayward Journey

By Nathan Hale Jefferson

Abundant Future Media
www.AbundantFuture.net

I0542065

Visit our webpage at www.abundantfuture.net for updates and other great content! Follow the author on Twitter (@NateHaleJeffers) and like us on Facebook www.facebook.com/NathanHaleJefferson

Sign up for the email newsletter at www.abundantfuture.net to be updated on the latest publishing news and to find out about prizes and giveaways as well as the latest in preparedness and survival news!

Stay tuned for Part II and Part III of The Wayward Journey: *Fires at Home* and *Winter Without Walls*

Thanks to Nobody, Joe Nobody, for providing inspiration and guidance on how to make this book become a reality!

Thanks to the many other great authors in the Dystopian, Post-Apocalyptic, Survivalist, and TEOTWAKI genre.

Thanks especially to James Wesley Rawles for the great pointers he gave me and for writing my favorite book, <u>Patriots: A Novel of Survival in the Coming Collapse</u>!

Foreword

While this is a work of fiction and many liberties may have been taken with the events contained in these pages, there is still a great danger posed from earthquakes in large portions of our country. During two months in 1811 and 1812, three of the ten strongest earthquakes that hit the continental United States were produced in the New Madrid seismic zone. This fault line is still active, and while there have been only smaller shakes in recent years, the chance of another large event to occur still exists as an ever present danger.

Because of the dangers posed by earthquakes in this region, it was the scenario used in the 2011 National Level Exercise, the first national exercise to simulate a natural hazard. This multi-state exercise simulated a 7.7 earthquake along the southern segment of the New Madrid Fault, which was followed by a 6.0 magnitude earthquake in the Wabash Valley Seismic Zone.

For more information about earthquake hazard programs, please visit:

http://earthquake.usgs.gov/prepare/

According the USGS records, since 2000 more than 55,000 people on average have died due to earthquakes each year. Here are a few notable examples:

May 12, 2008, China: 7.9 earthquake left nearly 90,000 dead and over 5 million people homeless.

January 12, 2010, Haiti: 7.0 earthquake left over 316,000 dead, 300,000 injured, and 1.3 million homeless.

March 11, 2011, Japan: 8.3 earthquake left 15,647 dead, many more homeless, and kicked off a series of nuclear tragedies that will haunt the world for years to come.

Please prepare and be safe!

Chapter 1

Radio Broadcast: Tonight, we bring you an update to one of the ongoing stories that we've been reporting. So far, both New York City and Chicago are being affected, and garbage is really starting to pile up, now that the strike is into its second week. Now, there are talks of this strike moving to other cities as an act of solidarity. These are just some of the latest responses to the strain caused by the rampant inflation facing our country. As you are aware, with the continuing oil shortage, prices continue to rise, causing many people to make hard decisions on which bills to pay.

The President released a statement assuring that the shortage will be under control within a few weeks and that the government is doing everything they can to stop the economy-crippling inflation. They are working with the Federal Reserve Chairman to tighten standards and should have a decision on whether to raise interest rates. Hopefully a solution is found soon. We will continue to follow both of these stories here on your nightly news.

"Do you really have to go?" Margaret asked as she started clearing the dinner table and loading the dishwasher. "I don't know if your going on this trip is the best idea with all the problems popping up everywhere."

She was never very vocal in sharing her concerns about John's new job because she knew it was the best option for their family. But with the new problems facing the country, she was even more nervous than before and her gut told her that something about this trip was going to be especially bad. The nightmare she had had for the past few nights didn't help either, but she dismissed it for what it was: just a dream.

"I don't want to have to deal with the swamped grocery stores and gas stations without you. They are swamped. It's crazy. It will be especially hard since I don't have anyone to help watch these kids now that mom can't come over." The financial problems and oil shock facing the country had been causing traffic jams and lines at gas stations to become common occurrences.

Normally, Margaret's mother would come over several days a week to help watch the kids so Margaret could run errands and have a little time to herself. But, for the past two weeks, Margaret's mother hadn't been able to make the trip, and it was starting to take a toll on Margaret. She had been watching the two kids while looking hard for a new job, not getting any breaks ever since losing her job several months ago. It didn't help that her husband John took a job where he had to work at least ten to twelve hours a day, seven days a week and was on the road four or five days a week.

In addition Margaret had a special resentment for John's new job. Since he was a salaried employee, he was not getting extra compensation for his increased time and effort, while the company he worked for—one of the largest oil drillers in the country—was raking in more money than they ever had, thanks to the ongoing gas shortage.

Ever since Margaret was let go from her job as a highly paid attorney, John had tried everything he could to bring more money home for the family. He finally took this job that had him flying across the country weekly while still working extremely long days when he was home. With the sudden boom in oil prices, there was an increasing need for engineers to oversee and sign-off on the work being performed across the country. While it was possible to run the heavy machinery and drill holes with skeleton crews or crews brand new to the industry, without reviews from certified engineers like John, work could only proceed so far.

"I promise it will only be for a few days, and I'll be right home. It will be a whistle-stop tour of about a dozen different sites, but I will have the crews work around my schedule and I'll be in and out faster than last time," John said. He tried to make his wife feel better about his latest assignment to fly out to the middle of nowhere near the Montana and Wyoming border to approve the work on some new wells they were drilling, but even he knew his explanation wasn't going to help.

He had been out to that region a few times this year, surveying and preparing the sites. Now the wells should be ready to go, drilling and setting up the pumping equipment, to start bringing up the oil that the geologist promised was there.

After a few moments of silence, John continued, "You know it's very important I get out there to help with this. Every new well that starts producing helps alleviate part of the shortage problem. I'll demand a vacation or something for all my extra time. Besides, heaven only knows how much profit we are going to make this quarter, and a big profit is going to lead to a big bonus!"

He purposely left out the part where he was supposed to remind her that ever since she lost her job, it was getting harder to maintain their lifestyle. Even though they were frugal with their money, and the only debt they had was their mortgage, the loss of the larger of two incomes was hard on the family's finances.

Not satisfied, Margaret replied, "Well, I still don't like them forcing you to work so much, and under these conditions." She shut the dishwasher door, headed upstairs to start getting the kids ready for bed.

Alone in the kitchen, John grabbed his laptop, popped it open, and shot off a few emails. He laid out the agenda for the next week, trying to squeeze as much action into as short a time as he could. He knew he would have to find a driver to take him from site to site while he slept in the truck—there might be little to no time for him to sleep in a real bed. He then booked his flights and sent the itinerary to his co-worker Bill, who would need to know when to pick him up from the airport.

Just as he started closing his computer, he remembered what he told his wife about getting a bonus or a vacation for his extra work and travel. He started crafting an email to his boss, asking for a little something that would help with household expenses, especially since gas, groceries, and other necessities had gone up considerably—at least by a double digit percentage—since his last raise 6 months ago. He hit writer's block when he got to the point where he wanted to suggest a number that was adequate and fair for his time, effort, and expertise. He wanted to be careful with his request because prices for most basic goods changed almost daily. Not sure what to write, he decided to sleep on it. He shut down the laptop, loaded it into his bag, and began packing for his flight, which was leaving early the next morning.

The kids were cleaned up and ready for bed when John made it upstairs. They were both eagerly waiting on the couch, sitting in the small loft at the top of the stairs, with a pile of books between them. John spent the next half an hour reading some of children's favorite bedtime stories to them before giving them each a kiss goodnight and tucking them into bed. A few tears welled up in his eyes at the "I love you, Daddy," and "I'll miss you while you are gone" that he got from each of them.

As he walked to his bedroom he thought, *I'll miss you, too, but right now, it's important that I work hard so I can take care of you the best I can.*

"You're lucky you're such a good father; otherwise, all this traveling around might make me rethink our situation," Margaret said coyly as she lay in a slightly provocative pose on their bed.

She was trying to liven the mood by giving him his favorite compliment of being a good father. John grew up as an only child to a single mother, and above everything else, he strove to be a good father. And by all measures, he was doing a fantastic job.

"I'm lucky I have such good kids!" he replied with a smile. Not wanting to let her get away with her last comment, he continued on, "Now if I only had a good wife, too."

Margaret laughed at him and then gave him a playful shove.

"Alright, that's enough from you, young lady!" John said, grabbing her into his arms and hugging her tight. He kissed her on the forehead and then lay down in bed next to her.

That night Margaret had another nightmare of her and her kids stranded alone in the dark. She didn't know exactly what was going on, but they were in danger. John wasn't there, and he was the only one who could save them.

When she woke in the morning, she dismissed the dream again. Unfortunately for her, and as she was to soon find out, dreams sometimes offer a prediction of what is to come. This was one of those times.

Chapter 2

Radio Broadcast: We're here live inside the loop in Chicago where the teachers union just walked out this morning because of, what they say are, completely deplorable conditions. Conditions they say wouldn't even pass for acceptable in the poorest countries of the world. For the past few weeks, the Chicago school system has been out of money, even though the school year has just started. It has not been able to pay vendors, and because of this, several of the vendors have stopped supplying the schools with necessary materials including supplies, food, and in some instances, electricity.

Now, to be clear, the schools that had power turned off weren't completely shut down. The power company just turned off the regulators installed on air conditioners and what they termed other nonessential hardware, while still leaving on the lights, computers, and other necessities in the classroom. The spokesman for the power company only had a short statement, in which he confirmed the details and assured the public that the utility provider will continue to work with the schools to ensure the safety and education of the students. He also clarified that the company had been working with the schools to solve the electricity issues for months. It has been over a year since the schools have paid a single penny for electricity, and it is with deep regret that they have to rely on such drastic measures.

Stay tuned for our continuing live updates as they unfold.

At 3:30 a.m., the alarm on John's phone went off, forcing him out of his half-sleep. He reached over, hit snooze, and muttered under his breath about not wanting to get up. Five minutes later, the alarm went off again. This time, he begrudgingly turned off the alarm, slid out of bed, and headed to the bathroom for a quick shower. After getting ready, he grabbed his packed roller-board suitcase, threw it along with his backpack into the back seat of the car and jumped into the front seat to begin his trip to the airport. About 45 minutes later, he pulled into the parking garage and took a spot close to the end, several hundred yards from the entrance to the airport. Luckily, he had woken up early and hadn't run into any traffic but he was cutting his timing as close as he could.

Walking into the terminal, he glanced at his ticket and headed toward the security line leading to his gate. The lines were short today, a situation probably due to the extra fuel surcharge and higher ticket prices that had been imposed over the past few weeks. Smaller numbers of people were flying now. Fewer passengers was a good thing, at least for a business traveler like John—shorter lines, better seats, and less hassle getting in or out of airports.

As he stepped up to the TSA agent to have his boarding pass and ID checked, John realized that a soldier stood behind each agent. He didn't notice the soldiers when he arrived at the airport, as members of every branch of the military were always traveling in uniform, so they didn't stick out. But now, he realized that about a dozen extra men and women wearing BDUs, the standard military camouflage clothing, were standing in strategic positions in the security area.

***

"Good morning, how are you today?" John said cordially as he handed the agent his papers.

"I'm pretty good, except that this is going to be a long week, which I'm not really looking forward to," the agent said as he started ticking off details on John's boarding pass.

Not one for subtleness, John went on, "What's with the army men all around here this morning? Is everything ok?"

The agent started to respond, but the young man in camouflage interrupted him. "Sir, we are from the National Guard, not the army, and we are just here for a training and readiness exercise. The Governor has issued an order to call up all guardsmen for an additional training exercise."

Slightly annoyed, the agent rolled his eyes as he nodded his head. "Yeah, just a training exercise. This has happened a few times in the past, but this week, it's going to be happening all day long for the whole week. Before, it would be half a day at most."

"Oh .... Ok. You guys have fun with that. Have a good week!" John quickly interjected, as he took back his papers from the agent.

"You too, and safe travels."

After getting through security, John had just enough time to grab a coffee before boarding his plane. He normally wouldn't pay the crazy prices charged for coffee at an airport, but while on a work trip, he was paid expenses for things like that.

The flight to O'Hare was short and uneventful. When he got off the plane, John wasn't surprised to see several Chicago police officers who looked as if they were ready to handle a riot in their black, bullet-proof vests worn over their uniforms. Some officers even had helmets, complete with face-shields, and one or two even had large plastic riot shields that up until now, John had seen only in movies or news clips.

Running to his next gate, John was just in time for his connection. This flight was going to be about two and a half hours, so he immediately put on his headphones and turned on his MP3 player, and went to sleep.

He wasn't disturbed to power down the device as the plane took off.

***

"Sir, you have to turn your electronic device off. We are about to land," the flight attendant said, gently touching John's shoulder to wake him up.

He grudgingly obliged, moving his seat to the upright position, powered down his MP3 player, and tucked it into his pocket.

The plane touched down and taxied to the gate of the small regional airport. As soon as the plane stopped, John hopped up, grabbed his roller-board from the overhead compartment, and stood in the short line to deplane.

He then shot a quick text to his ride, Bill, letting him know he had landed and was ready to be picked up. Next, called home to let Margaret know he had safely landed.

"Hi, sweetheart! Just wanted to let you know I'm here safely!"

"That's good. I'm glad you are *there* safely ... Sorry ... I just wish you were here right now. You know it's hard without you around. They just canceled school for the week and are working on a new plan to cut down on busing."

"Well, I'm sure they will have it all resolved before Jane starts kindergarten next year," he said sarcastically.

"John, don't get smart. Just get everything finished and come home. Please?"

"Got it. I'll be back as soon as I can. I love you."

"Love you, too. I'll talk to you later."

John made his way to the baggage claim area and waited for his backpack. He hated checking his bag, but his tools always received extra security attention. Once, TSA threatened to throw away a $2,000 rotary laser level. After that incident, John started checking the bag and took the opportunity to pack a few other items that he wanted to have on hand but that were against the carry-on rules. By the time he made it to the carrousel, his bag was out and making its rounds.

Service is really quick when only a dozen people are on the plane, he thought.

He grabbed his bag and headed outside. He quickly found his ride, a large company truck with tool and equipment boxes built into the bed, among the four other vehicles waiting to pick up passengers.

If I have to travel, this is the way. Traveling sure is a lot easier when there is no one else to contend with!

***

John opened the passenger door and greeted Bill with a warm "Good morning!"

"Good morning, boss. How was the trip?" Bill asked.

"Not bad. Weird, but not bad. Mostly, I just hate waking up so early, and it's going to be a long few days for you and me. Did you get the agenda I sent?"

"Yeah, got it. We'll make it work. But what was so weird about the trip?"

"Well, other than the armed National Guard and police decked out in riot gear at the Columbus and Chicago airports, not much," John said, drawing an odd looking scowl from Bill.

"Yeah, weird stuff is going on all over, but it's good for business ... at least for us. With all the overtime I'm pulling, I'll have the old homestead paid off in under a year."

"Well, if you can keep up with these hours for that long, you sure will deserve it! Now, let's get moving so we don't lose any time," John said as he threw his luggage into the back of the extended cab and hopped into the passenger seat.

Bill was happy to pick John up from the airport, even though he had to drive several hours out of his way. Bill never could put his finger on it, but like all the others on the various crews, he liked working with John. He wasn't sure if it was his no-baloney attitude or his willingness to get down into the mud and muck to help solve problems, something no other engineer or supervisor would do. Or maybe it was something entirely different that he didn't recognize. But Bill did know that he and everyone else that worked with John held him in great respect.

***

Not wasting any time, they started going over the itinerary John had laid out. The plan required them to make a run from the airport on the west side of South Dakota up to Helena, where he would depart from three days later.

With five stops along the way, each requiring an 8- to 10-hour inspection, the duo was going to be very busy. The job was to go to each site, validate the installation and setup of all the drilling and pumping equipment. This wasn't necessarily a hard job, but it was tedious, and because of different regulations and laws, only a certified professional engineer could authorize and sign off on a completed inspection. Even though Bill wasn't a certified engineer—not having had enough experience yet—he could help by validating measurements and setups, cutting down the time at each site, thus allowing the compact schedule to be accomplished.

A few hours later, they pulled into the first site and spent the next half-hour just trying to find someone to talk to. They eventually located a lone worker sleeping in the cab of a truck parked behind several trailers.

"It's about dang time you got here." The guy said as he, handed over several binders full of documents. A few days ago, the rest of the crew finished all the setup and moved on to another drill site because work was at a standstill until John and Bill approved moving ahead. This guy had thought he was lucky, but three days spent sitting with nothing to do, stuck in the middle of nowhere, wasn't the vacation he'd imagined.

"Yeah, sorry. Hopefully, we can knock this out, so we can all get on our way," Bill said trying to diffuse the situation.

"Well, everything you need should be in the binders. Here are the keys to the office, the trucks, and everything else you will need. Here is my cell number, but if you have any questions, I won't be able to answer them anyway. Now, if you don't mind, I'm going to go home for a few hours and then catch up with my crew," the man said.

He waited a couple of seconds to see if they had questions. When none came, he curtly tipped the bill of his ball cap and jumped back into the truck. He quickly started it and drove off without looking back.

The next few hours went by rapidly. Both engineers checked dozens of specs and setups and recorded all the results on their itemized checklists. After the lists were completed, the two men climbed back into their truck and headed for the next site. John sat in the passenger seat again and went through each line of the papers, double-checking the data and the initials of whoever validated the spec. He always double-checked everything because any missed point could cost thousands in noncompliance fines and tens of thousands in stopped or delayed productions, neither of which he wanted to be at fault for.

Pulling into the second site, they found the crew, who were working on several platforms that held generators and other equipment to run the heavy machinery. Grabbing the binders, they set to work, repeating the process they'd completed earlier in the day. When they were halfway through, the foreman came over and got their dinner orders, giving them a choice among a burger, two different cold cut sandwiches, and pizza from the local store, which was about a 20-minute drive away.

Discussions with the crew at dinner spun around many news topics, none of them good. The main discussion was the President's latest announcement that he was releasing more of the nation's strategic oil reserves. This would be the third sale from the reserves in the past two months, and the total held in reserve was already down by more than 75% from a year earlier. The latest release would leave the country with as little as a week's worth of oil in reserve. The mainstream media had ignored this fact and focused only on how great it was that the administration was taking such drastic steps to relieve the country's suffering.

Other discussion topics included rampant inflation and the strikes that had spread to most major cities. Gas prices alone were up over 50% in the past 2 months, and things people actually needed, especially food, had risen 20% to 30% in the past few weeks, a situation which was upsetting a lot of people.

Individuals of all types—teachers, construction workers, people who collected government assistance—banded together to demand a solution to their problems. These groups grew in number and started to break off into splinter groups, many trying to blame each other for their economic woes. These factions clashed, causing riots, most of which were small scale at this time, in a dozen cities.

As soon as John and Bill finished their sandwiches, they returned to work and finished up shortly after the setup crew left to go home for the night. They jumped into their truck and decided to stop at the nearest motel for the night; it was already past 10:00 p.m., and they still had to finish today's paperwork and talk to their wives who were hundreds of miles away.

After checking in to a small motel, John put his Bluetooth headset on and called his wife.

"Sorry that it's so late, honey. We just really wanted to finish up the first two sites today. If we didn't do that, it would be impossible for me to come home on Wednesday night, and I'd be stuck here until Thursday."

"I know. You're busy. I just wish you had called earlier. It is getting worse here at home. Did you know police had to shut down the interstates going downtown? People were protesting and blocking traffic all around downtown, and the protestors turned the interstates into a parking lot with people waiting for hours to get on or off exits. The news said that some people just got out of their cars and walked away. It was so bad. And then people started setting those abandoned cars on fire."

"Well, it's a good thing you never go downtown anymore!" John joked, but he immediately knew he shouldn't have. His attempt at a joke just rubbed salt into the wound still left open after Margaret had lost her job.

"You know darn well I'd still be going down there every day if I was working. It's not my fault I lost my job. Everyone in my office lost their job. If you hadn't noticed, the unemployment rate is still over 15%. And for another thing—"

Interrupting her, John apologized repeatedly. He knew the job loss was still a sore spot and would be for some time to come. Margaret had poured her heart into her work and was a rising star in her company. She was also the family's main breadwinner before the entire company had been purchased by a foreign competitor and shut down with no warning. The loss of her job was a major blow to her self-esteem, and even though she was taking it very well on the outside, he knew she was hurting on the inside.

He apologized again and promised to call earlier tomorrow. He followed up with the standard "I love you's" before hanging up and heading to bed.

Chapter 3

Radio Broadcast: Today we are following up on the story of the President's address last night. The President has called for patience and solidarity and for Americans to come together to help weather and solve this crisis. He discussed his plan to ensure law and order by sending the National Guard units from across the country, at the state Governors' requests, to California and several states along the east coast to help maintain law and order amid the many protests that have turned into riots.

Over 30,000 members of the National Guard will make it to California tonight from various states and 15,000 more are heading to the Northeast and there will be almost that many more making it there by tomorrow night.

The President has also detailed a special tax rebate program that will be paid to everyone in the country. Private employees should be able to expect a rebate check within three weeks, and public employees and those who receive government benefits like social security or SNAP will be given an extra month's payment, which will show up sometime tomorrow.

Waking up at 5:30 a.m., John took a hurried shower and threw on his clothes, meeting Bill at the truck just 15 minutes later. With a two-hour drive to the next site, and because they knew it was going to be a long day, they wanted to get there early and decided to eat breakfast on the go. John got behind the wheel, giving Bill a break since there was no paperwork for John's review.

"So how was your night?" John asked.

"It was ok. Actually it was good. I got some great news last night,"

"Oh yeah, what's that?"

"My wife picked up a couple of presents for me yesterday, and for next to nothing."

"She already ruined the surprise, didn't she?"

"I think she was just proud of the deal she got," Bill said, with a hint of pride in his voice. "She just happened to be at the pawn shop looking for coins when a guy came in trying to sell a pair of custom 1911's, a full size and with the matching compact. They offered him only $500 for the pair and all accessories. They were trying to blow smoke about the law limiting the purchase to that much and they wouldn't separate the items to different tickets to get around the law. The guy stormed out, and my wife followed, and picked them both up for $500, even though she offered to pay more. He was just so pissed that he wanted to sell them for that just to spite the store."

"Wow. That is one heck of a deal. I have always wanted a nice .45 like that, but I never did want to spend that much money on a show piece," John said, clearly jealous of the new toys Bill had waiting for him at home.

"Yeah, you and your cheap little plastic guns. You can keep them. With these new .45s, I can finally get rid of the little toy I keep in my truck and replace it with my current .45."

John said in a sarcastic tone, "Hey, careful there. I'd call your shiny hunks of steel toys! They are like spoiled little models—they look great, and you love showing them off to your friends. Maybe they are a lot of fun if you don't have to put up with all their whining and demands. But my plastic toy is tried and true."

"Yep," Bill interrupted him, laughing out loud. "I get it. I can ride my Harley while you fart around on your Honda. Hooray for gas mileage!"

They both laughed at the jokes and turned the conversation back to work.

***

A couple hours later, they pulled into the worksite and got to work. This site was also abandoned except for the one lucky guy who was assigned to meet the engineers.

This time, the man left behind had waited for only about an hour. John had known for a year or so that being left behind was a coveted position. Guys left to wait for the engineers would set up shop with a radio or portable television and treat the day almost like a day off, but now, the crews were getting a bonus for every milestone they completed on a site, and everyone wanted to work as fast as possible. The guys taking the day off were ribbed pretty hard and goaded into working more to make up for the lost time. As soon as the paperwork was handed off, the guy on site jumped into his company truck and drove off.

John and Bill worked together very well, performing their third inspection in just over 24 hours, knocking it out about an hour ahead of schedule. It didn't hurt that whoever was in charge of documenting all the details made sure everything was legible and provided extra information where he thought the inspection crew would want it. John made a note to provide this feedback up the chain—whoever did this deserved a pat on the back.

On their way to the next site, which was a few hours away, John decided to check in at home.

"Hi, sweetheart. How is everything going today?" John asked in his sweetest voice.

"It's ok, I guess. I can't help it though, I can't turn off the TV."

"Well, don't get too wrapped up in everything. There isn't really anything you can do at this point."

"I know ... it sounds as if things around here are at least a little better. The protests have quieted down, and the rioting is under control, but from what I'm seeing in the news, almost all of southern California is going crazy."

"Well, I'm glad things are getting better. I told you everything would work out!" John said compassionately, purposely glossing over her last piece of data.

"I know. I know. But this is only one day, tomorrow is another, and who knows how that is going to be. I mean could you have ever dreamed that there would be over a dozen riots yesterday?"

"No. No, I can't say I could. But anyway, how are the kids?" John asked, in an attempt to change the subject.

"Today? They are both acting like their daddy—stubborn and strong-headed!" Margaret said with a playful tone.

"I'm sorry, sweetheart. But I don't think I'm the only one to blame."

"Well, until you get back, everything is your fault. Even the grocery prices." She paused for a second to laugh at her own joke. "Mom just called and said she is coming over to take me and the kids grocery shopping. She just did her weekly shopping, and the prices she paid were appalling. Now, she is making us go and buy a few weeks' worth of food. She says it's to stay ahead of the prices."

John replied, "Well, I'll have to agree with her this time. A blind squirrel and all ..."

"Haha ... Mr. Funnypants over here."

"Hey, I've got to take my openings when they come! But seriously, I think you should take both cars and stock up on as much as will fit. Actually, definitely fill up. Worst case, we will donate it to the church's food drive at Thanksgiving. That will save us a trip then."

"Ok, I think that sounds like a good idea. I better start making a list. I think I'll need a legal pad instead of a notecard for this one," Margaret said.

Knowing that she thought she was being funny, John feigned a few laughs before telling her how much he loved her. After that, he spent half-hour talking to his kids and telling them grand stories about the wild, wild west. They knew he was making up the stories and loved them the more wild and outlandish he made them. He finished the last story, telling them he loved them and that he would be home soon.

***

When John and Bill were almost to the next site, they stopped at a small highway gas station to grab lunch. They usually passed by such places since they filled up from the tanks at the worksites per company policy. But this time, they had no idea where else they might get food in this sparsely populated area.

Going down the aisles of junk food, John didn't find anything appealing for lunch, and he had to settle for some not-so-fresh-looking fruit, a bag of beef jerky, and a bag of pretzels. He was trying to maintain the healthy eating habits that he'd developed over the past year while preparing for the half marathon he'd completed a few weeks ago.

John looked at his watch. He figured that they would make it to the worksite just as the crew there would be about ready for lunch, so he decided to buy a bunch of snacks for the guys. He and Bill ended up spending over $200 on chips, jerky, drinks, and other snack food, but because of the previously high convenience pricing and the recent rapid increases from inflation, the snacks filled only five plastic shopping bags.

When they arrived at the site a few minutes later, they put out the spread of goodies and marveled at the speed with which the food disappeared. Even though the company paid all of its employees well—very well, in fact, especially many of the "roughnecks" who easily made twice what they would working for a different company— the men were happy to save a little money on lunch. Everyone said thanks and was grateful, and by the way they acted, an outsider might have figured they hadn't eaten in days. After John and Bill finished their lunch, they set to work, inspecting and recording details. They sped through the work and were able to pack up and head out shortly before sunset.

They stopped for dinner at a greasy spoon and checked into another roadside motel for the night. The call to Margaret that night revolved mostly around shopping—how much things cost and how much she'd spent. After making one trip with her mother and being shocked at spending over $1000, Margaret had dug up the food pantry wish list and sent her mother back to the store, spending over $1000 again on the usually cheap staples on the list.

Even though the family now had more food stacked up than she knew what to do with, she felt more stressed by the current situation than the news of protests and riots had stressed her the day before. She fretted that if they, an upper-middle class family, had to spend this much for food, how could people making less or feeding a larger family to get through this. The reality of what caused the riots hit home.

John's story for the kids that night described the scene from lunch, where mud and slime-covered monsters—a description not too far from the truth for some of the men—climbed up out of the ground and devoured their meals before slinking back to the depths . The kids ate it up and laughed and giggled the whole time.

"When will you be home, Daddy?" Jane asked.

"Soon, sweetheart, very soon. Daddy loves you. Good night," he replied.

Chapter 4

TV Broadcast: On your screen, are some of the video feeds that are trickling in showing the mass confusion in response to the special rebate payments that went out as part of the President's package outlined yesterday. An error gave peoples' accounts ten times the amount they should have received, effectively giving recipients almost a year's worth of pay or benefits instead of a single month's worth. Many are blaming this accounting error for the renewed protests and mayhem that has broken out across the country.

Along with the confusion from the mistake in the much-needed benefits, renewed actions of violence and looting are spreading throughout LA. In reaction to the increased presence of the National Guard attempting to subdue aggression in many areas previously hit, coordinated flash mobs are now descending into affluent shopping districts, destroying some of the most upscale shopping centers in the world.

To top off the day, the Northeast and Canada have experienced rolling brown-outs attributed to record-setting high temperatures.

Waking up at 5:30 a.m. again, John performed his ritual of showering and getting ready in a hurry. As he repacked everything nicely and neatly in anticipation of his flight later that day, he laughed, noting the exercise clothes and shoes he always packed. *Carrying around a lot of dead weight,* he thought and wondered what else was stashed in the suitcase that he would never use on his trips.

John and Bill grabbed breakfast at the greasy spoon and ordered to-go meals for lunch to shorten their down time. They arrived at the site early and went to work. Before long, they realized it was good that they had gotten there early: the paperwork was incomplete and illegible, and the crew was frantically working to complete the last steps needed to pass the inspection. John and Bill spent almost the entire morning rewriting and filling in the blanks on the documents.

By lunchtime, it was evident that this site wasn't going to pass inspection that day. The engineers met with the foreman and laid out a plan to get everything inspection-ready by the next morning.

A call to the company's travel agent and John's flight was rebooked for the same time the next day. Those were the easy problems to solve. Next he had to resolve the most important and pressing issue at hand, how he was going to break the news to his wife.

"Hi, my love! How are you today?"

"I'm just counting the minutes until you get home tonight. The kids and I are very excited. Plus, I've got a special present for you!" Margaret said cheerily.

After a short pause and no response from John, she continued, "And you are calling to tell me that you aren't coming home today, aren't you?"

"Well, no, I'm sorry. We won't be able to finish up today. But we will have more than enough time to get everything ready tomorrow."

She replied in a very sad tone, "You promised ... I can't stand this. I really wish you were here!"

"I know, I'm sorry, I'll make it up to you. Somehow."

Working through the rest of the afternoon and evening, the site was almost completed by the time they headed out for the night.

***

Waking early as normal, John got ready, and he and Bill headed to the site to help with the work. Working alongside the crew, they installed piping and wiring for the pumping equipment. By the time lunch rolled around, they were able to begin working through the sign-off process. Making good time, they spent three hours finishing all the validations, ensuring the site was ready for the next steps of breaking ground.

After packing up everything, Bill drove John to the airport and dropped him off at the gate. Going to the counter, John checked his backpack full of tools and headed to the security line. Lines were short here at the tiny Helena airport, and he zoomed right through. He thought the TSA agents seemed different than they did back in Ohio: friendlier, less authoritarian, or maybe just more accommodating instead of combative.

After going through the metal detector, he walked to his gate and waited for his flight that was due to take off in two hours.

Watching the news running on the screens throughout the airport, he could barely believe what he was seeing and began to regret not being at home. Stores across the country were madhouses as people blew a year's worth of government subsidies in a single day. Even though it was announced that the bonuses were going to be clawed back, people tried to spend them before that happened.

The TV showed people stuffing their carts full of junk food, steaks, and anything else that hit their fancy. News stations also showed people offering to trade their bounty for cash, cigarettes, booze, or other items that they couldn't buy with the standard allotment. Even knowing that TV cameras were on them, people boldly hawked their benefits—possibly even more boldly—as they wanted to get their fifteen minutes of fame by showing how cavalier they could be while "getting theirs."

Looking to the flight status board, John noticed that his flight was now delayed by 45 minutes.

The delay is a good thing for everyone else because I'm the only person around this gate area waiting for a flight, he thought. Even with the scheduled flight over an hour away, several other people would usually be waiting nearby.

Returning to the TV, he saw the continuing coverage now showing the shelves, almost completely bare, inside the store. The news cut through different feeds to many areas across the country showing the same outcome, whether it was downtown Chicago or backwoods Kentucky. Getting antsy, he decided to call home and see how things were going.

"Hello, my love, how are you?"

"We are ok. We just miss you."

"Well, the good news is that I'll be home soon! I can't wait!"

"Neither can we. We've been hanging out here all day playing games, reading books, and telling stories about what we are going to do with Daddy when he is home. But don't worry, I kept my plans to myself. The kids don't need to hear what I have in store for you!"

"Well I'll be home in just a few hours. I'm sorry it's been ...," John paused for a second as he noticed the newly updated flight board; his flight was now delayed two hours.

"John? You there?"

"Sorry, the board just updated, I'm delayed two hours now ..."

"You're joking, right?"

A long pause took over the conversation as the reality of the situation set in. In their experience, almost every time his flights had two or more delays like this, the flight ended up being cancelled, usually due to "mechanical" problems.

Margaret picked back up, "Are there any other flights out? Any other options?"

"No, there are only two other flights out for the rest of the night, one to California and the other to Texas. And that one isn't until 10:30 p.m. I'm sure I can't make it home tonight after that flight ..."

Silence took over the conversation before John continued, "I'll give you a call back as soon as I know more. I love you. Tell the kids I miss them and kiss them for me."

"I love you, too. I hope we have some good luck today. I'll talk to you later. Love you."

John then called Bill, telling him the situation and letting him know he might be hanging around town. Bill was still in the city doing some shopping and was actually planning on staying the night before heading to pick up his own truck in the morning.

Twenty minutes later the flight was cancelled. A few phone calls to the travel department, and he was booked on the first flight out in the morning.

Bill drove up, and John jumped into the cab, tossing his backpack and roller-board into the back seat. Seeing that the senior engineer was distressed at the turn of events, Bill turned the conversation straight toward dinner, and how he knew of one of the best steak houses in the country, located only a few minutes from where he was staying. On the way to dinner, they stopped at the motel and got a room for John, and he dropped off his luggage.

Dinner was great. They each ordered the house special: a 44-ounce porterhouse steak with corn hash, au gratin potatoes, and creamed carrots. They finished early and headed back to the motel to try and get a good night's sleep.

After another call to the Mrs., with an extended chat with the kids, John turned in. His new flight was supposed to take off at 6:00 a.m.

Chapter 5

"What the heck was that?" John nearly shouted as he bolted upright from sleep.

He looked around the room and didn't see anything out of the ordinary. He stood up, turned on the light, and looked around. Nothing.

He walked to the door, and he heard a car alarm going off outside. He put on his pants over his boxers and stepped outside to look around. He didn't see anything out of the ordinary.

Just as he was about to turn around and head back inside, another patron a few doors down stepped outside, asking, "What the heck are you doing out here? You scared the crap out of me!"

"I don't know, I just heard something and came out to see what it was," John replied.

A few other patrons stepped outside, trying to find the cause of the disturbance. They all stood around chatting for a few minutes and looking around, but did not find the cause.

The consensus of the group was that the noise must have been a car crash, probably by a drunk person who backed up and drove off.

It was just after 2:00 a.m., and at this time of the night, this explanation was good enough, and John went back to bed.

***

The earth started trembling, then violently shaking, and within twenty seconds tens of millions of people were roused from sleep, and entire cities, with millions of inhabitants, were left utterly devastated.

In St. Louis and Memphis, almost all buildings were damaged so badly that they would have to be condemned. In other nearby cities, some high rises were at best cracked in their foundations, while others lost large chunks of concrete and glass. A few close to the epicenter collapsed, taking out other nearby structures in their demise.

Almost as soon as the vibrations stopped, fires broke out all across the region.   Explosions from natural gas spewing forth from ruptured lines compounded the fires.

The power grid that covered the entire central region of the United States went out as dozens of conventional and nuclear power plants went off line and transmission lines fell to the ground like dominos.

Bridges and dams crossing rivers and lakes, especially the mighty Mississippi River, cracked and fractured, causing chunks to fall into the water below and allowing previously held back water to flood into farmland and cities lining the waterways.   Hundreds of barges sank as waves caused by the quake or the deluge from broken dams flooded the barges with water.

Seconds after the shaking stopped, people, who could, fled their homes and apartments to the safety of the outdoors.   Those trapped in ruins desperately tried to escape. Others tried to free trapped loved ones. The only sounds louder than the rampant fires were the cries of children seeking their missing parents and the shouts of parents trying to find their children.

Chapter 6

Radio Broadcast: The latest details are still flooding in from all across the country. Too many to share, but here are some of the more dire items we've been notified about from the effects of the 8.2 magnitude earthquake that struck along the New Madrid fault line last night. The entire city of Memphis, Tennessee, with about 800,000 residents, is in complete ruin after the effects. Few, if any, structures larger than two stories remain in the entire city, according to reports. St. Louis is also reeling from major damage, and we have reports of catastrophic flooding in the city of Chicago.

The President will address the nation regarding this in the early morning. No time is currently scheduled, as the President and his entire administration are putting every effort into mitigating this devastating catastrophe.

Rolling out of bed at 4:00 a.m., John grabbed his luggage and tossed it in the truck. A few seconds later, Bill came over and got in the driver's seat. John hated that Bill had to get up this early to drop him off at the airport, but he needed the ride.

They arrived at the airport and instantly recognized that something wasn't right. The small terminal was much darker than it normally was at this time. The majority of the lights were off, and no one was in sight except for the two uniformed police officers leaning against their car in the middle of the lane. The police waved them over as they approached.

"Guys, all flights are canceled because of the earthquake," the first officer said.

"Wait, what?" John replied.

"There was an earthquake last night. Turn on the radio. The whole Midwest is messed up ... bad. Sorry guys, but we don't know if or when they will start flights back up," the officer said as he started walking slowly back to his position next to the car, signaling the conversation was over.

Dumbfounded, Bill drove on, not knowing where to go next as John pulled out his cell phone and began dialing home. He got an "all circuits are busy" message. He hung up and tried again, same message. Again, same result.

"What's wrong?" Bill asked.

"I can't get through. All the lines are busy," John replied.

"Alright. Well, how about we grab something to eat and figure out our next steps," Bill said as he turned the car down the road to a favorite diner of his.

On the way there, they turned on the radio and tuned to a news station, which was actually the local hip-hop station broadcasting the same information that every station was currently sharing: a massive earthquake had struck the Midwest. The death toll was already in the tens of thousands, an initial estimate based on a few of the affected areas, and the number was expected to increase exponentially over the coming days as more details became available.

Pulling into the diner at 4:30 a.m., they noticed it was already packed. They took a corner booth to get away from the patrons discussing what they'd heard so far as well as from those glued to the TVs at each end of the bar. As they sat down, John tried the cell phone again and got the same response.

Not wanting to give up on air travel yet, John found a pay phone that was connected by a landline. His first call was to his wife, but he received the same all-circuits-busy message. Next, he called the travel department and got through. They assured John that everything was okay and that flights were already being resumed. They found him a flight leaving later that day that would take him to

Detroit where he could fly to Columbus the following day or rent a car and drive home.

It's the best I'm going to get for now, so I need to take it.

John and Bill sat in the diner taking in the news while Bill waited with John for the airport to open and start flights again. After watching the news for hours and putting down lunch, they were ready to leave for the airport. They returned the bill to the waitress, who laughed a little bit when she opened it up.

"Hon, didn't I tell you cash only, today? Our machine is down, and we can't run plastic right now."

"Oh, sorry, didn't know that. Let me take care of that," Bill said, as he pulled out his wallet and handed her a pair of twenties.

***

John and Bill didn't feel it, but on the way to the airport, a large aftershock earthquake—even stronger than the first—struck, further devastating the already affected areas. The radio reported the bad news within minutes.

***

When the aftershock struck, the roadways had been clogged with millions of refugees fleeing by car and foot, trying desperately to make it out of the impact zone. The debris and ruble from the first quake had compounded their problems, leaving the majority of people moving forward at a crawl. The renewed shaking threw people to their feet and tossed cars from roadways. Thousands more were trapped and killed as roadways and bridges fell apart above and below them.

By the time the shaking stopped, almost 200 of the 221 bridges crossing the Mississippi were total losses. Any oil and gas lines that survived the first quake were sheared, leaking their contents into the wild and severing the entire eastern half of the country from getting much-needed fuel. Waste-water treatment centers leaked raw sewage into flooded reservoirs and water ways, contaminating the drinking water for millions of people. The iconic St. Louis arch that had remained standing after the initial quake toppled over into the now flooded park below it.

At the last functional gas station for hundreds of miles, hundreds of people were milling around when the aftershock ruptured the tanks which caught fire and exploded. Hundreds were killed; hundreds more were horribly burnt.

Many of the looters robbing refugees and looting broken buildings became casualties when already damaged buildings came down around them. Thousands of relief workers in place or in route now required assistance to help save themselves instead of providing aid to those in the affected zone.

Luckily, the death toll from this quake, even though it was stronger and more violent than the first, was much lower. That's because the majority of the population was outside fleeing. The infrastructure and buildings weren't as lucky; buildings from Wisconsin to Louisiana were damaged.

***

Pulling into the airport again, John got out of the truck and headed in for his flight. Bill insisted on waiting until he actually saw John's plane take off. After hearing the same song and dance of delay and then cancellation, John was very happy at Bill's insistence.

***

It was dinner-time and not knowing anything else or anywhere else to go, John and Bill headed back to the greasy spoon for the third meal of the day. As they walked in, Bill saw John's brow furrowing at the new bright, red sign on the door: CASH ONLY. No credit card was a slight problem right now, but every hiccup that happened now would become a bigger problem further down the line.

The local news came on. It showed local gas stations and grocery stores that had been smashed and looted, some by those fleeing the quake zone and some by those who either couldn't afford food because of the rapid inflation or who just wanted to get their share of free stuff. The news also described travel restrictions that were being put in place and warned that officials were on the verge of enacting marshal law.

With little hard information to go on, John and Bill started devising a plan to get John home. The airport was a no go. All flights had been cancelled. The landline still worked at the diner, but John and Bill could only reach people on the same branch of phone lines, which included phones in about a ten-mile radius. With no other options they could think of, John was going to have to drive back.

Bill still needed to pick up his truck from the worksite where he had switched it for the company truck. That site was about a six-hour drive from where they were. Luckily, it was in the right direction for John. They decided that instead of leaving the truck there, John would drive it home and worry about getting it back to the proper location at a later date. They figured that worst-case scenario; John could pay to have it shipped back west. That would probably cost less than a plane ticket anyway.

Their main concerns were about gas and clear, passable roadway. Gas shortages were happening across the country, so John wasn't sure he could get enough gas to make the trip without waiting in long lines or dealing with the odd/even rationing schemes that the government had created. These schemes, which had been put in place in different locations, limited the ability to buy gasoline based on the last number of the car's license plate. Now that mass devastation had occurred throughout the heartland, no one knew how hard it would be to find available gasoline.

The second concern hinged on how John would get across the Mississippi River. From what they heard on the news, the worst destruction ran right along the river.

The news reported downed bridges, new lakes, and even some instances of the river flowing backwards.

They grabbed the atlas from the truck and continued planning John's route home as they ate breakfast. From their current location in Helena, they were going to drive back to the worksite in northeast Wyoming to drop Bill off, gas up both trucks, and pack John's truck with every gas can they could find. From there, John would need to hop on I-90, drive east, cross the Mississippi on I-90, turn south on I-39 until he could get on I-74, and then get on I-70 and drive all the way back to Columbus.

Easy enough. No problem. John choked on the water he was drinking, nearly spitting it out, in response to the sarcasm he had running through his head.

By this time, the sun was starting to set, and both men agreed that driving at night in this situation wasn't the best plan. Getting a room at the motel was hard, but the clerk recognized them as patrons from the previous two nights, and snuck them to the front of the line. Dozens of people had lined up, looking for a place to stay, having just fled their homes because of the earthquake.

Because of the demand for rooms, the clerk gave them one room, but charged them the price they had paid for two the night before. John didn't mind since the clerk pulled out an old carbon copy machine and let them use their credit cards, preserving their precious cash.

***

John tossed and turned all night and didn't feel as if he got any sleep. He didn't know how his family was doing or what was going on.

They need me now, and I'm way out here where I'm of no help. I need to make it home, and fast.

They got up at 5:00 a.m. and jumped straight into the truck to begin the journey. Before leaving town, they stopped at several banks, trying the ATMs at each one. On the third try, they were finally able to get cash out. John withdrew the maximum amount he could on his debit card and credit cards, giving him $900 in cash in addition to the $74 he already had in his wallet.

Bill pulled the maximum amount out as well, but he only had a debit card, which got him $300 in addition to the $150 and change he already had. *I always knew I was supposed to carry cash in case of an emergency, but that's a lesson I'm learning a little too hard right now.*

They then began the long trip through the great wide-open "Big Sky Country." As they drove down state highways, they passed cars and trucks stopped along the road that had run out of gas, most of them packed full of belongings. Sometimes the occupants were seen hanging out nearby, sometimes they would try to flag down the truck, and sometimes the cars looked completely abandoned.

A little over an hour later, they were running low on gas. Pulling into the first gas station, they noticed that the prices weren't listed, just as they weren't at all the other stations they had passed along the way. A man in blue coveralls ran up and told them, "Cash only, $15 a gallon, limit of ten gallons a person." They took a second, looking at each other, trying to gather themselves. Ten gallons would get them about half the way to the site where Bill's truck was.

Bill wanted to kick himself for not filling up earlier, but company policy was to fill up from a company tank whenever possible, so he had been trying to wait.

"Alright, I'll take 10 gallons," John said and then he smiled really big and cheesy, "and he'll take 10 gallons too."

"Sorry, no can do. 10 gallons per car," the attendant said, rolling his eyes. This obviously wasn't the first time he heard that today.

"Well, I'll tell you what. I need at least 20 gallons, and I've got $340. Why don't we make a deal?" John said, giving a wink with a big cheesy smile.

This got the attendant's attention, and he looked around real quick and said, "Ok, you got cans in the back? If I get caught selling more to you, I'll get my butt chewed. So you hop out and head over behind that truck, and I'll set it up. Just wait for me to give you the thumbs up."

Carefully, John took $340 from his wallet, making sure that the attendant couldn't see that he had several times that much—he didn't want to get bid up in price and spend more of his precious cash than he had to. Luckily, most people didn't have enough cash to buy the 10-gallon limit, and the chance to make a few extra bucks was all it took to get the attendant to play along.

Bill hopped out and grabbed the two gas cans from the back. They had a few gallons of gas in each, so he put that in the tank and then headed over to the pump the attendant had indicated.

The attendant called over the radio and told them to put ten gallons on the pump where John had pulled up. Then, the attendant slowly walked to where Bill was standing, waited a couple of seconds, and told Bill to put 10 gallons on that pump.

A stern reply could be heard coming over the radio, "You already sold them their 10 gallons!"

The attendant started cobbling together a story about how it's for the guy who walked up with the gas cans and told the lady inside to look out the window and see. A few other quips back and forth before the gas was authorized and Bill started pumping.

Before walking away, the attendant told Bill to walk across the parking lot and get in the truck when he's out of the manager's sight. Bill nodded and as soon as he finished filling his 10 gallons, he started hoofing it across the parking lot.

John, not clued in to what happened, spent a few minutes waiting for Bill before he saw him about 150 yards away, sitting on a sidewalk. After jumping back into the truck, John drove over and picked up Bill. Since the truck was about 2/3 full, he decided to wait until later to put in the remaining 10 gallons to avoid overfilling.

Back on the road, they kept driving and stopped only once to refill the tank.

***

Around noon, they arrived at the worksite. There wasn't a soul to be seen, and the site eerily reminded John of what a real western ghost town would be like, with everything intact but completely abandoned.

They filled up the truck, the gas cans, and Bill's truck from the bulk tank at the worksite. Then, they spent about fifteen minutes scrounging up gas cans and anything else they could use.

They found three more five-gallon cans and filled them up. Next, Bill put two in the company truck John was going to drive and the other in the back of his truck. He apologized, telling John that even though he had a bulk tank back at his farm with several hundred gallons, he might not have enough to make it all the way there, even with a full tank and the extra five gallons.

As they were getting ready to part ways, Bill went to his truck and came back with a small black canvas bag.

"Hey buddy. How about you take this piece of junk back with you? I can't stand looking at it anymore," Bill said, handing him the bag.

Looking inside, John saw a black handgun, several extra magazines, and a couple boxes of ammo along with other standard range gear, like earplugs and safety glasses.

"Bill, I can't accept this ..."

Bill interrupted by holding up his hand, "I've got my sweet new pieces at home, and I'll be home in a few hours. Besides, it would be illegal for me to sell this to you, so I'm just loaning it to you for a few weeks until you come back out here. "

John started to reply, but Bill cut him off, "Boss man, just take it. Please? It will make *me* feel a lot better knowing you've got it with you on your trip home. We've been dodging it all day, but we both know it is probably going to be a lot harder than just a 20·hour drive, even if nothing else goes wrong."

John looked down at his feet, "I know. I just can't believe this is happening ..."

"But it is, so take this," Bill said as he handed him the canvas bag, "and this for the gas you paid for earlier. I would have had to do that anyway, and I'll go ahead and put in an expense reimbursement form for it," Bill said, as he handed John the $300 he had withdrawn earlier.

John thanked him and promised to bring back the gun. He wasn't going to get rid of it that easily. The men shook hands and drove in opposite directions.

Chapter 7

Radio Broadcast: For those who are just tuning in, we have been covering the unfolding of events. FEMA has been activated, and all states' National Guard and army reserves have orders to call up all available personnel. Unfortunately, the ability to contact reserve members has been difficult due to power outages across the country. The international community is making preparations for thousands of relief workers from around the world to help in the heartland following the devastation caused by the earthquake.

Death toll estimates are already over 100,000. And almost 20 million people have been displaced from their homes as a result of the structural damage, flooding, and security factors, such as ruptured gas and sewage lines.

Stay tuned for all the latest updates and for the live broadcast of the President's address later this evening.

John was on the road cruising down the highway at a steady 75 mph; there were hardly any cars in sight, especially going his direction He could easily speed up, but he didn't want to use more gas by going faster. He periodically tried calling home, but every time he tried, he got the same message that all circuits were busy.

He turned the radio off since he was not getting anything worthwhile from the news—just more scary details from the major cities that were affected. The information wasn't something he thought would be helpful since the news wasn't giving any specific information regarding which roads were open or closed, or anything else that pertained to his travel. Luckily, he hadn't heard any mention of his destination, Columbus, Ohio. That, at least, made him happy, and he hoped that there wasn't too much damage since the city was about 400 to 500 miles from the quake's center.

A few hours into the drive, John came to Chamberlain where he had to cross the Missouri River, and everything looked fine from what he could see. He did notice several crews that appeared to be surveying and inspecting the large bridge that I-90 took over the river, but the road was open.

Even though he didn't face any problems here, a pit started welling up in his stomach at the thought of getting across the Mississippi. He knew this would be his biggest obstacle as he had heard news reports that most bridges were damaged, many completely closed and impassible, if not outright collapsed. Although he planned on taking the bridge on I-90, which was around 500 miles north of the epicenter, he was still very worried.

The news stories had described how the river was flowing north from some point along the southern half of Illinois. Many of these bridges were designed and built to manage the flow of the river, but were reinforced in one direction only–the natural direction of the river. Understanding this design flaw, the reversed flow of the river was washing away what remained of many bridges crossing the mighty river, along with more of John's hope.

Seeing that the gas gauge was getting below a quarter of a tank, John started looking for somewhere to fill up. Of the first three exits he tried, two didn't have gas stations that he could find and the third was closed with cones and barricades blocking the way.

On the fourth try, John found an open station, but the attendant wouldn't sell him any gas. The Governor had ordered rationing by your license plate number, and according to the gas station attendant, today wasn't John's day, but John was more than welcome to spend the night in the lot and buy gas tomorrow. It was already a little after 5:00 p.m. and John didn't have time to waste. So, instead of waiting until tomorrow to buy gas at $30 a gallon, he emptied two of the gas cans into the tank and drove on.

He continued to try exits. But now, he was more selective and took only those where he saw definite signs of a gas station. He reasoned that every extra bit of gas he burned looking for gas was that much less he could use toward getting home. Finding two more stations, he got the same reply—no gas until tomorrow. Luckily, the attendants told him this before he waited in the 50-to-60 car-long line. He tried bribing the employees, but this time, his trick of offering cash didn't work. Evidently the attendants had been warned about people running random stings to catch anyone who was breaking the law.

About 7:00 p.m., John came to the outskirts of Sioux Falls, which he thought might be a good place to spend the night and get some food. Sioux Falls was one of the larger cities around for at least a few hours drive. Although the thought of sleeping in a hotel instead of being home made his stomach turn, he knew he was going to be stuck sleeping somewhere since he was low on gas and needed to wait until tomorrow to buy enough gas to keep going.

Before getting to the first exit, he saw a construction sign blinking a message: "All Local Exits CLOSED" and then it flashed "All Exits to I-229 CLOSED." Sure enough, as he passed the first exit, he saw a line of orange and white barrels blocking the path, as well as what looked like chains running along the ground in front of and behind the barrels. He figured the chains must be tire puncture devices to help dissuade anyone from driving through the barrels, even though the exit looked deserted and anyone could have easily moved everything from the path. The next few exits looked the same, but he did notice that the westbound lanes were manned by at least one, and sometimes, two police cars.

Since he obviously wasn't wanted by the police, he decided to motor on. He would pick a lonely field somewhere to get a few hours of sleep while waiting until he was allowed to buy the needed gas. He was a few miles from the South Dakota and Minnesota state line, and decided to just play it safe and stay in the state he knew he could get gas in the next day. For all he knew, Minnesota was rationing gas, too, and their days might be reversed from South Dakota.

Throughout the day, he had seen more and more cars that had run out of gas along the road. They all seemed to be fleeing the area where he was heading. Not wanting to bother—or be bothered by—anyone, he decided to hide. A few miles east of Sioux Falls, he pulled off on an exit for a northbound road and started looking for a quiet place to park for the night. The population density of the area was about 10 people per square mile, making it in the bottom five states population-wise, so finding a spot was pretty easy, even with the addition of the new inhabitants who were fleeing the ravaged areas.

By now, it was little after 8:00 p.m. and John realized that he hadn't eaten anything since morning. He looked around the truck and was surprised to find a bagful of food, left from the gas station spread he shared with the work crew a few days earlier. A few sports drinks, several bags of different chips, and a couple other odds and ends were packed into the plastic shopping bag. Normally, he wouldn't touch most of this stuff, but after the day he'd had, he was giddy at the idea of wolfing down the over-processed starches and grease. He figured he had enough food to last him another meal or two, allowing him to spend more on gas if needed.

Not knowing what time gas stations would open John set his alarm for 3:30 a.m., and planned to get to a station by 4:00 a.m. at the latest. He thought that if he didn't have any delays getting his gas or on his drive to the station, he could make it across Minnesota in time to have a victory breakfast on the eastern shore of the Mississippi.

Rolling down the windows to let a breeze through, John eventually dozed off into a light sleep.

Chapter 8

Radio Broadcast: This just in. In addition to the devastation from the earthquake putting the heartland into chaos and affecting supplies of electricity, food, and materials to the Northeast, there is now renewed and more frequent unrest in the southwest where power is intermittent in many areas. The National Guardsmen has pulled out of those areas to help with the earthquake relief efforts. Reports estimate that as much as 90% of the country is currently out of power or under brown-out conditions. We hope that even those without power are still able to hear us and the emergency broadcasts being sent out by the government.

John slowed as he approached the stop sign and looked both ways. Not seeing anyone coming from either direction, he slowly started into the intersection. In the small parking lot across from him, he noticed two men getting out of a beat-up old truck—why didn't notice them there before? Come to think of it, he didn't even notice the parking lot or building when he came to the stop sign.

Suddenly one of the men raised a gun in John's direction. Everything slowed. He could see the muzzle flash, and what seemed like a lifetime later, John watched as the windshield became an intricate pattern of spider-webbed glass. He swore he could actually see the bullet as it came toward his face. His head jerked back violently, and everything flashed bright white.

***

Jumping awake, John looked around—darkness—and wiped cold sweat from his forehead, feeling for a wound. Trying to calm down, he scanned his surroundings again. The windshield was fine. *A dream.*

Hitting the button to turn the light on, he glanced at his watch, 2:00 a.m. He had been asleep for several hours and decided that was enough. He started the engine and slowly drove back to the road. A few minutes later, he pulled into a gas station.

The light inside the store was on, but none of the lights in the lot were on, and John couldn't see anyone or any other cars in the lot. He pulled up close to the door and turned off the engine, figuring he would wait until someone showed up—at least, he hoped someone would show up.

Within a few minutes, John saw someone moving inside. It looked as if the person was trying to not be noticed as they moved closer toward the windows. John sat up and leaned forward and raised his hand to wave, trying to convey friendliness. Taking the hint, a small woman with gray hair stood up inside. She was holding what looked like a shotgun. As he opened the door to get out of the truck, John heard the unmistakable sound of a pump action shotgun being racked right behind him.

"Slow and easy," said a voice from near the back of the truck's bed.

"All right. No problem. Take it easy," John replied as he froze in motion.

"Go ahead, step out, and tell me what you want. Or were you just looking to bust in and take what you want?" The voice said.

"Just gas. I'm here to get some gas and maybe food." John replied as he slowly stepped out, keeping his hands on the door and easily visible to the person behind him.

The man standing behind him came up and lightly probed John's waist with the barrel of the gun, evidently trying to find any weapons.

"You have cash? Card machines aren't working, and we wouldn't use it anyway if it did," the man said after the probing.

"Yeah, I have cash. Are we ok now?" John said, turning around to see his assailant, a man who looked to be in pretty good shape and probably in his mid-30s.

"Yeah. Just stay out where we can see you. There won't be any gas for another hour. We have to run the generator for the pump. If you want anything from inside, we can go on in. Just keep your hands out of your pockets."

The two men walked to the door as the lady inside held the door open. With her shotgun in a low ready position, holding it diagonally in both hands pointed at the ground. The man kept an ever-watchful eye on John, and held his shotgun tight across his chest. He introduced himself as Matt and said he was the son of the owners. He introduced his mother, the lady already in the store, and said his father would arrive shortly to open the pumps.

The food prices were all hand-written on post-it notes throughout the store. Figuring he should grab as much food as he could afford while still leaving himself enough cash to fill up on gas, he walked down the aisle of packaged food. There he saw several post-its stating that everything on the shelves was "listed price x 4," and, of course, underneath that was the obligatory "cash only" post-it. He balked at those prices. Even though he had over a thousand dollars cash in his pocket he knew he had to save as much as possible for gas.

Matt noticed John's reaction and pointed out that if John wanted cheap food, he should look in the refrigerated section, as prices were still as marked. He told John they wanted to get rid of the cold food quickly so they could stop wasting gas running the cooling unit. He led John to the back of the store and showed him the racks of food, still cool but obviously warmer than normal. John picked out a few packaged sandwiches that, under other conditions, he would have joked about running to the toilet after eating.

Grabbing a couple of bottles of water—the cheapest he could find—he went to pay. He figured he had enough food and water to get him through two days of driving, more than twice the time required under normal circumstances. He figured he had two large meals, or three small meals, a day, and he should be able to find places to refill the water bottles if need be. The total came to $44. Just a few weeks ago, he would have been able to pick up a couple steaks and some beer for that much.

John went outside and lowered the gate on the truck bed and sat there opening up one of the sandwiches. Matt came out asked John a few questions about who he was and where he was headed. More importantly, he asked John how in the world he thought he was going to get there.

Matt then provided information that began to cast a dark shadow over John's plan. Matt explained that they expected to run out of gas in the tanks today and that they were informed yesterday, before the power went out, that there was a zero chance of resupply in the foreseeable future.

He described how they had lost power yesterday morning, and according to the local radio broadcasts, the shutdown was planned to relieve stress on the grid. Power companies were turning off rural areas to keep the cities going.

He described in detail what he had heard about the quake zone. And he mentioned how he thought John's plan for getting home to family was an honorable ambition, but it was one that he thought was near suicide at this point. He described what he had seen on TV before the broadcasts had gone to a recorded loop from the emergency alert system. They showed entire cities, of hundreds of thousands or even millions of people devastated, of buildings on fire, and of people fleeing in droves. The cities had no electrical power. They showed the response that was being mounted in a few select locations. Even then, the response was completely overwhelmed. He recounted footage showing a couple of dozen National Guardsmen and a few FEMA agents among tens of thousands of refugees, all fighting for help.

By this time, Matt's father had shown up in a small import car that looked as if it belonged in a junkyard instead of on the road. A few other cars and trucks started to trickle in, all waiting for gas. Matt let John go first since he was there first, and they were running only one pump on the generator.

The price was a "low $25 a gallon" since it was probably the last gas available for miles around, and Matt knew places back in town were charging $40 to $50 a gallon. He reasoned that his parents needed enough money to cover mortgage and taxes for the next year, so they did some calculations and priced the gas to hit that number. They just wanted to sell the entire inventory as fast as they could, and close down the shop until the resupply runs were back.

John put a hair over 20 gallons in the tank, and then topped off the four gas tanks for a total, rounded down to 31 gallons. This gave John 46 gallons of gas, only enough to get him a little over 2/3 the way home and left him with a little over $200 in cash. From what he'd heard, getting more gas before he reached his destination might be impossible. He brainstormed ideas, but kept coming back to one: sell or trade everything in the truck, bolted down or not. There were several lockers full of tools and other equipment. He could even sell the lockers themselves.

Selling and trading went on until about noon, and some deals were very one-sided, but John acquired another pair of five-gallon gas cans full of gas, a CB radio, and some more food and drink to tide him over. To get these items, he sold or traded everything in the truck bed. The tools alone had cost close to $10,000 new. He figured that by getting rid of as much as he could, he would help increase his gas mileage, too.

With the extra gas, he could make it to Ohio if he didn't hit any big snags. But he would still need to go another 100 miles to 150 miles.

After going through the zone, when I make it that far, 150 miles will be like a cake-walk.

Digging into another one of the sandwiches for lunch, he pulled the truck onto the highway and started driving east.

Chapter 9

Radio Broadcast: This report comes straight from the local emergency management agent, who is asking people to stay in their homes if they are habitable, even if utilities are out. There are mass exoduses happening in many major population centers, causing logistics problems that cannot be handled. FEMA is coordinating transportation, housing, and food for as many people as possible, but the supplies are limited and it may take several days to reach all affected areas.

The President is requesting additional help from former members of all branches of the military. Because of desertion and lack of response the number of members of the military forces available to respond to the crisis is dangerously low.

Driving I-90 at a slower pace this time, keeping the speedometer at 55 mph to try to conserve gas, John noticed more and more cars coming the other way, and more and more stopped along the road. He figured that the number probably wasn't even as many cars as normally seen on this stretch, but the traffic was more than he had seen for the past day or so.

The look of the cars had changed dramatically, too. Instead of sedans and pickups—the latter being very popular around here—he saw more mobile homes and trucks with campers or tow-behind trailers. All the cars and trucks were packed to the gills, and many of them showed rifles and shotguns, either held in passengers' hands or propped up in the seat next to the driver. He saw only one other vehicle going west, a pickup that passed him like he was sitting still, only to pull off the next exit.

After a few hours of driving with no incidents, other than the new stream of counter traffic and the occasional blocked exit, John rolled up to the clover leaf crossing of I-90 and I-35. Before getting to the overpass, John saw barrels as well as signs flashing "Road closed · Take ramp for detour." This was the first quake damage John had encountered so far on his journey home.

Going down the long exit ramp, he followed the few detour signs that lead him to I-35 and then pointed him back to I-35, forcing him to drive in the wrong direction. He stopped for a minute, scanning the roads, trying to see what the traffic situation was like. He wondered why the detour directed vehicles to drive the wrong way on the interstate.

Seeing that the road was also blocked going both ways under the bridge he made the turn and found the next detour sign directing him to cross the median where a gravel path connected the lanes. The gravel had been originally placed there for police and other emergency vehicles to make U-turns. From this spot near the bridge, he could see large cracks and fissures throughout the structure and a number of concrete chunks littering the ground below.

He followed the remaining detour signs, which instructed him to drive the wrong way on I-90 to the I-35 exit. Back on the interstate, he resumed his slow steady pace, and turned on the radio to catch up on the news and find out what was happening. He didn't want to know, but his better judgment said that he should learn as much as possible about the situation. All stations he found played the same messages on a loop, asking people to stay home if at all possible or head to the nearest FEMA relief station. Everything would be fine as soon as relief workers could get to everyone. Since that was an exercise in futility, he turned the radio off and enjoyed the drive in silent anxiety.

After a few miles, he came to another overpass, this time going over the interstate. Barrels were lined up and signs were posted again, but this time, a lane's worth of barrels had been knocked over and rolled around on their sides beside the highway. Not seeing anything blocking his way and figuring the chances of anything actually falling on him were pretty slim, he drove on through. This scenario presented itself several more times in the next few hours. Two of those times required him to drive around or over large chunks of the fallen bridge. From what he could see, this bridge, hundreds of miles from the worst hit areas, would require a lot of work and time to fix the infrastructural damage.

After driving another few hundred miles, he was finally nearing the Mississippi. A few miles away, the road was blocked, by a row of cement dividers backed up by a police car. He had noticed similar blockades on a few of the exits, but they were all for traffic heading west. This was the first blockade he had seen for east-bound traffic and the first that just popped up in the middle of the road. A large sign read, "Road closed," which was followed by "I-90 Bridge out."

Slowly coming to a stop a couple of hundred feet from the blockade, John tried to figure out his next move. Before reaching a conclusion, two officers decked out in black on black riot gear and holding rifles, stepped out of the car and waved him back. John hesitated for a few seconds, trying to comprehend this, but quickly got the hint as one officer again motioned, this time quite violently, to back up, and the other laid his rifle across the hood of the cruiser as if he was lining up a shot.

John put the truck in reverse, did a three-point turn, and drove about a mile up the road where he pulled off to the side. He dug through the atlas to see what other options he might have.

Trying to think, he refilled the gas tank, completely emptying three of his six gas cans and most of a fourth in the process. He had a full tank and probably 12 gallons left in the cans, so he was right where he had estimated he would be. Too bad he had no idea how far out of the way he was going to have to go.

Even though he wanted to head south to find another crossing point, he figured he had a better chance of finding an intact bridge further north, away from the quake. Looking at the atlas, he saw that an exit he'd passed about 10 miles back headed north to a small town and a bridge across the river. And if that bridge was out, too, there was a state highway running along the river that he could keep following until he found one that he could drive across.

Since he was already stopped and it was almost 7:00 p.m., he went ahead and ate dinner, a delicious pre-cooked, vacuum-sealed burger that he'd bought from the refrigerator at the gas station.

While he was sitting there, he noticed lights driving up behind him. He turned in his seat and could see what looked like at least two or three dozen cars driving on the interstate in single file, with a police cruiser in front. It was a long line of cars, trucks, campers, and more, just like he had been watching drive by all day. As they passed, he saw two more cruisers, flanking the procession and another taking up the rear. The car at the rear slowed to a stop parallel to John's truck. A few minutes later, another car came back from the convoy to join the one already waiting. Out of the two cars stepped five men, all dressed in riot control black and carrying rifles.

One of the men lay out in front of one of the cars, deploying a bipod on his scoped rifle and pointing it right at John while the other four slowly walked across the median. The two leading the group carried their rifles in low ready, but the two slightly behind and to the outside kept their rifles up in firing position and pointed in John's direction.

Thinking that he needed to get the heck out of there, he fired up the engine. Putting the truck into drive, he saw the men sprinting toward him, all guns up now. One man was running to intercept his path, holding his hand up for John to stop, and another was running straight toward his passenger side window, motioning him to kill the engine. With five guns pointed at him from less than 50 yards away, he decided to comply. He put the truck back in park and turned off the engine as the men surrounded the front of the truck.

"Hands up where we can see them!" shouted the man nearest him.

John complied, raising his hands above his shoulders.

"Now I'm going to open your door, and you are going to step out. Keep your hands where we can see them!" the man continued shouting as he stepped up and yanked the door wide open.

Slowly, John climbed down from the cab of the truck, stepping forward as the man kept motioning him.

"All right, hands behind your head," the man continued. At least this time he wasn't shouting at the top of his lungs. One of the other men came around the truck and frisked John while the others kept their guns leveled.

"Anything I can cut or stick myself on?" the man patting him down asked.

John shook his head no, and the man patted him down, top to bottom, and then the man who had been shouting a few seconds earlier did the whole exercise again, this time reaching into John's collar, pockets, and waistband. He pulled out John's wallet and cell phone, which he laid on the ground a few feet away.

"Anything in the truck we need to know about?" He asked next, heading over to the truck.

John said quietly, "Just my pistol, a map and a little bit of food and water." This drew an icy glare from the man asking the question.

"SO ... You're packing? I'll bet you wish you had it right now don't you? You want to fight back? Shoot us? I can see it in your eyes!" he said, and then turned to rummage around in the truck.

He came back with John's backpack and pulled out the range bag containing the pistol and ammunition and laid it next to his wallet.

"So you stole a truck and a gun from someone, and now you want to come into my town and steal some more, right?" The man continued getting close enough to John's face that John could feel the hot air of the man's breath.

"No, no ... No. I'm just trying to get home," was John's stuttered reply.

Looking to the other guys, John noticed their rifles were now pointing down to the ground and at least one of them looked as if he was trying to hold back a smile.

"All right. Cut it out, Tom," another man said, half laughing.

The questioning officer, who was apparently Tom, turned and snapped that man an icy glare and snarled, "You cut it out! Cut out your bull crap! You think he's all innocent, and I shouldn't press him?"

The other man raised his hand indicating that Tom should stop. "Tom. Cut. It. Out. NOW."

A few seconds passed and the man continued, "Go back to the car and get on the radio and make sure everyone knows everything is ok, and find out where the escorts are."

Obviously still angry, Tom stormed off toward the cars.

The other man introduced himself as Chris, the sergeant and ranking officer of the group, and apologized for Tom. He then made a joke about Tom's "little man's" syndrome.

Only then did John, at 6'1", realize that he stood a good head taller than the man who was trying to get in his face. Chris said that Tom probably thought his action was necessary because of the recent robberies and looting. People fleeing the worse hit quake areas were taking anything they needed or wanted in their trek across our small town.

The road closing was a ruse to steer people away from town. And the group didn't know what to do with someone approaching from the west since no one had come that way since the men had blocked the road. The bridge was still up and currently passable, but large cracks were seen throughout, and in several places, huge chunks had fallen into the river below, limiting the width to about one and a half lanes.

Chris explained that on the east side of the river, they were running two blockades. One was several miles outside of town, and had been setup to get people to turn away down other roads. The second blockade was right on the outskirts where they stopped all cars, secured any weapons, and then funneled the cars across the bridge, one at a time. Then several times a day, they escorted all the cars about ten miles down the road and returned any weapons that had been held. They told the drivers not to return.

Their actions were in response to several factors. First was the dangerous condition of the bridge, which might not support too many cars on it at the same time. Second, looting had gotten bad very rapidly: people tried to hold up the gas stations in town, drain gas from parked cars, and even invaded a home the night before last. No one was seriously hurt in these crimes, but the looters did take food, weapons, and all the gas from the homeowner's car and garage. After that incident, the police officers decided the outside world could fend for itself. They were going to do what they could to protect their families, friends, and community. That was when the roadblocks went up.

Since it was late, the officers weren't planning any more runs across the river. They told John if he wanted to cross on the bridge, he had to check his gun and ammo with them and sleep in his truck on the highway down by the river. The directive was put politely, but in a very non-negotiable way: if John didn't like this arrangement, he was free to turn around and not come back. Thinking this was a better choice than back tracking and trying to find another route, John agreed to the terms.

The sergeant picked up John's range bag and walked back to the cruiser. John followed them down to the bridge where he parked at the foot of the bridge. He opened another sandwich and washed it down with a warm 20-ounce soft drink. Rolling the windows down to let some air through, John wondered how he was going to sleep, or otherwise pass the time, until he could cross sometime tomorrow morning.

Homesick , John barely slept that night, but when he finally fell asleep, he dreamed of a weekend trip the family had taken earlier in the summer to a small cottage on a lake. He remembered it as one of his favorite trips, where he taught his kids how to swim.

Chapter 10

Radio Broadcast: Today's updates: the death toll continues to climb, and the official count is now over 150,000. The number of displaced people also continues to climb. And utilities continue to fail all across the Midwest and there are portions of the Northeast that are without power and other basic utilities, even though the Northeast suffered only light structural damage from the quake.

Sanitation is a major concern, so please drink only clean water to reduce the spread of waterborne disease. Boil advisories are in effect for most of the country because of cracked and damaged pipes. Without electricity or piped natural gas, the majority of people are unable to clean the water properly.

John woke up shivering in his T-shirt and rolled up the windows in an effort to keep the warm air from flowing out. He dug into his suitcase and pulled out one of the button-up shirts, which he had worn when working at a drilling site, and pulled it over himself like a blanket.

It was early morning and several hours before the sun would rise. He spent the next few hours staring out the windows, trying unsuccessfully to fall asleep. From where he sat, he could see the lone watchman posted at this end of the bridge. Across the water, several lights were visible. There must be more watchmen near the town itself.

His thoughts raced to his family and wondered how they were faring while he was gone. It had been four days since he last talked to his wife, and he had no idea how she or the kids were doing. Even before the earthquake, people had been rioting and running out of gas, and from what he had seen, these troubles were increasing exponentially.

Luckily, they had plenty of food. After Margaret's last trip, the family probably had enough food to last at least three months. The kids, and Margaret for that matter, might not like everything, but they wouldn't go hungry. That was the biggest shopping trip she had ever been on, and then the return trip that her mother went on had to have provided even more food. He didn't get a breakdown or description of that second trip like he did of the first trip, but he knew it was mostly comprised of cheap bulk foods, like large bags of rice, flour, sugar, lots of canned goods and other staples. These bulk foods would greatly extend their ability to feed themselves, even though when they were purchased, they fully intended to donate them to the local church when things quieted down.

Thinking that the family's food situation would be okay for several months, John started thinking about water. Both bathrooms had large water bladders he hoped were full and he thought they still had a gravity filter purchased a few years ago when Margaret was pregnant. The idea had been to drink only the purest water and these filters were the ones they found that also removed fluoride. If they filled the bladders, and used that for drinking, they could be all right at the house for several weeks or months.

Security shouldn't be a problem, at least at home, since they lived in a nice upper-middle class subdivision and knew most of their neighbors.

Having been afraid of getting run over by the price increases at the grocery store had put them in a much better position than they would have been in otherwise. Someone or something had been looking out for him and his family during the past few days to help them be prepared for this storm.

As the sun started rising in the east, he ate his last sandwich purchased from the gas station's refrigerated section. He thought that it probably was still okay because of the nitrates and other preservatives, but he wouldn't want to eat it any later than now. He dug through all his food and drink and realized he had a little more than he had thought. After trading the $10,000 worth of tools and equipment, he was still light on gas, but he did get plenty of junk food.

Probably worth about $50 before everything went to crap. Over $10,000 for $50, and I made out like a bandit. He laughed out loud at how he had actually thought he did well on those trades.

After the sun was all the way above the horizon, the guard walked over and motioned for John to roll down his window.

"You ready to go?" the officer asked.

"Ready and waiting," John replied.

"All right, well I'm going to ride in the bed. Keep it SLOW, like below 5 miles an hour. There are a lot of cracks and a few big fissures. Just steer clear of them," the man said as he started to scale the side of the truck to sit in the bed.

John fired up the truck, put it in drive, slowly crept to the bridge, and started across. He wondered if this was the right choice. The bridge was visibly in shambles, and he wasn't sure whether driving across it was safe.

This is going to be a total loss for a bridge. He couldn't imagine how much replacing it would cost, especially as he observed its length. It didn't go straight across the river, but it hopped across several small islands and one large island that had numerous houses and a small airport on it before touching down on the eastern shore.

They passed ramps leading to the airport. Barrels and cars and trucks parked sideways blocked the ramps and were backed up by two men sitting in a police cruiser. A short distance later, they were on another bridge that was just as bad as the first, but luckily shorter. On the other side of the bridge were a few more on-and-off ramps, blocked by parked vehicles, but John didn't notice anyone stationed there. He guessed that police probably had someone at the other end of the ramps. At the officer's direction, John sped up to about 25 mph when they were on solid ground, and he drove for about two and a half miles before they came to a large roadblock in the middle of the highway.

There were barrels, concrete dividers, police cars, a fire truck, a few shipping containers, and a couple of dozen cars and trucks, all parked and placed in strategic places across the road, median, and all the way down the shoulders for a few hundred feet.

Impressive for such a short period of time, they didn't spare anything to block this off. The blockade even continued over to the access roads that paralleled the highway and across those roads until a small forest took over the work. In the area, he could see at least a dozen men and a few women, in strategic spots, armed with some type of long gun.

One of the men directed John to pull to the side and stop. As soon as they stopped, the officer in the truck bed hopped out and commented about how they really have upped the game since yesterday. The man who directed them told a story of how a group had become rowdy and threatened to run the blockade—two vehicles even tried. They had rammed the cars blocking the road. He pointed to two fancy SUVs—both now riddled with bullet holes— and stated that those SUVs had been the first additions to the new blockade, which they had worked on all night long.

The officer told John to pull over to the first opening and wait there while the officer retrieved John's wallet and gun. About three minutes later, he returned with the range bag and tossed it into the truck bed. "Just leave it there until you get past the second roadblock." Then he slapped the truck on the side and waved goodbye.

John slowly weaved through the blockade. The winding path was four layers deep and required him to slowly snake through a double S pattern to get out the other side. About 100 yards further out, he could see another pair of cars parked sideways to create a buffer for traffic. On the other side of the road, several hundred cars had lined up, two or three wide, waiting for their turn to cross the river.

Evidently more and more people are trying to get out of Dodge.

Driving between the two cars, John waved at the men posted there. They waved back, waved him through, and urged him along. Since he was driving the wrong way, and now heading directly into traffic, he quickly cut across the median and onto the open road heading east. He had to dodge a few parked cars and a few makeshift camps that were setup on the road, and then he was on his way. Looking at the westbound traffic, he passed an estimated 400 or 500 vehicles.

A few miles down the road, he came to another roadblock of two cars and a sign flashing "Road closed - Bridge Out." John smiled at the setup. It had been conveniently placed where it was easy to turn off the interstate to medium-sized state highways.

About a quarter mile past the last roadblock, he pulled over and grabbed the range bag from the back of the truck. He checked the pistol to make sure it was loaded. It was, with a round still in the chamber.

Good to go.

He checked the other contents of the bag, something he hadn't done before in earnest, and found two loaded magazines, two boxes of ammo—one of cheap full-metal jackets and another of expensive hollow points that looked like the rounds already in the magazines. There was also a cheap, padded, nylon holster for the gun, a spare magazine, several sets of earplugs, safety glasses, and a small cleaning kit with a bottle of lubricant. In the side pocket, he found pens, a pocket-sized flip notebook, and a crumpled boonie hat.

He decided to keep the pistol at hand, just in case, so he threaded and fastened the holster onto the center seatbelt and then fastened the seatbelt, securing the holster to the seat beside him. Then he put the pistol and an extra magazine in the holster and returned the other stuff to the bag. He figured that would be the easiest way to secure the holster in case he had to swerve, stop, or do anything that might make it slide off the seat. Wearing the cheap holster would not be comfortable. Then John took off again, keeping his speed at a steady 55 mph, and drove for about half an hour before coming to the end of the interstate, where it merged into I-94.

He had seen numerous cars along the way: some of them had been abandoned, some had people in them, and some were charred remains. He cruised through the merge and could see several manned roadblocks going north and west. These roadblocks seemed strange since they didn't look as if they were protecting a city or anything. He hoped the roadblocks hadn't been setup to rob or loot people who drove by, but John's guess was that was exactly what was happening. Luckily, setting up such a roadblock heading east, the way John was going wasn't as profitable, and the lanes were open.

Over the next few miles, John kept the speed at 55 mph but decided to drop to 35 mph after he had to slow down when coming up on random groups of people or cars. He slowed enough to stay vigilant but fast enough to keep anyone from rapidly sneaking up on him. Many cars were heading west and more had been abandoned or parked and the owners were milling about. Some people had setup makeshift campsites. Other cars had been burned out or ransacked or were full of bullet holes and no one was around.

John saw more people walking, most were dragging luggage or carrying bags strapped over their shoulders. The loaded trucks and RVs that he had seen the past few days were few and far between. He could tell that the people he was passing now weren't nearly as prepared and were trying to leave without a plan.

Occasionally, he passed more exits, some of which were blocked by debris that had fallen from nearby overpasses. By driving up the exit and back down the on ramp on the opposite side of the road, he was able to get around the debris. Most of the roads beside an exit were manned by armed men and women, not always in uniform so he tried to not stray from those roads. A couple of these people pointed their rifles his way, and while no one shot at him, he would accelerate for a few seconds to speed away.

It was late in the afternoon when he came to the junction of I-90/94 and I-39, which lead into Madison. John didn't know how much damage to expect there, so he had no idea if the interstate would be passable. After seeing the damage he'd seen all day, he figured it probably wouldn't be.

The damage John saw became worse as he continued his journey. Looking at his atlas, he thought there may be quite a few large overpasses and elevated exit/entrance ramps likely to be in shambles.

He pulled to a seemingly safe spot to review his options. From where he sat, he determined that there was still at least one more exit before the interchange. But if the past exits were any indicator, he probably wouldn't be able to drive through the exit. He saw that there were a few small roads close to the highway, so if he couldn't use the road at the next exit, he could bypass it and do a little off-roading until he came to a side road to drive around the interchange.

He didn't particularly like the idea, but he couldn't think of anything better. At least he knew the truck could handle it. All the company trucks had been upgraded with four-wheel drive and off-road package enhancements. To get to several worksites, he had had to drive these trucks over terrain much scarier than the current setting. But he still didn't like the idea, knowing that it increased his chances of encountering trouble.

Getting ready for the next adventure, he grabbed a bite to eat and topped off the fuel tank with 10 gallons of gas, an amount close to full without overfilling. After filling the tank, he tied all the cans together with a piece of rope that was in the bed and then lashed them to tie-downs so they wouldn't tip or bounce out while off-roading. He also tied the plastic shopping bags of food and drink closed and, for extra measure, stuffed them and the range bag into his backpack, stretching it to its fullest capacity. Satisfied that everything was ready to be jolted around, John started the truck and drove slowly toward the next exit.

Just then, he noticed a group of men, at least 100 yards away, walking his way. John was sure that they were heading toward him. The hairs on the back of his neck stood straight up as he saw the men, and he didn't know why. There was no quantifiable reason for them to scare him, but they did. He stomped the accelerator, hurtling more or less straight toward them. He turned the wheel slightly to the inside shoulder, enough to visibly avoid a collision path with the men, but not enough to really take him off course.

The truck didn't accelerate nearly as fast as he had hoped, but in the few seconds it took for him to close the gap, he saw the men spreading out to cut off his new angle. John laughed as he saw them raising their hands, trying to flag him down or slow him down by standing in his path: a handful of guys standing on the ground versus a ton of V8-powered steel. This was a game of chicken he knew he'd win.

As the truck got up to speed, he saw several of the men's arms swinging wildly. Maybe they were trying to warn him not to go that way. Before he could react, a loud crack pierced his ears as the first rock slammed into the hood of the truck. If they were hoping to stop or slow him, the rock throwing didn't work. Instead his reaction was to push even harder on the accelerator, even though it was as far down as it could go.

As he passed the men, the few that were in his direct path jumped out of the way at the last second. The others kept throwing rocks, and he continued to be pelted until he was safely out of range. After a few hundred yards, he slowed down to 35 mph. He didn't realize right away that he had been going over 90 mph in his panic to get away. He cursed at himself a few times for going so fast.

How could I let those men get that close without knowing it? I need to be more vigilant. He thought he was being careful and had only stopped for about 10 minutes, maybe 15 minutes, but that was all it took for someone to find him. He cursed at himself for being so lax.

He knew the danger of driving on the highway, but he didn't know any other way to go. He could take hundreds of smaller highways and side streets, but doing so would slow him down and use a lot of the gas that was in short supply. Besides, taking those smaller highways and side streets could potentially expose him to more places where others might jump him.

The next thoughts in his head cursed what was happening, it has only been four days since the earthquake, and already, things seemed to be falling apart faster than he ever thought possible. Then again, things were already falling apart too quickly before the earthquake, the shaking just helped hasten the fall and destroyed the infrastructure that was needed to get everything back on track. His last thought, before banishing the whole train of thinking, was that he was lucky they just had stones.

A few minutes later, he arrived at the last exit before his most likely off-road trip. He slowed as he approached, realizing this was going to be more difficult than anticipated. The exit was on the other side of the cross road behind the fallen overpass. He surveyed the area, looking for a way around, and saw lots of faces looking back at him. Dozens of people were milling about. Some were setting up tents or campsites now that it was near sunset, and some were congregating in cliques that reminded him of his run-in a few minutes earlier.

Not wanting to give anyone time to start in his direction, he put the truck into four-wheel drive and drove off the side of the road. He cut across a field heading toward the exit ramp to get back on the highway. No one seemed to be on his side of the road and the distance between him and everyone on the northbound lanes seemed adequate. He wished he could have cut straight and gotten further away, but small clumps of trees blocked his path. He could navigate through the trees if he needed to, but only at a much-reduced speed that would leave him open to being easily overtaken.

Many eyes followed him, but no one seemed to care enough to do anything about his driving by. He made it to the ramp a few seconds later, running over a wire mesh fence, which luckily slid under the truck and didn't slow his speed.

Now the sight before him was something wildly new. He had grown accustomed to seeing cars parked and abandoned or parked with people camped out around them, but here, on the far side of the overpass, backed up for as far as he could see, were cars, trucks, vans. The road was blocked, the median was packed, and the shoulder was overrun. Thousands of vehicles were stuck in a huge unmoving parking lot. He wouldn't even be able to get on the highway itself for several hundred yards because the southbound lanes were also flooded with cars.

Uncountable numbers of people were standing, walking, and building camps. Everyone who heard his truck was staring wide-eyed, many trying to wave him over and some of the closer ones came darting toward him. Not wanting to have another repeat of a few minutes ago, he kept moving ahead, running down the outside of the shoulder, driving as quickly as he could while dodging the occasional car or truck that was in his path.

Pulling around a truck that was blocking his way, he slammed on his brakes as a small child stood in his path. Behind her was the rest of her family, sitting in their little makeshift campsite on the other side of the truck.

Coming to a complete stop, just inches from the little girl, John mentally said a little prayer that he was able to stop in time and that the girl wasn't hurt. He thought of his own daughter, hundreds of miles away. This girl was probably a few years younger, but just as cute and sweet looking. John could feel tears start to well up in his eyes as he realized the hardship this girl was going to face. He hoped the family had somewhere to go instead of waiting here for help to arrive.

A clicking sound to his right snapped him back to reality. Someone was trying to open the passenger door, which was locked. Looking over, he saw a man, probably this girl's father, trying desperately to open the door. No matter how much John felt sorry for them and no matter how much he wanted to help, he knew he had to keep driving. If he stopped here, he wasn't going to start the truck again. He was one man versus hundreds. At best, he figured only his gas would be stolen, and he would be on foot. The situation would most likely be worse than that.

John slipped the truck into reverse and gunned the engine, breaking the man's grip on the handle. He yanked the selector into drive, and in his haste, he dropped it all the way down to D1, and gave a strong push on the accelerator. He noticed his options were shrinking as additional people flocked his way. He picked a path that would let him sprint about 50 yards before making another turn and nearly ran over three people in his path. He felt bad, as if he was cold and uncaring, but he knew he was doing what he had to. After his 50-yard sprint, he kept going. Luckily, the cars were fewer on this side of the highway, and he was able to keep up speed and stay away from anyone else who might slow him down.

Slowly, he worked back up to the highway, only to see another downed overpass ahead of him. This was a much smaller bridge, and somehow, the northbound lanes had been cleared letting the train of cars through.

This one probably came down with the first quake.

He knew he couldn't get through to the other side since it was full of parked cars, even though the path was clear of debris the cars were blocking his path. He ran off the outside of the road, off-roading until he hit the pavement of the road that once crossed the highway but now dead-ended at a broken bridge. Figuring he was, at most, a couple of miles from the next large interchange, which was an obstacle he decided to steer clear of. He decided to stay on this road, speeding away from the interstate and the downed bridge.

The road took him on an angle back toward the last exit, but he decided not to stop to find a better route. He kept driving until he came back to the state highway and turned south, going even further from the interstate. He drove for a few minutes and took a smaller county road, trying his best to get away from all the people and chaos. After putting a few miles between him and the highway, John found a secluded section of road and stopped to look at the atlas.

He didn't like his available options. Before, he figured that his only problem might be the interchange where the two interstate highways met, and he didn't look further ahead. Now, he realized that a few miles away was another river to cross, and he had no idea how he was going to cross it.

He scanned the atlas for a few minutes and found a route that looked as if it would take him in the right direction and away from civilization. The sun starting to set, so he needed to find somewhere to spend the night. The sound of his truck was enough to alert people to his presence, but the bright headlights would act as a beacon for as far as the eye could see.

A few minutes later, he was alone in the middle of a small clearing off of a small county road. He turned off the engine and walked around for a few minutes, listening. Not hearing anything, he grabbed a few snacks from his backpack and cozied up in the bed of the truck.

He didn't sleep much, constantly checking his surroundings and listening for anyone approaching. The night went uneventfully, and the little sleep he did get was better than none.

Chapter 11

Radio Broadcast: This is the BBC reporting live from London with a breaking news report. Russia has banned the export of all food and beverages, with the exceptions of vodka and caviar. Even though that country has pledged to aid the United States, which has been stricken with the largest natural disaster in US history, Russia has already stopped food aid from being sent. The official message doesn't provide any reason behind the move, but looking at some statistics, it's easy to determine the cause.

The United States is the largest food exporter in the world, accounting for about 10% of all food exports globally. Because of the earthquake-caused disaster, the amount of US exported food will drop dramatically. The future markets in Europe and Asia reacted with wild speculation, the cost of most food commodities for trade have gone up huge percentages, wheat and soybeans leading the way, both increasing at over 200% in a few hours.

The world's number one economy is in shambles, and we are now starting to see some of the more drastic effects this will have on the world stage.

John woke up and looked at his watch. It was only 4:00 a.m., but he knew he wasn't going to be able to fall back to sleep. He replayed the events of the previous day over and over. He felt bad for the people he'd passed on the road, and his eyes filled with tears, remembering the little girl he had almost ran over. He worried about what would happen to them in the next few days. Things seemed to be getting worse, not better. Despite his concern, he couldn't have helped those people. The best he might have done was to give them his food or gas, both of which he needed. Both were very temporary solutions.

It was still too dark out to l read the atlas, and John wasn't going to risk turning on a light. It was perfectly dark and quiet. No lights, no cars, nothing except for the sounds of the forest around him. Anything he did now could easily draw attention to himself. He knew he was part of an ever contracting few, people who had gas in their cars and that fact painted a big target on his back. Luckily, as long as he had that target on his back, it would be extremely hard for someone to catch him.

He tried to figure out his next steps. He had another decent-sized river to cross, and he didn't have much hope of finding an intact bridge.

Even if I can get across this river, what about the next one? Or the one after that?

He wondered how many more times he was going to run into the same predicament. He had figured that once he got across the Mississippi, most of the bridges would be small and not badly affected. But he hadn't expected to see so many overpasses collapsed on the interstate, nor had he expected to see wave after wave of cars broken down and blocking highways.

He started worrying about what he would do when he did run out of gas. He began to realize that it might be impossible to get more. He needed to formulate a plan for that outcome. He mentally went through what he would need and what he had on hand. He had a pair of high quality running shoes and a couple pairs of good wool running socks as well as shorts, t-shirts, and a pair of sunglasses to complete his exercise outfit. Several pairs of thick cotton work pants and shirts, a few undershirts, a few pairs of underwear, and cotton socks rounded out his clothing. In his backpack, he had stuffed his food and water, and under that, he had a small set of tools, most of which wouldn't be of any use if he were on foot, except for perhaps his multi tool and flashlight.

His next thoughts were about food and water. He had enough food to snack on for probably three or four days if he ate light. But before, he and a buddy could down the amount in one sitting while watching a single football game. Either way, he wasn't too worried about food, even though there wasn't a whole lot of it. Everything he had was packed full of more fat and sugar than a person really should eat, which meant enough calories to keep him going. Also, he knew he could go for quite a few days without eating at all: though, the idea of having food to keep him going was nice.

Water was a little tighter than he would have liked. Three cans of soda, three 20 oz. bottles of water, and two 1.5 liter bottles of water were a lot for now, but if he had to start walking, his water wouldn't last long without a resupply.

He grew tired of thinking, since every new topic made everything seem harder. John decided to get up and exercise to try to lift his spirits. He spent about 10 minutes doing a stretching and warm up routine. He hadn't walked more than a few hundred feet in the past few days, and he was quite stiff. By the time he had stretched every muscle group in his body and was warmed up, he had decided to keep the exercise slow and simple, and did a few sets of push-ups and sit-ups, not even breaking a sweat. The workout lasted about 5 minutes, and he followed it with another 10 minutes of cool down stretching. He knew he had to keep active, but was afraid that if he did too much, he could easily fall into a situation where he would need that extra bit of food or water.

By this time, the sky was starting to turn lighter shades of blue. It would still be a while before the sun came up, but the sky was slowly getting brighter. John had a little snack from his larder, and then changed his clothes, which he realized smelled horrible, having not been changed in several days. After putting on fresh clothes, he put his dirty clothes into a shopping bag, tied the bag shut and stuck it in the bed of the truck. No need to smell it up here with me, he thought.

A short wait later, enough light was available to start reading the map. John found a couple more rivers blocking the path he planned to travel today. Luckily, most were smaller, at least on this map, than the one in front of him here. When he started tracing the river he faced now—the Wisconsin River—he realized it wasn't very large, but as fate would have it, it was much wider where he was currently than anywhere else on the map. He traced a route, taking him along the river and around Madison. He hoped to get on a highway somewhere that was at least somewhat straight and fast. Even with the experiences on the interstate yesterday, he knew an interstate would probably be safer than traveling on the back roads.

After deciding on a route, a backup route, and the backup to the backup route for the next 50 miles or so, John stretched then started the truck. The sky was just starting to turn pink, but it was light enough to see without turning on the truck's headlights.

He left the clearing and pulled onto the narrow county road at 20 mph. At the first possible crossing, the bridge was down, crumpled into chunks of stone submerged in the river below. He backtracked to avoid the small town ahead, and turned to the backup route. Even though there were at least two other bridges, between the first one and the backup, both were closer to small towns than he wanted to go. He had no idea what would happen if he drove into one of them.

Another hour later, the sun was up, and he came to the backup bridge. Normally, the trip would have taken about 20 minutes, but he was travelling extra slowly and cautiously. The river was narrow and shallow here, and this bridge was also out. But, by the way the partitions had fallen, and because the river was shallow, the bridge remained above water. Not seeing anyone around, he got out of the truck to survey the damage. He quickly realized that there was no way to get across, but as he turned back toward the truck, he saw what looked like another bridge a few hundred feet to the north. Returning to his truck, he looked at the atlas but didn't see anything on the map.

Backtracking to go to the third route he'd identified earlier, he noticed a set of old dilapidated train tracks that he had crossed before. He'd studied them in both directions when he crossed them, but he hadn't thought about their need of a bridge, too. He didn't want to drive the truck down the track and chance getting stuck, but even more than that, he didn't want to leave the truck on the road while he checked the bridge so he decided to just go ahead and try driving.

He pulled onto the tracks and realized getting on was easier than he thought it would be. He hoped he wouldn't have to backtrack, not only because he hoped the bridge was still good, but because he didn't know how he'd get the truck off the tracks without chancing a flat.

A few hundred feet down the tracks, he crossed a small bridge over a stream. About a quarter mile and several hundred bumpity-bumps later, he stopped at the bridge he'd seen. It looked pretty sound. He got out of the truck and surveyed it closer, walking almost half way across to inspect it. He noticed a few broken beams and supports, but overall, it looked solid. It had been built to withstand trains weighing several thousand times more than his truck, so John figured driving across it would be ok, but he wouldn't want to drive a train across it now. He got back into the truck and a few minutes later, he was on the other side.

Back in his truck, he drove to the other side, and pulled onto the first road he came to. Luckily, the tracks were flush with the road so pulling onto the road was simple. He wasn't sure which way to go, but he cut a hard right and headed back to where he figured he could return to his planned route. He would have liked to verify the direction, but there were a few houses around and he didn't want to stop close to anyone. A minute or two later, he turned onto the highway he had planned to use if the backup bridge had been intact.

The highway was a two-lane state highway that ran east to west and he planned to go a few miles on it before taking another highway south. He made a snap decision not to use interstates now that he was close to Chicago.

The number of people he had seen yesterday didn't register with him until he decoded the situation later. The number of refugees and broken down cars was staggering. There had been easily several thousands in that small area, across several natural barriers that had to have stopped even more from making it across.

How many people were fleeing Madison? Chicago?

He remembered hearing about flooding and other problems in Chicago immediately after the flood. Several million in the city and its suburbs must have been affected. How many people lived even closer to the center of the quake? He couldn't recall exactly, but he knew both St. Louis and Memphis were referred to by name and had to have millions of residents each.

Next break, I need to check the atlas to see what major cities had been in the vicinity of the quake.

He slowed and stopped the truck along the side of the highway. He scanned the area; then, scanned a second and third time even more slowly.

No cars or buildings. Should be good for a few minutes.

Flipping open the atlas, he turned to the national map and took a few measurements. The situation was worse than he had thought. He measured the distance between where he first encountered serious damage and the quake center. It was about the same distance from the quake center to his home in Ohio. If the damage is this bad here, it could be just as bad in Ohio. Unbeknownst to him, several of the bridges he had seen down had been slated for renovation and replacement. But for the past several years, work on the bridges had been neglected, as the state didn't have enough money necessary repairs in its budget.

He sat for a few seconds to compose himself. He then mapped out a few possible routes and pushed the gas pedal. He accelerated to 55 mph, faster than before, caring less about scanning surroundings. He couldn't drive slowly anymore—his family needed him. He reasoned that other families along the way also needed what he had, and he didn't want anyone to take what he had or slow his trip home. The faster he drove, he reasoned, the less time anyone would have to interfere.

He blew through many intersections and by small clusters of houses while breaking pretty much every traffic law in the books. Near sundown, he stopped by the side of the road somewhere in Illinois. Although too mentally exhausted to continue driving, he couldn't stop the day's images from replaying. He saw hundreds of abandoned cars side streets and small highways. He saw groups of people on foot, usually walking down the center of the street. This image especially gave him pause. He had hit at least two people hard enough to severely injure them.

The accident had occurred as John approached a gathering of 50 to 60 people walking in the street. They had refused to move as he approached. He'd slowed to about 25 mph and laid on the horn, but they seemed intent on stopping and surrounding him. Gripping the wheel with his left hand, he buried his right elbow into the center of the steering column to sound the horn. He didn't know why but he'd thought that if he pushed harder, the sound would be louder. As he sounded the horn, he floored the gas pedal. The truck started to pick up speed as fast as the eight cylinder engine could push it.

Most of the people jumped out of the way at the last second. But one person was a split second too slow. The truck struck his lower body, and he cartwheeled to the side. Another person didn't budge from his spot directly in front of the truck, playing chicken with the much larger machine. John heard the impact as the man hit the hood of the truck, forcing him directly under the truck. John felt the bumps as the rear wheels went over him.

John chewed on a couple pieces of jerky, not enough to fill him, but he didn't feel like eating anyway. After the sun went down, he burst from the parked truck just in time to clear the cabin as he threw up the contents of his stomach. He didn't sleep that night, his mind replaying what he had seen and done. And he feared what still might prevent him from getting home.

He wasn't willing to admit the fear of not being able to make it home, so he made a different excuse to stay awake: he didn't want anyone to find him while he was asleep.

Chapter 12

Radio Broadcast: This is BBC finance reporting on the ongoing problems in the international markets. Most exchanges are in turmoil as embargos and trade restrictions appear across the globe in response to the earthquake in the United States. Russia's restrictions on food and gas trades have exacerbated the situation. And OPEC has unanimously voted to no longer accept dollars for oil, moving to accept only the Chinese Reminbi, Russian Rubles, or Euros at a penalty discount up to 20%, or to accept gold at a fixed rate of an ounce per barrel. The gold exchange rate has skyrocketed, raising the cost of oil from the OPEC countries over 500%.

It has been five days since the earthquake hit and three days since the power went out and stayed off. It was off immediately after the quake but came back on for a few hours here and there over the next two days. Each time the power went out it stayed out longer, until it never came back on.

Luckily, John and Margaret had installed a generator in the garage and connected it to the freezer and refrigerator for such emergencies, and Rick, a neighbor who lived a few houses away, was happy to help Margaret start it.

Rick and a few other men in the neighborhood have really stepped up in the past few days, Margaret thought.

They were helping with not only starting generators to keep freezers and refrigerators going, but cooking and getting water and other necessities. Since the power has been out for the past three days, they have started conducting nightly meetings near the playground and were helping to keep the neighborhood functioning. Being in a nice upper middle class neighborhood, you would think this was easy, but everyone could see the large cracks forming in the community around them, but Rick and his team were doing a good job of holding it together.

Margaret was especially grateful for her neighbor's assistance since John wasn't home.

John, why did you have to go? I really miss you and hope you're okay. That theme kept playing in Margaret's head. She cried herself to sleep each night, wondering if her husband was ok and when he would be home.

At the previous night's meeting, everyone had agreed that gas and electricity needed to be rationed and that food should be consolidated in one or two large freezers and refrigerators. Today, Margaret and the kids would be busy consolidating everything from her neighbors' freezers and refrigerators into John and Margaret's refrigerator and into the large standup freezer in the Goldsmith's garage. They spent the morning marking food with stickers, donated by a neighborhood schoolteacher to indicate whose food was whose, loading the kids' radio flyer wagon, and hauling food between each house. This is what finally won over a few of the families who were hesitant about "sharing" food with others.

***

When lunchtime rolled around, all the food had been moved, so Margaret made lunch for her kids and neighbors. She was distressed at seeing how little food the Goldsmiths, a retired couple living next door, had. They had always been nice to her and John and sweet to the kids.

She was also scared at how little food the Rogers had. They had three kids, and their food would last only a few days. But all three of the kids were picky eaters and complained all morning about there being nothing to eat because they didn't like their food options. Little did they know, those few options they currently had were shrinking.

The Rogers' kids' main topic of conversation, other than their picky eating habits, was how their game systems and MP3 players weren't working and how if their parents really loved them, they would find a way to get them up and running again.

The lunch Margaret provided came from some of her food, giving each person a choice of salami, ham, or peanut butter and jelly sandwiches. She had plenty of each and figured the meats might go bad before she and her kids could eat them. She also opened a bag of chips and filled a pitcher with water plus ice that didn't fit in the consolidated freezer. The Rogers kids complained about their lunch the whole time while their parents scolded them to no avail. But they wolfed down their sandwiches, grabbed seconds, and polished off the chips before everyone else got any.

Getting the idea that's how kids were supposed to act, Sam, Margaret's 4-year-old, started complaining, too. Jane, his older sister by two years, giggled at him. Her giggling encouraged the behavior, making Sam think he was cute or smart, but in reality, she was laughing because she knew as soon as the guests left, Sam would find out that he was not supposed to act like that.

Initially, Margaret gave Sam two polite warnings; then, she sternly told him to stop. After that, she let Sam blend in with the other brats. After the second warning, Jane's face became bright red as she bit her tongue trying to hold back her laughter. She loved her brother, but there was something extra funny to her about seeing him act out then act out more after he had been scolded. It was as if he was begging for a spanking.

After lunch, Margaret said goodbye to the neighbors and cleaned up the mess. Once the kitchen was in order, Sam got two swift swats to the rear end. He got the message. Even though he wasn't hurt or in pain, he started to cry.

His sister giggled at his misfortune. She knew better than to act the way he had and thought it was funny when he started to cry. She knew the spanking didn't hurt.

***

That evening's meeting started with bad news. Three houses had been broken into last night, and someone had tried to force his way into another house in the middle of the day. Luckily, no one had been hurt beyond a few bruises and scrapes, but the thieves had made off with a few easily replaceable electronics. Rick told them the police haven't been notified yet, since the landline and cell phones have been out for days. They intend to have someone drive to the police station first thing tomorrow morning to file reports.

After sharing this news, Rob, one of Rick's new companions, stood up and outlined steps that should be taken:

A.) Supplies and volunteers were needed to fix a few broken windows and doors from the robberies.

B.) Volunteers were needed to setup a neighborhood watch. For tonight, they already had several volunteers, but they wanted everyone to start thinking about keeping everyone secure *around the clock*. (He said that last part very loudly, as if he was trying to scare people into action.)

C.) A set of rules for people living in the neighborhood was needed. They needed a curfew, and they needed to prevent people from coming in.

D.) A trip to the stores to get more food and supplies was needed, but it needed to be coordinated, since several people who had left to go to the store previously hadn't returned.

After this, people started muttering among themselves, and the meeting was effectively over. But Rob made closing comments, shouting above the noise of the crowd. He said that everyone had to think about his points and that tomorrow they would stop by house by house to discuss the ideas.

Chapter 13

Radio Broadcast: Tonight, we bring you some good news. At the President's request, Mexico is mobilizing all resources it can spare to help with the unrest embroiling Southern California. In order to help maintain order and peace and enhance public safety, government officials are going door-to-door collecting all registered firearms. According to the President, these measures are necessary to help bring order where there is massive rioting. In those areas, the National Guard is moving resources into position to support FEMA, which will provide relief aid to those who have been displaced by the New Madrid earthquake, which has crippled the center of the nation.

The sun rose, but John could barely see the daylight because of the heavy clouds and pouring rain. His stomach still felt queasy, so he drank a little water and started the truck to defrost the windows. The damp air and his breathing all night long left a layer of fog inside the windows.

He took a few minutes to find his location on the map and to plan a travel route for the day. He was disheartened when he found he was almost directly west of Chicago. The heart of the city was 40 to 50 miles east of his position, luckily people fleeing the city didn't seem to be flooding this area. The realization that he was at least 75 miles or so further north than he thought didn't sit well with him.

He couldn't believe how much he had driven to get not very far on winding back roads and small state highways. He hoped to get farther today. Rain, though, would play in his favor, so at least one thing was looking up for him. After a few minutes and a few slides across the muddy field he had parked in, he was driving along a state highway heading south.

He passed several houses, but didn't see any signs of life. The heavy rain was keeping people indoors. The first sign of civilization was a pair of houses a couple hundred feet away on opposite sides of the highway. Fires were burning brightly through the rain. People were running around outside both buildings. At first, John couldn't tell what they were doing.

Surely they are trying to put out the fires.

As he got closer, he could see there were no buckets or hoses, no efforts to put out the fires that engulfed both houses. Instead, people seemed to be fighting over boxes and bags. And a few people seemed to be violently kicking a few unlucky people on the ground. *So much for friendly help.*

He stomped on the gas, picking up speed as quickly as possible. No one seemed to have noticed him until he was a few hundred feet away and going 75 mph. The delayed reaction didn't stop a few people from trying to run after him, and a few others produced flashes from gun barrels pointed at him. He didn't hear any bullet impacts and kept speeding on through. The raging fires pierced the rain and darkness, providing a vivid and horrifying portrait. At least five people lay on the ground, completely motionless, two others were surrounded by part of the mob, and were being kicked and beaten with bats and other clubs. Other groups were fighting over the spoils salvaged before the fires took over. John could see a few small clusters of women and children huddled under tarps, watching the show before them.

John slowed after passing the burning houses, but the rain and the lack of light—he had decided to drive without headlights—made driving fast hazardous. He realized that if he'd had headlights on, he probably wouldn't have gotten nearly as close as he did without being noticed. A few minutes later, he passed another house. The yard was littered with the contents of the house, and he wondered if the same group had looted all the houses.

How many more houses might they loot?

A few abandoned cars, several tents, and makeshift campsites later, John turned down a side road and started looking for a bridge to cross the Rock River. He thought there had to be dozens, if not hundreds, of bridges crossing it in this highly populated state. His task was to find one that was traversable and not blocked by damage or two legged varmints.

Driving down a small county highway, he noticed a small construction site. It was too dark for him to see much, but he saw a backhoe, a bulldozer, and several other implements as well as the requisite cones and orange barrels. He slowed down to check it better. He couldn't see anything awry. He didn't have enough time to stop when he saw a large steel drainage pipe laid across the road.

He hit the brake hard and could hear and feel the ABS system shudder as he slowed. But he didn't slow enough and he hit the pipe with enough force to jar him forward and cause the truck to lurch. Immediately, the backhoe's lights flipped on, illuminating the silhouettes of three people coming toward the truck. He hadn't regained his composure when he saw the first flash, followed immediately by the windshield shattering into thousands of pieces and a baseball size hole appearing in front of the passenger seat.

Ducking below the dash, he tried to figure out his course of action when the windshield was hit again, creating another large hole right where his head had been a split second earlier. After what seemed like ages, he found the pistol strapped to the seat beside him. He pulled it out of the holster and grabbed the spare mag with his other hand. He chanced looking out the window, but he couldn't see anything through the windshield. Out the passenger side, he could see two of attackers coming his way. Luckily, they didn't notice him. He didn't see anything on his side of the truck.

He popped open the door and rolled to the ground, landing hard on the wet pavement. He drew more gunfire. The sound rang in his ears as the buckshot peppered the truck. He scooted back to the rear wheel well and crouched low as the first person came into view.

He saw a second person. Both were pointing long guns in the direction of the cab, making small sweeping motions, and looking for their quarry. John reacted first, unconsciously raising the pistol, lining up his shot, and firing off a string of rounds. He couldn't tell if the man dove under his own power or fell from being shot. The thing that mattered now was that the assailant ended up on the other side of the tail pipe.

John looked around and under the truck. Then, he sprinted to the side of the road and dove into a muddy drainage ditch running along the road. Rolling to a prone position with the pistol pointed toward the truck, he waited until he saw movement on the far side of the truck and responded with three rounds. Flashes responded from the other side. But none of the impacts were even close to John's position.

After a few seconds, the firing stopped, and John didn't see any more movement. He didn't hear anything except for the rain, so he decided to try to back up further from the truck and the guns. He moved about 50 feet away when he saw three figures running across the field. Not wanting to take any chances, he kept creeping away from the truck and moved in a wide circle, coming in behind the heavy machinery. No one was in sight, but he kept up a very slow pace as he rechecked every detail.

Finally, he made it to the truck and was relieved there was no more contact. He thought they might be watching him and be back soon.

Why set up a blockade like this and not be more organized or determined?

If for no other reason than to prove it to himself, he tried to start the truck. No dice. It didn't really matter since the windshield was shattered, the front end had curled up under itself, and the driver side tire was flat. So he grabbed his backpack and the range bag and threw them over alternate shoulders. He then grabbed his roller-board out of the back seat and ran. He hoped to put distance between himself and the firefight. He ran for about 10 minutes before he slowed down and started looking for some shelter from the rain. He needed to rest and regroup.

***

In the opposite direction, the three conspirators hobbled across a bean field, one on each side of the wounded third being carried by the arms. The leader was wiping tears from his eyes, from the throbbing pain in his head where he had landed after tripping backwards over their barrier and from the realization that his best friend had just stopped breathing. They had been out there that day, shaking down people fleeing the city. They hadn't expected anything bad to happen to them. He wondered how everything had gotten out of control so quickly. Just a week ago, the only thing on their minds was the next freshmen football game.

***

John ran into a small copse of trees and found an oversized beech to lean against. The free was so large that even though several inches of rain had fallen, the ground near the trunk was barely damp. He slouched, gasping for breath, his body shaking. He had never felt an adrenaline rush like this before. He leaned back against the tree, using it to steady his shuddering body. His mind raced at the possible consequences— what would his fate be?

I shot them, at least one. Why else would they have run?

He focused on the memory and recalled the site picture from his first shot. It was squarely lined up on the upper chest of the dark figure. He couldn't remember "calling" the second and third shots, but he knew at least the first one hit home.

It won't be hard to link the truck to me. I did properly sign it out of the lot, and my finger prints are all over it. Even the most backwater police station will be able to put me at the scene. So what? The shooting was self defense, clean and clear. Those guys ambushed me. They got what they deserved. My family needs me, and I will make it home. No matter what.

A few minutes later, his breathing had slowed, and he took inventory of his situation. He was soaking wet and caked with mud. He had a few days of food and water left, but nowhere to sleep and no means of transportation, other than his two feet. His shoulders slumped heavily at that last realization. Walking would mean many more days of travel. But at this rate, it might be safer than driving.

Luckily his roller-board suitcase and backpack were water resistant, and the contents were only slightly damp. He pulled off his muddy garments and exchanged them for a clean set of clothes. As soon as he was relatively clean and dry, he opened a soda and downed half of it before tearing open a bag of chips. Walking around the area, he found the river he was attempting to cross was less than a hundred yards away. He washed down the chips with the rest of the soda and started making a mental list of what he needed.

1. Food
2. Water
3. Shelter
4. Transportation
5. Protection
6. Money

He return to his makeshift base under the tree and transcribed the short list onto a notepad from the range bag. Food and water: he had enough for a few days, but not enough to get him home, though.

Shelter: That was a problem. He had been sleeping in his truck, but it was no longer helpful. Even though it was mid-September and the temperature was in the high seventies, it would probably drop to the sixties tonight. Wet and cold was not how he wanted to spend the night. Getting sick, or worse, wasn't an option.

Transportation: Two feet. Maybe he could find a bike, but as he'd found, driving was out of the question.

Protection: He had that and had proved that he knew how to use it.

Money: He still had a few hundred dollars but he didn't know if it would be worth anything.

It was late afternoon, and he didn't realize how much time had gone by since the incident—it still seemed as if it was just minutes ago. Since the rain wasn't letting up, he decided to try to find somewhere to sleep. He wanted to wait for darkness in order to enact his plan.

Chapter 14

"What was that? What the heck did you do?" Garret said, shouting at the top of his lungs, shoving his wife who had been sleeping beside him.

"... I... I didn't do anything. Is somebody breaking in?" she replied fearfully.

"Dumbass picked the wrong house to break into!" He said, getting up from bed. He launched into a tirade of the most vulgar expletives he could conjure up.

He reached behind the headboard and pulled out a shotgun stored there for emergencies. He continued cursing loudly as he walked across the room. He opened the bedroom door with a snap of his arm, and quickly racked the shotgun. .

"Hey asshole, I'm coming for ya!" he shouted into the dark hallway.

He flipped the hallway light switch, but the lights didn't turn on.

Smart one, cut the power before coming in, he thought.

Stepping into the hallway, he thumbed the pressure switch to turn on the flashlight mounted on the front of the shotgun. Quickly, but deliberately, he swept the hallway with the bright light as he slowly cleared each section of the house. A few minutes later, he had cleared the whole house inside and out and found nothing out of order.

"I don't know what that was, but something ain't right," Garret said, walking back into the bedroom.

He grabbed his cell phone from the nightstand and tried bringing up the Internet, but he couldn't get any websites to load. Next, he decided to try calling his friend across town to see if they heard the noise, too. All he got were "all circuits are busy" messages. After making his way down to the garage, he pulled out his radio scanner and powered it up. He then turned on the emergency radio he kept next to the scanner.

The scanner started chattering as soon as he had it on, and he could tell the dispatcher was overwhelmed.

Evidently the noise, whatever it was, woke up the whole city, and these idiots don't know what happened.

He flipped the scanner off and tuned into the emergency station on the radio.

No news on what had happened. All right, something hit us here, don't know what. If it's real big, it will be on this station, but it might take a while. I should go ahead and fill up the gas tanks like I meant to yesterday, just in case.

A few minutes later, he drove down the road and pulled into the first gas station with lights on. The first two were completely dark, like the rest of the buildings he had passed. Two other cars were already getting gas, which was abnormal for this time in the morning. He tried putting his card into the machine to pay, but the machine wasn't working.

"Cards won't work out here. Have to go inside," a man at the pump across from him said.

"Nothing works anymore, right?" Garret said, with a laugh. "Do you know what happened?"

"Best guess is earthquake. That or we got nuked. I mean, could be a bunch of things, but I'm betting on one of those two."

Garret stood there, dumbfounded for a second.

Earthquake. Ok. But nuked? I know people hate us, but who is that stupid?

He shook his head and walked into the store to pay for the gas. The man behind the counter had a manual card machine for making carbon copy of Garret's card for payment. He said the owner bought it a few years ago so they could keep the store running when power and phones were out.

Carbon copy, I don't even remember ever being charged on one of those things. If we were nuked, that carbon copy isn't even going to matter. Heck even if we weren't, my interest rate is probably lower than inflation. Might as well stock up.

He spent the next few minutes grabbing all the empty plastic gas cans in the store, along with a few armloads of food. He went outside, and filled the truck, the gas cans brought from home, and the new ones. By the time he was finished, the parking lot was almost full. As he sped home, he noticed more cars on the road.

He unloaded the truck into the garage. Then he hurried back out, speeding at over double the speed limit. This time he headed to the big box store up the road. He was late to the party. A crowd had already formed at the front doors, and a police car with its lights flashing was parked on the sidewalk next to the entrance. He pulled into a parking spot close to the front and turned the truck off. He debated what to do next. He turned on the radio and scrolled through the channels until he found one that was broadcasting.

The broadcaster didn't say much except that an earthquake had occurred in the middle of the country and that several large cities had massive damage.

Not good. Really not good, but this is what I'm good at, making the best of bad situations.

He watched the crowd at the front of the store shuffling about.

Zombies. All unprepared and needing food. I need food, too, but I'm going to make sure I get what I need.

He grabbed a ball cap from behind the seat and put it on. Next, he pulled a pair of aviator sunglasses from the visor and put them on even though it was still dark outside. Then, he pulled leather gloves from the glove box and slid them on. Finally, he picked up his pistol, which he always kept underneath the gloves in the glove box. He slid the pistol into his jacket pocket.

Ok, ready for anything now.

He walked up to the crowd and shoved his way to the front, where he could hear a desperate store employee begging people to stay calm. He told them that the store, which was normally open 24 hours a day, would reopen as soon as power returned.

That could be hours from now, or it could be never. I'm not waiting.

He shoved his way to the outside of the crowd and looked for his next move. The crowd was loud and upset, but with the police presence, they were orderly enough. So, he looked for another way in.

I could start a problem, but I don't want to be caught as the one instigating.

He walked back to his truck and drove around to the back of the store. He first checked the loading docks where a few trailers had backed up. All the doors were shut.

Those will be locked tight.

Next was the garbage compactor. The door beside to it looked promising, but he held out for one more.

Bingo.

On both sides of a single door, picnic tables had been set out for an employee break and smoke area. He backed the truck up near the door and got out. He tried the door handle. It was locked, as he expected. He pounded on the door three times. No response. Three more times and still no response.

He started looking for the best way to take the door off its hinges when he heard someone call from the other side of the door.

"We're closed, go away!"

"I know we're closed, I just got pushed out from up front and need to get back in," Garret lied.

"What? Who are you?"

"It's Steve."

"Who? Who's Steve?"

"I'm Steve from receiving"

"And how'd you get out there?"

"I was up front looking at the crowd and, uh, having a smoke break. The door locked behind me."

"I let you in, you gonna let me bum one off you?"

"Sure thing. Just let me in."

The door opened a few inches, and Garret pulled it the rest of the way open.

Offensive jerk, I'm not letting this little twerp question me!

"What are *you* doing back here?" Garret barked at the young man standing inside the door, taking him by surprise.

"I'm, wha—"

Garret interrupted him, "Are you taking the whole night as a break because the power is out?"

"No, I ..."

Garret cut him off again, "I've still got trucks to unload, what are you supposed to be doing?"

"I am sup..."

Garret cut him off by shoving past him. "Man, I'm gonna get back to work. Don't get us both in trouble."

The helpful employee stood dumbfounded trying to think of something to say when Garret produced a pack of cigarettes from his jacket pocket and popped two into the younger man's hand.

"Just don't get us both in trouble," Garret said as he stomped away.

A few seconds later, with a pallet jack in hand, Garret was walking the floor of the store stacking hundreds of pounds of food on a plastic skid. He went completely unnoticed the entire time. Everyone was too busy milling about the front doors, watching the spectacle, or hiding in the break room, shirking their duties in the darkness. He filled two pallets in the span of fifteen to twenty minutes. Not wanting to be short-changed, he went back and filled another pallet with more food and booze. He transferred this last pallet onto the scissor lift in the back of the store, and used the remote to raise the pallet all the way up. He then disconnected the battery so the lift wouldn't operate.

I'll come back for this later.

He rolled up one of the dock doors, jumped down, and ran to his truck. He then backed his truck to the open door. A few seconds later, he had the first two pallets loaded into the bed of his truck and covered with some thick plastic sheeting. He headed down the road toward home.

As he pulled into his neighborhood, he noticed a few lights on in houses.

Candles? Flashlights? Still no power. Whatever. They are all suckers. I'm going to pull this rig into the garage and no one will be the wiser. I'll be set like a king.

Pulling past a particular house, a few doors down from his own, he slowed a bit and tried to peak inside as he always did.

One of these days, one of these days, I'll catch a glimpse of something nice. Sarah, you sure are a fine piece.

He spent most of the day moving the stolen goods from his garage to multiple caches throughout his house. What was left of his day was consumed with listening to radio reports of what had happened and trying to estimate the extent of the damage.

Need to know what happened, so I know what to do.

Later that night, Garret returned to the big box store, driving slowly without lights on to prevent drawing attention. He smiled as he passed store after store and building after building. Even in the dark he could see they had been victims of looters or other criminals. When he arrived at the big box, he saw that the store's doors had been smashed and the store had been looted. Scraps and destroyed merchandise littered the ground.

It's amazing what can happen in a single day.

He snuck to the back of the store and found the scissor lift as he had left it.

Figures, no one is smart enough to simply put the wire back on the terminal.

He hooked the battery back up, lowered the lift, and then reloaded everything onto another plastic skid. A little while later, he headed home with enough booze to last several lifetimes.

The radio made it sound bad, but I didn't think it would be this bad. Not here, so far away. An evil grin crossed his face. *This is going to be fun.*

Chapter 15

Radio Broadcast: Today, we bring you some updates on the continued unrest in the southwest. Power is out in most of California and in large parts of its neighboring states, and there has been massive rioting and chaos. And the departure of various National Guard units to aid in the areas devastated by the earthquake has meant there has not been a force large enough to quell the fires. Luckily, a plan to regain control is being built with the help of the Mexican army. The President of Mexico has pledged full support of the United States, and has said he is willing to do whatever it takes to help its closest ally get back on its feet.

Before the sun was up, Margaret had already been up for hours preparing for the day. She ran the generator to keep the refrigerator cold, prepared an oatmeal breakfast for the kids, and as soon as there was enough light to see, she was out in the garden pulling weeds and picking the harvest.

It was a small garden, grown as a hobby. The fresh vegetables were small supplement to the food they ate, and because of the garden's small size, she easily noticed the missing tomatoes. Several of the largest, ripest fruits were gone. Not on the vine, not on the ground, and not strewn about, half-eaten like they would be if eaten by raccoons. She didn't like thinking that someone had taken her vegetables. Now, since the stores were closed and food couldn't be bought, every bit of food she didn't get from this garden was food she and the kids didn't get to eat.

Not wanting to condemn people just yet, she found the wire cage-like trap in the garage and set the cage next to the garden. She then went into the house to find the dog treats used to bait the trap in the past. She found them in the back of a drawer—almost two years old and extremely stale, but the bacon smell was strong and completely unmistakable. Tossing a few treats into the back of the cage, she propped open the door and set the trap just in case her intuition was wrong.

By the time Margaret had finished, it was time for the kids to get up. She yelled upstairs to wake them and after a few minutes, she went up and helped them get dressed for the day. Their cold oatmeal breakfast was low on their favorite foods list, but they were hungry and ate it all. Even at their young age, they knew, at least somewhat, how lucky they were.

A few books and games later, Margaret heard a knock at the door. Sarah, Rick's wife, was there. Margaret and John didn't know everybody in the neighborhood, but everybody knew, or at least knew of, Sarah and Rick. It's not that they were overly social, super friendly, or the bad neighbors people liked to complain about. Actually, it was Sarah herself. She frequently went for runs through the neighborhood and walks with her children, providing a chance for everyone to ask, "Who was that?" She was six feet tall, had blonde hair and blue eyes and looked as if she had stepped out of a Victoria's Secret catalog. Looking at her, neighbors would guess she wasn't even 30 years of age, much younger than the other women in the neighborhood, who ranged in age from late 30s to 50s. Because of her stunning good looks, many neighborhood women gave her the cold shoulder, even though she was an outgoing, sweet woman.

"I'm sorry for bothering you, but we are trying to get to everyone's house today and go over what was talked about last night," she said.

"No, no, that's ok. I was expecting someone. Why don't you come in? Is Rick coming too?" Margaret replied.

"No, he is busy with some of the other families, and he wanted me to talk to you and a few of the other single women in the neighborhood," Sarah said.

Realizing she made a misstep, she continued on, "Sorry, I don't mean to say you're single, but—"

"It's ok. I understand. I know what you mean. I think that's a good idea. Thank you for coming," Margaret interrupted, trying to save the woman any embarrassment.

A little flushed, Sarah continued, "Ok, I really am sorry. But back to the topic. Since you are here alone, we figure it won't be necessary for you to help out with most of the duties." Noticing that Margaret's facial expression changed, she added, "I want to be clear that we aren't saying that because you're a woman, but because you have kids, and you need to take care of them. There are a few single dads in the neighborhood too ..."

As Margaret's facial expression softened, Sarah continued, "There will be ways you can help. We want everyone to be part of the neighborhood watch. There were more incidents last night, and we need to do everything we can to keep everyone safe."

Noticing that Sarah was fishing for feedback, Margaret told her about the situation in the garden and how she was willing to do what she could to help out. Margaret noticed that the news of food being stolen drew a frown on the woman's face.

She genuinely does care and wants to help, Margaret thought.

For the next few minutes Sarah explained the steps they were taking and laid out some rules they wanted to put in place. Most of the rules were regarding the curfew and visitors. The curfew was to be from 8:00 p.m. until 7:00 a.m., roughly dawn to dusk. Anyone outside after that time would be considered unwelcome and would be stopped for questioning. And if need be, the individual would be escorted away from the neighborhood.

As for visitors, the watch group was going to setup checkpoints around the neighborhood, especially the entrances and exits, to make sure anyone coming or going was supposed to be there. Visitors had to know the name and address of whom they were coming to see. An escort would take them to the address to verify.

"Do you have any objections to this, Margaret? We don't want to just go around doing things in the neighborhood without everyone being on board," Sarah said.

"No, I think these are good ideas. I just hope it will be enough," Margaret replied.

A few pleasantries later, Sarah was out the door to the next house on her list.

***

Time passed slowly recently, Margaret noted. She realized that it wasn't even lunchtime, and she felt as if it should be dinnertime. Not that she was bored. It had more to do with how much more she was able to get done without interruptions and distractions. The kids were playing with toys on the floor—a pretty normal occurrence—but there was no TV, Internet, emails, or phone calls. Without all the noise, she was getting a lot more done than before the quake.

Later in the afternoon, there was another knock at the door. It was Rick and Sarah, with kids in tow.

"Hi, Margaret," said Rick. He reached out presenting two of the largest tomatoes Margaret had ever seen. "I heard about the mishap over here, and I'm sorry that happened. And since we have extras right now, I figure you could use them."

"Thank you. These look amazing!" Margaret replied.

"And the kids have something for yours, too," Rick continued as he nudged his two daughters forward, both several years younger than Sam and Jane.

In unison, with huge smiles, they said, "we brought these!" And each held out a chocolate chip cookie.

Margaret called her kids. Both were delighted to get a fresh baked cookie. Sarah reached into her purse and pulled out two more cookies, handing them to her girls with instruction to play with Sam and Jane while the grown-ups talked.

Rick asked to see the backyard and garden. A waist-high cedar fence enclosed the yard on all sides, leaving a view of the entire garden. He walked around a few times. He said he was looking at different angles for views and places to enter or exit. He wasn't happy with what he saw: there were too many places to hide and too many places to get in or out. It would be hard to prevent another theft without watching the garden all night. But he knew of a few things to help.

"Any empty soft drink cans, or soup cans? We can use those to make an alarm system to surround the garden, and if we can get enough cans, we can set some along the fence in key areas, too," Rick said.

"We've got plenty of both, especially since trash hasn't been picked up," Margaret replied.

"Lead the way," Rick said as he followed Margaret inside.

"We do a pretty good job of sorting our recyclables, so there shouldn't be anything too gross in the bag, but we haven't been rinsing everything as we normally do," Margaret said, as she opened the door to the mud room, leading to the garage.

"Whoa, wow. Look at what you've got here," Rick blurted, as he stepped into the mud room and noticed the stacks of cans and other food filling up about half the room. The supplies were the majority of the large hauls she'd made a little over a week ago.

He continued a second later, "I'm sorry. I don't mean to be rude, I just have verbal diarrhea sometimes. It's good that you have that, I'm glad you do have it. Pretty much everyone I talked to today is already running out of most things."

"Yeah, we normally don't keep a fraction of this, but somebody was looking out for us when I made a few *large* shopping trips just days before the quake. We've actually got more in the garage that was set aside for the food drive," Margaret replied, a slight smile on her face.

"Ok. Great," Rick replied. He tried to speak, but it took him several seconds to find the words, "It's great that you have this, but like I said, most people are already running out of stuff. Sure they have enough to last them a few weeks when you start getting down to brass tacks and cook stuff. I mean everyone has five pounds of flour, five pounds of sugar, and a host of condiments, so I don't think people are going to turn into skeletons, at least, not for a while."

He paused for a second, and Margaret tried to interrupt, but he held his hand up. "Who else knows you have all of this?"

"Just my mom, and John," Margaret replied quizzically.

"Ok, good. Keep it that way. I don't even want to know about it, ok?" Rick said. When Margaret gave an awkward nod, he continued, "Don't let anyone know you have this. I suggest sticking most of it in a closet upstairs. If people know you have all of this ... you *will* be a target."

Shocked and not knowing what to say, Margaret nodded again, "Ok ... I'll do that."

Her head was spinning, thinking about everything. It was starting to become too real.

I trust Rick and Sarah and feel that he was speaking in my best interest, but did he have to be so blunt about it? Yes. He knows what might happen if things don't start moving again, and every indication is that everything is slowing down, not speeding up. Today, it was just some of my tomatoes, but if someone takes this food, we have nothing else. I need to try to help my friends and neighbors. Everyone needs to pitch in to make it through this storm, but I need to think of my kids and me first though. I need to care for them first and foremost.

A little while later, they had constructed a makeshift alarm from fishing line and soft drink and soup cans filled with gravel. The alarm surrounded the garden and ran along the fence in a few spots. Soon after completing the alarm setup, Rick and Sarah left. Margaret had just enough time to move the majority of her stores to the guest closet upstairs before she and the kids went for the nightly meeting.

The meeting covered the same topics discussed with each individual homeowner earlier that day. The rules were put to a vote and were passed unanimously. The men who had gone to the police station had returned, with many wild stories, and the direction to note the time, location and details of any crime and have a witness sign the document. They were assured these details would be suitable to file insurance claims when the dust settled, but in the meantime the police were unable to respond to anything that wasn't a life or death situation.

Margaret put the kids to bed reading them story after story. Picking the next story was her trick to change the subject whenever they asked, "When is Daddy coming home?"

Chapter 16

Radio Broadcast: This is a BBC international breaking news alert. After reportedly taking fire from a Taiwanese patrol boat, China has launched a full-scale invasion of Taiwan. Tensions had been building for weeks, but in the past few days, with the United States out of the international picture, China had preemptively been amassing troops ready for a potential invasion. Overnight, hundreds of transport ships were launched from mainland China, and China has established dozens of beachheads on the island state.

John rolled from under the downed tree he was lying under.

Bad idea, he thought.

Lying under the tree had kept him pretty dry, but he was stiff from the hard ground, and he could feel a couple of dozen bugs crawling under his clothes. Finding a way around the discomforts would be great, he thought. Being sore and tired wouldn't make the hundreds of miles ahead of him easier. He gathered up his belongings and started working his way out of the forest, back toward the direction of the truck he'd fled hours earlier.

The rain was only a drizzle now, and John used the darkness to sneak his way back to the truck, stopping every few seconds to look and listen. He figured that whoever set the ambush ran away when he did, but even the remote likelihood of anyone being there was enough to make him go slowly. It took him almost half an hour to traverse the area that took him only minutes when running.

A few hundred feet away, he could make out the outline of the backhoe, and he paused, unsure if he should continue. The idea was to sneak back in, grab the gas cans and use them as barter to get what he could to help him get home. But now he was second-guessing his plans. He didn't even know if gas was still there. He knew that surely, if anyone had come back, the gas can would be the first thing they would take. If someone was there, he'd have another fight, and that wasn't worth anything he could barter.

He had a feeling that he should turn around and head on his way because maybe the chance he was taking was too great. He paused, taking in all the surroundings, hesitating.

Hesitation will get me killed.

He pulled one of the stones from his pocket. He had scrounged it from the forest for its size, and hurtled it toward the motionless hunks of metal. A sharp clang rang out, not very loud, but definitely enough to alert anyone lying in wait. No movement, no response. Not wasting any time, he kept walking in a low crouch toward the implements.

Still seeing nothing, he pulled a second stone from his pocket and chucked it toward the truck's windshield, smashing out more of the glass and making plenty of noise. Still no response. He broke into a quick jog, making a straight line for the truck. He was committed now, and all he could think was to get in and out quickly.

Coming up beside the truck, he pushed off the top of the truck bed, vaulted in, and pulled the gas cans loose from the tie down. He jumped down with two full cans in tow. Just seconds later, he was sprinting back toward his remaining gear. A few seconds later, he was balancing the five-gallon can on his roller-board and holding the smaller two and a half-gallon can in his free hand. He had hoped to take two five-gallons, but the other five-gallon can had a through and through bullet hole half way up the can. The can was mostly empty now.

***

Carrying the gas was more awkward than he anticipated, and he was forced to stop several times to readjust the larger can. Eventually, he pulled his mud-soaked shirt from the suitcase and put the can inside. He used the shirt's sleeves to tie the can to the suitcase's handle. He had to walk about five miles to the next small town. He figured it would take him about two hours to walk the distance in the rainy darkness.

On the outskirts of town, he came to a sports complex and lay down to sleep until sunrise in a baseball dugout.

This dugout is cozy, dry, and has a roof. I'll be lucky to find something like this next time it rains. He shook his head in disgust. *I've made a few mistakes, but I've gotten lucky. Any one of my mistakes could have ended my journey, left me injured ... or dead. I've been lucky. Now it's time to quit playing on fate and step it up. My family needs me.*

Looking around the diamond, he saw the small building that looked like it normally held a concession stand. The side door laid flat on the ground and several boxes and bags were strewn about the area.

There will be no food, but I'm sure there is something I could use. He walked over and looked inside. It was a total wreck.

People not only took whatever they thought was valuable but smashed, knocked over, or destroyed everything they didn't want.

Sure, the earthquake started it, but the footprints on top of everything help to paint another picture.

Digging through the rubble, he found a few things that he quickly added to his possessions: several large black plastic trashcan liners, paper packets of salt and pepper, plastic utensils, and a few big handfuls of wet wipes. He grabbed plenty of wipes because he could clean up a little, using most of what he'd grabbed.

Heading back outside, he walked around the building and found the bathroom. Its door had also been ripped off the hinges and the toilet inside broken into pieces. The sink was still intact, although hanging at an angle from the copper piping supporting it from below. He tried the water. No joy. The cinder block wall sported a few cracks, but the mirror, probably acrylic or some other plastic, was still whole and firmly attached to the wall.

John spent the next few minutes using his wet wipes to clean his exposed skin, underarms, and a few other extra smelly spots. Happy with the cat bath rejuvenation, he turned to walk out when something caught his eye.

OH MY. Lucky, lucky day. I can feel it now. Today's going to be good!

A smile spread across his face as he reached down and picked up three rolls of toilet paper sitting behind the yellow mop bucket.

Some luxuries are worth their weight in gold, he thought with a smile on his face.

Back at the dugout, he resituated his belongings, adding the new finds and doing his best to hide the gas cans. This was pretty easy to do now with the large bag liners. The garbage bags not only covered the gas cans but also added to the refugee effect he wanted to personify.

After packing everything, he headed into the town. It wasn't long before he started to see signs of life—armed and dangerous life.

The town was pretty small, but probably had a few hundred, maybe even a few thousand inhabitants. Several of the houses and buildings looked newly abandoned, with broken windows and doors ajar, and a few houses had visible, large cracks and crevices in the exterior. A few others had collapsed completely. A few of the better off houses were definitely occupied. "Looters will be shot!" and similar signs were posted on several houses, and a couple had men sitting in front of them, sporting rifles or shotguns in hand or within reach.

Discarded belongings littered the front yards of some houses, and more piles were around abandoned cars lining the streets. There were several campsites with three or four tents or lean-tos built from tarps in a group. All were utilizing the same fires, storage, and security.

People were milling about and poking through the refuse on the ground. Anything that once had value was mostly likely ruined from the previous day's rain.

Even after changing clothes last night and cleaning up in the bathroom, John smelled bad but seeing the others milling about the town, he knew he wasn't the worst off. People glared at him and at one another. Everyone looked tired and on edge, and no one seemed to be welcoming. Most people quickly averted their eyes whenever he returned their stares, even though he tried to smile and look friendly.

Yesterday, he wasn't sure how this was going to play out. And now, he feared his heroic plan of liberating his gas was not going to work. Food, water, maybe a sleeping bag—these were the thing he'd love to get, but now it looked as if he might not get anything. The extra time and energy used to carry the gas wasn't much, but the risk he took to reacquire it was. He knew gas had to be one of the most important and valuable commodities; even before the quake, the shortage was hurting many people. He also knew food and water would be worth their weight in gold, but gas was going to be scarcer. He needed to find the right people to sell it to.

Walking down one of the main streets, John stopped by a small group of people sitting around a fire and cooking on a cast iron skillet.

"Which way to the bridge? I'm looking to get across the river," He called out, carefully keeping about 50 feet away.

One of the men set down the child who was sitting on his lap and stood up. He motioned in the direction John was heading.

"Keep heading that way. You'll hit the river. The bridge is three blocks south," the man said, lazily returning to his seat.

John noted that another man and a boy, who looked to be in his late teens, had shifted into ready to respond positions from their previous laid back positions.

Not too friendly, but I might as well try.

"What are you guys cooking up?" John said. He could see the group rolling their eyes and making faces of mild disgust, obviously they were getting tired of people asking this question.

"If you have extra, I have money. Would love a hot breakfast," he added, figuring he might as well finish the attempt.

"Yeah? How much money?" the man responded in a sarcastic tone.

John paused for a few seconds and thought to himself.

Enough, not enough. Doesn't matter, I'm not telling you. I've played this game before.

Before he could respond, the man continued, laughing, "We could use some money, but it doesn't burn as well as newspaper."

"I know you're hungry. So are we, but I wouldn't trade my breakfast for $50,000 cash."

John knew the man was right. Even before the earthquake, the few hundred dollars he had were quickly becoming worthless. Now it likely wasn't even worth the paper it was printed on—it didn't burn well.

"Thanks for the directions," John said, waving to the man, who nodded in return.

He kept walking a few more blocks and passed more campsites. He saw a few people on their porches and a lot of people wandering about. People seemed to be coming from everywhere—cars, damaged buildings, tents, and boxes. Some even looked as if they had probably been holed up in dumpsters.

What a sad state of affairs, and I get to walk through this for a few hundred miles.

He didn't feel too threatened walking by himself, but he did keep his pistol tucked into his waistband, loaded and ready to use. He consciously switched from side of the road to the other to avoid the people who were starting to crowd the street. He even made a couple of turns when he felt as if people might be following him.

Nobody continued to follow him after he made the turns, since he appeared to be like all the other people, covered in dirt and seemingly aimless.

If they knew I had gas and food, they would probably tear me apart.

He knew they could do it, too. Even with his pistol, he was no match for a large crowd. There were too many people, and they were armed, too. About a third of the adults, mostly the men, had a gun of some sort visible. And pretty much everyone else had a baseball bat, large knife (many just large kitchen knives), or some other threatening device.

A few minutes later, John was at the foot of the bridge, or at least what used to be a bridge. Even though there wasn't enough of the bridge left to drive a go-cart across, let alone a car, there were dozens of people making the trek on foot. All were coming toward him. None were going his way. They were walking in an almost single file line. Families walked together with the kids sandwiched in the middle.

Refugees. It would be the saddest thing that I've ever seen, if I wasn't one of them. And I'm walking right into the place they are fleeing from.

Starting across the bridge was easy, but he was making a lot of people angry when they had to stop to let him cross at the choke points. Many times they wouldn't let him through, and he waited for gaps in the human wave to make his move. Twice, he thought he would be pushed into the water when the counter flow of human traffic just kept coming, right toward him. The first attempt may have been an accident. The second attempt clearly was intentional.

While slowly balancing on the only still-standing, metal I-beam, two men at the lead of the second group sped up, in an attempt to cut off his progress.

They are up to no good.

"Hey guys. You might want to slow down. This part is tricky," John called out to them, holding his right hand up, motioning them to stop.

They looked at each other, and one said something to the other that John couldn't hear, but they kept coming closer and a little faster.

Been here before, too. Opportunity is knocking, huh, guys? You don't even know what I have, but you're willing to jump me to take it?

"Hey man, I think your kid back there needs some help. You should stay together," John called out again. The men paused for a second to look back, but when they did not see anything wrong, they came toward him again.

"No, they are fine. YOU need help," the first man said, pointing toward John with a knife that looked as if it had come straight out of a Rambo movie.

You don't even care that your kids will see you doing this? Plus, that looks like the cheapest piece of junk knife I've seen in a long time.

John methodically pulled the pistol from the holster in his waistband and pointed it in the man's direction. By the time he got the pistol leveled, the man was about 10 feet away and closing fast.

"Drop the knife."

"Screw you!" was the reply, as the man continued to charge forward.

Less than half a second later, the man started a blitz straight ahead. A fraction of a second after that John fire the pistol and the man was falling into the water below, his screams could be heard all around.

I don't know why I did that. What was I thinking? Why? Why did I shoot him in the leg ...?

Leading with the pistol, John forced the other assailant back and made his way across the rest of the bridge, watching closely the families who rushed after the fallen man. They seemed to have lost interest in John after realizing he was armed and in control of the situation. They were now completely absorbed with retrieving the screaming man and quieting the crying children. Even though everyone heard the gunshot, no one other than those directly affected seemed to care, and no one said or did anything to John.

The city on the other side of the bridge was larger than the one he had come from, but just as dreary. More people were wandering about or sitting, aimlessly and helplessly. It was mid-afternoon when he wove his way to the outskirts, and he was getting very hungry. But, he didn't want to chance stopping to eat. He didn't see anyone eating in the open, though he did see a few trying to hide behind tents while they ate.

***

A little past the outskirts, John walked by an all-stone, ranch-style house when the man sitting on the front porch hollered at him, "You're going the wrong way!" He pointed at the groups of people walking in the opposite direction.

John stopped for a second and reaffirmed what he noticed on the bridge: refugees were streaming through in large quantities, but in one direction only.

John yelled at the man, "I guess that just depends on where you are heading. And I'm heading that way," as he pointed east.

"Well there is less that way than where you are coming from, so no sense in heading that way. You'll just find trouble that way."

"Home is that way, and if there is trouble, then I need to get back as soon as I can."

"How far?"

"Far, pretty far." John didn't want to give him too much information.

He noticed that this man, probably in his 60s sat leisurely on the porch of his house, rocking back and forth on a dark wood rocking chair, a glass in his hand and no weapon in sight.

That is a first today.

The house seemed to be in much better shape than any of the others around, and the yard was clean and free of debris and refuse that littered most of the others.

Might be worth a chance.

John continued as he slowly walked up to the porch, "Further than I've got food and water for, but I've got money, or I can trade if you have food to spare."

"Food to spare? That's a riot!" The man was laughing.

He continued, "Even funnier than wanting to pay for it, I'll bet you have a couple hundred bucks, tops. You know how many thousands some of these folks coming from shitcago were offering for a single meal?"

John couldn't help but laugh at the potty humor name the man used for Chicago.

"Yeah, cash is worthless, but I can trade you for it."

"That's close enough, just wait right there," the man said when John made it into the front of the yard. "You come any closer with that pistol at your waist, and you're asking for trouble."

He's pretty good. I think only one in a hundred people I've passed even know I'm packing.

"So your goal is to talk me into disarming, then mug me for my cash?" John said in his most joking tone.

"You got me!" The man said, laughing. By this time, a few other people were starting to walk up behind John. "You guys keep on moving. Ain't nothing here for you!"

The small crowd milled about for a few seconds and then shuffled on, obviously used to the treatment.

John started to step away also.

"Not you. You can stay, for a minute. Just leave your bag and piece right about there." The man said as he pointed to the middle of his yard.

"No, I best be on my way."

"I'll trade you a glass of lemonade for your story. It's not fresh squeezed but it's pretty good."

John stopped to think it over.

He's ok. If he wanted my stuff, I'm sure he could just take it. There are at least two guys behind those windows. And he is probably my best, if not only chance to trade off this gas. He has a good setup going here, somehow, and I'll bet he has food enough to spare.

John complied and left his bag and roller-board in the middle of the yard and slid the firearm into the backpack before walking up to the porch. John climbed the stairs and sat on the top porch step. He waited while the man went inside and returned with a tall glass of lemonade. The man took a large drink from the glass before handing it to John, trying to emphasize that it wasn't full of poison.

Over the next few minutes, John gave an overview of his trip so far and where he was heading. His host sat back and soaked it up. This was the first entertainment he had had in days. After he finished his tale, his host described the current situation.

The hordes from Chicago started heading out of the city a day after the earthquake. The pace of the exodus picked up on days two and three, and the number of people coming through on foot was staggering. About 10 million people lived in the Chicago metro area, and because this town was 40 or 50 miles away from the city, a huge portion of those people were heading directly toward them. None were prepared for travel: food, water, and shelter were all scarce. At best, some were equipped with their weekend camping gear. Most arrived on foot. On the first day, many people were driving, on the second day less, and by the third day, almost no one was driving. They either were out of gas or had been stopped in a manner similar to what happened to John.

The man didn't have much to worry about, according to him. He had plenty of food for his entire family and more than enough firepower to back it up. He and his two sons were all former Marines and they had a few neighbors staying with them. They were all armed. It wouldn't be until after the masses trudged through that he'd be concerned.

"Repelling these zombies is easy. Just yell at them with authority, and if that doesn't work, point the guns at them. If that doesn't work, I give them a spray of this and that works every time," he said holding up large can of bear pepper spray. "It's the wolves that will come out at night, especially when the numbers let up. Those are the ones to be afraid of. But it will probably be a while before we see them."

Another glass of lemonade later, John brought up the main reason he was there on the porch: to trade. The man laughed at the subject. That was until he found out that John was toting seven and a half gallons of gas. Then, he became excited. They had gas enough to run their generator, but they would need more. So a deal was struck.

John stayed for dinner, which was already being delayed because of his presence. He also got a box of protein bars and two cans of stew. Even more importantly, he won a small vial of water purification tablets, enough to treat 15 quarts of water. Not wanting to be cheap, but also not wanting to trade away more of his food, the man gave him a dollar's worth of dimes: silver dimes, he explained, and a knife.

"See this here?" he said pointing to the emblem etched on the blade. "Good knife. Normally, a week or so ago, it would go for ten times that much gas. Take care of it, and it'll take care of you."

After dinner, the family set him up with a bedroll in a tent in the backyard. And even though they left him disarmed at night, including his new knife, he knew he was safer there that night than he would be anywhere else around.

Homesick, John spent several hours staring at the ceiling and thinking about how he was going to make up his absence to his kids and wife.

Margaret will be ok, but I can't ever let Jane and Sam think I won't be there for them.

Chapter 17

Radio Broadcast: We interrupt the emergency management broadcast to bring you this breaking news. There are reports of dozens dead in a clash along the United States and Canadian border. A crowd of refugees walking from Detroit to the Canadian border was delayed and became restless. After several hours of waiting in line, the crowd suddenly charged the gates, trying to break through. After the first few people made it through, the officials on both the Canadian and United States sides were beaten, prompting an order to authorize the use of deadly force to break up the mob.

Before the bodies had even stopped falling, the Canadian Prime Minister, with the backing of Parliament, issued a stay on all entries into the country coming across the US border. He gave his regrets at having to institute this action, but he stated that until officials can assure the safety of their citizens, the border was going to remain closed.

The sound of stones rattling inside a soft drink can woke Margaret from a light sleep. The sound was so brief that for a moment, she thought she hadn't heard it. She hoped she hadn't heard it. Everything would be better and easier if she was simply hearing things.

Who could it be? Maybe it's just a raccoon. Maybe it's my imagination, I have been having way too many nightmares recently.

Bolting upright, she grabbed the flashlight that she had laid on the nightstand.

Walking down the stairs, she opened the living room window overlooking the backyard and turned on the flashlight. Flashing the light through the back yard, she couldn't find anything out of the ordinary except for the string of cans that Rick helped put up along the fence. The string now was laying on the ground, knocked down from whatever made the noise.

She was too slow. Whoever or whatever had been in the garden was gone. After a few minutes and still not seeing anything, she closed the window and went back to bed.

When the sun rose a few hours later, she checked the garden again. To her dismay, whoever had come in the middle of the night had come back. But this time, the person was quiet enough to not wake her during the pilfering. Almost half the garden was gone—not just picked, but entire tomato and bean bushes were gone. Whoever it had been didn't want to spend time picking, and instead, just yanked entire plants. Her stomach started to knot up with grief.

That means less for everyone. Each of those plants would have produced much more than what was on them! How could someone be so greedy and stupid at the same time?

She spent a little time repairing the noisemaker that had been knocked down and then went about her normal morning routine of making breakfast and spending time reading to and playing with the children. A few hours had gone by when a knock at the door interrupted them.

It was Linda Rogers, their next-door neighbor, coming to get food for lunch.

"Hi Margaret, how are you doing today?" She asked when Margaret opened the door.

"We are doing well. Just having some quality time with the kids."

"Oh yeah, lots of quality time over the past few days, huh? I don't know if I can take much more of this. Xbox this. I hate that. This stinks. I can't keep them from complaining! Trust me, I feel your pain!" Linda said before she paused to chuckle.

She continued, "Just coming over to grab lunch for the family. I know we still have a little bit left in your refrigerator and we might as well eat it up, especially since it looks as if we are going to run out of gas for the generator today if we don't find more."

"Yeah, come on in. There isn't a whole lot left, but I'm sure we have some extra stuff you can have. It will just end up going bad if we can't run the generator," Margaret replied.

She feels my pain? I love getting to spend time with my children. How can she be so heartless?

Margaret led her into the kitchen and helped pick out a lunch for the Rogers family. Almost everything was from Margaret's own supplies since the Rogers were down to nothing except for a few bottles of condiments left from when the Rogers emptied their refrigerator. Margaret knew the Rogers had already used all of their frozen food from the Goldsmith's freezer. In fact, some of Margaret's food seemed to have disappeared from the freezer over the past day or so. She knew the Rogers had taken it, but she couldn't bring herself to say or do anything about it. They needed the food, and she and her kids had plenty.

A few minutes later, Linda was on her way and Margaret packed a small grocery bag with a lunch for her other neighbors, the Goldsmiths. Even though they still had some stock in the refrigerator, it wasn't anything that really made a meal, so Margaret again combined some of her food to make a healthy meal for the Goldsmiths. She took the food to them and let the kids play with their dog, something that broke the monotony of the day.

After lunch, Margaret spent time cataloging the remaining food in the refrigerator and freezer. She noted that more food was missing from the freezer than the day before. Mrs. Goldsmith apologized profusely when she found out what had happened and promised to keep a better eye on the freezer whenever anyone was getting into it. She had been relying on the honesty of her neighbors, a strategy which didn't seem to be working. The rest of the day was uneventful until the nightly meeting.

***

Across town, trucks stopped in front of a crowd of people, all waiting for relief packages that had been promised. The sun was just starting to come up. Distribution would not begin for another six hours, but already well over a thousand people had crowded around, fighting for their position at the building's front doors. The crowd grew as the hours passed, and by noon, more than a dozen fist fights had occurred, in which two ended with guns being drawn. Luckily, no shots were fired and injuries amounted to bruises and scrapes.

A little after noon, the trucks arrived, and the crowd devolved into a mob. Even though the three semis were escorted by the National Guard, the .50 caliber machine guns and M4s might as well have been toys, sitting unused. The hordes of people simply pushed in and grabbed anything they could and then ran away. Several groups of men had anticipated the mob action, so they had networks of people grabbing and passing goods to runners, who took the relief packages they snagged to vans or trucks away from the crowd. They also knew enough to have a strong show of force with armed men guarding the vehicles.

Garret, who was bigger and stronger than most people around him, fought his way to the front of the crowd and snagged a box of MREs—meals ready to eat a pre-cooked ready to eat meal that the military typically ate—and started back to his group. When he was almost back two men stopped him. One punched him in the face with the butt of a baseball bat while the other pointed a pistol at him. From behind, small hands pulled the box from Garret's grip and a boy, barely in his teens, ran off with the loot toward one of the well-armed and organized groups.

After the boy was a safe distance away, the two men shoved Garret and told him to get back in line and try again. Both men laughed; then disappeared into the crowd. Garret looked around and finally saw the two men, who were holding up another man in the same fashion that he had just been.

Not wanting the men to get away with what they'd done, he shadowed them, watching their every move and seeing with whom they interacted. A few minutes later, he triangulated his path to cut off one of the boys working as a runner. As the boy came by, package in hand, Garret nonchalantly stuck his foot out and tripped the boy. Quickly reaching down and picking up the package, Garret tucked it under his arm and then used his other hand to help the boy up. A few apologies and questions later, Garret got the information he wanted from the boy, who was completely clueless of the man's intent.

I know what those assholes look like and what they drive. And now I know where they live. At least close enough to find them. I'll teach them not to mess with the wrong guy!

Fifteen minutes later, the crowd had dispersed, except for a few wrestling matches over the scraps. From the observation post on top of a hummer, a young private noticed that most of food made its way to the few select groups who aggressively ripped off everyone else. Rick and his group, like the majority of those who showed up, left mostly empty-handed.

***

That night at the neighborhood meeting, everyone felt dejected when they heard the news about the relief food. The aid that many of the residents were counting on wasn't going to be coming today. The other topics were glossed over, and the meeting was about to break up when a box truck pulled up alongside the gathering.

Garret stepped down from the driver's seat and flashed a big smile as he addressed the crowd. "Don't look so sad everyone! Rob and I were able to call in a few favors and we picked this up."

The crowd started moving toward the truck, and a cheer erupted as the gate was rolled up to display the contents.

"I think this should hold us for a few days at least!" Garret said, drawing cheers from the crowd.

Rick walked over and shook the man's hand, thanking him heartily.

He then turned and addressed the anxious crowd. "Garret, we all can't thank you enough! This is amazing! But we'll have to make sure it goes to those who really need it the most. And it will probably be best to wait until tomorrow so we can fairly distribute it to everyone. Is that OK?"

There were murmurs of acceptance, although a few people spoke quietly about not having food for dinner tonight.

Now, with a much lighter mood, the meeting was adjourned until tomorrow. In the morning, some of the men would go door to door to help update the list of residents, how many people were in each house, and their current quantity of food.

***

A dozen miles away, the lifeless arms of a father and son were wrapped around each other, buried underneath the bodies of their three friends who had helped gather food at the relief drop earlier that day. It wasn't the food Garret had been after, it was revenge. They should have known better than to attack him for the food he carried. He couldn't let go of being robbed and attacked. Serving up revenge, with extreme prejudice, was the only acceptable thing.

Rob, who accompanied Garret, was surprised at his friend's actions, but when push came to shove, he shoved right along with Garret. Garret was happy at the outcome on many levels. First was revenge. Second was a big pile of loot. Third was a new partner in crime.

Complicit in murder, reluctant as he might have been, poor Robbie will be under my control now.

Before dropping the truck off, Garret pulled to the side of the road and selected several cases of food and other goods. He hid them alongside the road as a prize for Rob to pick up later for helping out. With three kids at home who were hungry, Rob didn't decline the "blood food," and they arranged for Rob to pick it up the next day.

Hook, line, and sinker; my first toady. Overall, today was not a bad day.

Garret smiled as the wheels of his mind started turning, planning his next move.

Chapter 18

Radio Broadcast: Reports today indicate that all remaining aid workers have officially left the Chicago area, and efforts to help evacuate any remaining inhabitants have come to an end. These actions follow the inability to get supplies to aid workers and to protect the workers from rampant gang warfare and violent looters. The officials estimate that over 75% of the population has already been evacuated, and that those few remaining are actively participating in violent or other felonious conduct or require more assistance than can be provided at this time.

Startled, John woke up to the sound of someone opening the small tent.

"All right, time to get up and get going," a voice came from the darkness.

It was still several hours before the sun would come up, but John recognized the old man's voice.

John rolled over and sat up before he replied, "Yeah, I guess I best get going."

He was thankful for the accommodations and even though he had finally slept, he didn't want to wear out his welcome.

"We've got some oatmeal on inside. You're more than welcome to some before you go."

"I would love some. It'll be a great start to the day! I can't begin to thank you enough for everything."

"Don't worry about that. It was worth the conversation and the distraction. Heck, after you went to bed, I cleaned up that pistol of yours, and the women washed all your clothes, not machine-washed, but the clothes are at least presentable now. Funny things happen when you are bored out of your mind!"

Breakfast was plain oatmeal, no sugar or sweeteners, just plain oatmeal, and it was good. After finishing his helping and downing a large glass of water, the man escorted John outside and returned all John's gear. He took special care to show John the clean clothes and gun. But John knew that the man really wanted to show him that everything was still there to erase any doubt that anything had gone missing.

"I'd have loved to let you sleep longer, but you will want to get farther out of town before people wake up," the man said to John, who nodded in reply.

"You'll be safest traveling this time of the day before everyone wakes up. I suggest you hunker down around dinnertime and make sure you are well hidden by the time the sun sets. That is when bad things are most likely to happen."

John nodded again, and the man continued, "Good luck, I hope your family is OK. And most importantly, even though I know you would want to try, don't help. You see a problem, someone struggling ... DON'T HELP. Not if you really want to get home. Once you make it there, help everyone, pour your heart and soul into making everything right again. But you have to ask yourself, what is really the right thing to do? Help someone now? Or get home to your family?"

John nodded and said, "Thank you for your help and advice. A week ago, I never would have even thought about passing by someone who needs help, but I know you are right. My duty lies with my family, and I'll do everything I can to make it home to them."

"Don't forget that. Hold that with you and use it to drive you all the way home," the man said as he reached out and shook John's hand.

An hour and a few miles later, the sun rose in the east and John stopped to verify his travel plans for the next few days. He figured that the route he should take, giving a wide berth around Chicago and other larger cities. His trip would be about 450 to 500 miles. If he walked three and a half miles an hour for 10 hours a day, it should take him 13 to 15 days to get home and that was if he wasn't held up because of bad weather or anything worse.

It is what it is, he thought, but the feeling of despair was strong in the back of his mind. *Two more weeks until I'm home. A lot has happened in a week, so who knows what is going to happen in the next two.*

His stomach tightened with these thoughts, causing him to stop and take a short break.

A little water and a bathroom break later, he was back on his feet walking at a brisk pace. For the first few hours of the day, he didn't see much activity. He figured it was most likely because he was heading south on a small county road while most people were heading west or northwest on main arteries heading away from Chicago. He had planned his route and was trying to stay away from the places where he would be most likely to encounter other refugees.

Refugees. There's that word again. For the next few hundred miles, everyone is in the same boat, and that is no boat at all.

Over the next few hours, it was more of the same. If he saw a house, it was almost assuredly showing visible damage. He passed a few small subdivisions, two of which were completely in shambles. The third was still standing, but the houses were showing significant numbers of broken windows as well as cracked brick siding, and other damage. The sight was reminiscent of the news footage shown when a tornado hit a mobile home park, tearing it to shreds.

Cheaply built houses and earthquakes don't mix. Hopefully the inhabitants were able to make it out OK, but all of those cracker boxes, fly by nights, and McMansions sure aren't built the way a house should be.

Occasionally, he saw people poking through the buildings. He wasn't sure whether they were owners or looters. He figured at this point, it didn't really matter.

Even if they weren't the homeowners, anything left was fair game to whoever could use it before it deteriorated from weather or other damage.

Might be me in a few days, two weeks to go on the road and only enough food for one. Don't judge them; they are only doing what they need to do. Heck, who cares if they are digging for gold. It obviously isn't valuable enough to the former owners to stick around and collect it. Former owners.

He didn't quite know why, but he chuckled out loud at that thought. He valued a person's rights and the right to his property, but something out here, in the new wild, made ownership a funny, if not fluid concept.

He passed a few abandoned cars, contents strewn about and picked over for the most valuable items. Evidence of evacuees or other scavengers going through everything inside was obvious. No care was given to any of the contents. Expensive clothes, game systems, laptops, make up, luggage, and tons of other currently useless items were tossed aside as worthless trash. He even saw a small jewelry box with its contents strewn about, though it looked as if most of contents were missing. His favorite was the abandoned Cadillac and the two sets of golf clubs on the ground beside it.

Hopefully they just didn't have time to unpack before leaving; anyone who thinks golf clubs are important when bugging out is going to be in for a world of hurt.

Occasionally John passed other people walking the opposite direction. John gave them a wide berth, sometimes walking off the road to keep clear. The looks on their faces were mixed. Some were sad, some were angry, and some seemed completely mindless as if they were nothing but an empty shell, shambling down the road.

Zombies. Like I heard yesterday. These zombies aren't a problem, at least not yet. It is the wolves that will come out sooner or later, especially at night, that I need to be watchful for.

All of the refugees were dirty and carrying or dragging what they could. They stared at him as he passed. Several were visibly hurt and had bandages or blood on their body. Almost everyone was armed, usually a shotgun or rifle slung over a shoulder. They stared at him as he walked by. He wasn't sure whether they were sizing him up as a threat or as a target.

Friend or foe? I don't care. I'm just going to keep walking, and now you're history.

Along the way, he saw a few camps, but these were all far away from the road. Evidently, they wanted to be safely away from the travelers just as the travelers wanted to stay away from them. John could sometimes see cooking fires. But rarely did he see any of the occupants, and any he did see were grown men, no women or children.

Probably just in hiding, safer to keep them out of sight and not invite any trouble.

By time the sunset, John guessed he had walked more than 35 miles. He was tired and sore, much more so than he had anticipated. Even though he was in great shape, the walk was hard on him. He walked off the highway and down a side road until he found a collapsed house where he set up camp for the night. A short rest, then he worked on pulling some of the house's siding and large boards into a small lean to propped against the side of a collapsed wall.

He had a small meal and then spent the next hour stretching and massaging his feet and legs. Even though he was in good shape—exercising and running several miles multiple times a week—he had never walked this far in a single day, and it had taken a toll on his body. He rested for half an hour, lying flat and using a garbage bag stuffed with his extra clothes as a blanket. Then he repeated the stretching and massaging routine.

Sore, yep, and I'm going to be sorer tomorrow. But at least my wool socks have kept me from getting any blisters. That would be a much bigger problem to worry about.

With that last thought, he stripped off his boots and socks, turning the socks inside out and hanging them up to air out for the night. A little while later, he dozed off to sleep.

The next day went by much like the previous day, except that his pace was greatly reduced. He took more breaks and walked slower because he was sore. By the time he sat down for the night, he estimated that he'd walked only 20 miles—an optimistic estimate. Anyway, he was probably going to be sorer tomorrow, but he had to keep going. As long as he had no major risks or health concerns, he had to keep moving forward.

He went to bed early that night, so early it was hard for him to go to sleep. He wanted to get up early the next morning so he could to get the next few miles over with. According to the atlas, he was a couple of miles away from crossing another interstate highway and then another river. Either one of those would warrant extra care, but both of them at once required his full attention.

If I get up early enough, maybe I can just walk right on through without a problem.

That thought didn't help him get any sleep, but it wasn't the thought that kept him awake. That was reserved for his thoughts of his family and how much he missed them.

Chapter 19

Radio Broadcast: On the BBC today, we bring you updates on the food riots that have broken out across the European Union as food prices have doubled, and store shelves are left bare. Hoarding of needed food and medical supplies is becoming a huge and ongoing problem. Because of the protectionist policies being enacted across the world, many countries are trying to determine how to make up shortfalls on common staples such as wheat, rice, and soybeans.

First thing in the morning, the neighborhood was abuzz first thing, and a large crowd had started to gather at the playground where the nightly meetings were held. Food, free food. It was the topic on everyone's hungry lips. For many people, it had been several days since they had had a good meal. They had been eating leftovers and other scraps their pantries. With the arrival of Garret and the truck full of food he had delivered, food was the only thing people could think or talk about.

"We have to be careful on how we distribute this. There is a lot of food here, but there are even more people who need it," Rick said addressing the crowd.

"I don't know the best way to handle this, so any recommendations are welcome."

"We should give it out to the families with children first. Kids need it more than anyone!" said a woman in the back.

Several murmurs of agreement went through the crowd.

"That is an option. Any other ideas?" Rick replied.

"The kids do need food, but we should keep it fair. Have a soup kitchen type setup," an older gentleman said, to which a few other people agreed.

"The people without enough to eat need it the most! Give it to us, who are out!" Shouted a woman from the back. She followed up with "C'mon people, this is silly. Don't make it harder than it needs to be."

The crowd started getting out of hand, with people both agreeing and disagreeing with the last woman. More people disagreed, but those who agreed with her, wanted food for themselves and were extra vocal trying to drown out the others. It took a few minutes and several people yelling loudly to get everyone back in order and paying attention to the topic at hand. Eventually, Garret's booming voice got everyone's focus back to the meeting.

"People! I don't know about you, but a central kitchen to cook and feed everyone who is in need is my favorite idea. As a matter of fact, there is an empty house right down the road from my house. We can use that to store the food, cook it, and distribute."

The crowd murmured a little bit, many in agreement. Some were quiet, but no one wanted to disagree with the man of the moment. If it wasn't for him, they wouldn't even be having this discussion. Even the most greedy and selfish people had to admit that it was the best and most fair option.

"I'll let Rick lead the sorting out of the details," Garret said, turning over the attention to Rick.

A quick vote was taken; it wasn't a unanimous vote because many people decided not to vote at all. But no one voted against setting up the soup kitchen. Several rules were proposed and were going to be worked out over the next few hours. The most important one was to have one meal a day, at least until more food could be acquired. It wasn't preferred, but everyone figured it would be optimal since no one would starve on a good meal per day. Many people, however, wondered what they would do for the other two meals each day. Other rules addressed how to make sure everyone who wanted a meal got one, and only one. The rules also covered how to track what food was left, and who would cook, clean, and serve the food.

In addition, there were concerns about security of the food. There had been several more break-ins, and they had run off more refugees from the city and other suburbs. Many of the neighbors suspected each other of malfeasance, but wouldn't admit to it openly. A plan was needed for securing the house and cataloging the food. Garret was nominated and heartily accepted the task. He drafted a few assistants to help him with his tasks and then left immediately to implement his plans.

He first drafted Rob, his partner in crime. Then he selected another neighborhood father, who had volunteered, and two older high school boys. The high schoolers were "young backs to help with the heavy lifting," he said when he picked them. In reality, he picked them because he knew a bit about them, as most of the neighborhood did. Both boys had been picked up for different petty crimes, ranging from vandalism and petty theft to a few minor assault charges. Nothing that was too serious, but they did have quite a few hours of community service under their belt.

These two little punks, I hate them, but I'll be able to put the fear of God in them and they will do what I say.

He told all in the group to go home and change into work clothes and to look for any spare lumber they may have. When they return they should bring a hammer and nails if they have them.

Swinging by his house, he grabbed a set of lock picks and a couple of screwdrivers from the garage. After walking the three doors to the empty house, he picked the lock on the front door—a skill he had practiced a couple of times before and made quick work of the lock. He opened the door, he went to work removing the door handle and releasing the metal lockbox that contained the key realtors used for house showings. Sliding the lockbox and lock picks into his pants pockets, he surveyed the house. It was nothing special: four bedrooms, fully finished basement, two car garage, and all the other amenities expected in a house that size.

He rolled up the garage doors and waited for his crew to arrive and implement his plan to convert the house into a soup kitchen—and more importantly, into the capital for his little kingdom. He had a grand scheme planned, and this house was going to be the front for it. The house had it all—space and location. The house was in the middle of the neighborhood and only a few houses away from his own place. Best of all, it was available for the taking.

First, he would secure the site: board up windows, install strong locks on the doors, and build a neighborhood watch command center for coordinating the activities to keep everyone safe. Then, he would use it as a front to skim from the pot and consolidate his power base.

I have to get in early, make my name known, and take control. Most people think this is going to just go away and everything will be OK in a couple of days. Man, are they wrong. It's going to be a few months at best, but more likely a few years.

By mid-afternoon, the crew had been able to adequately secure the house. Garret then backed the truck into the garage, and they started unloading everything into the house. As the crew unloaded the food, they listed what and how much they had. They then assigned a storage location in the kitchen. Most of the food was MREs; canned foods like mixes of fruit, vegetables, soups, and stews; and a variety of other odds and ends; and dry goods like flour, rice, and beans. Large bags of dry goods were stacked along a wall in the kitchen and the cans filled the cabinets and the small walk-in pantry.

All in all, they had close to a ton of food. And this was minus the couple hundred cans and hundreds of pounds of dry goods that Garret had snuck into his house late the night before and added to his already substantial larder.

He sent the crew home, pushing the volunteers out quickly, so he could pull aside the two delinquents and

Rob. He took the notepad in which Rob had listed all the food and made a few adjustments of a couple dozen cans and bags of food for each man.

A down payment for my three stooges.

"These are for you, guys. You deserve it. What we are going to do is move it to the upstairs bedroom for now. Late tonight or tomorrow night, we can move it to your houses. And I'm sure you all understand this when I say, 'don't tell anyone ... or I'll kill you.'"

Garret walked to Rick's house to let him know the food had been stored and that whoever would be doing the cooking could go to the house. He was pleased to find that half a dozen women and a couple of men had volunteered to help prepare, cook, and clean for the first neighborhood meal, which had been planned for tonight.

That lousy crappy work, they can have it, he thought.

Down the street, Margaret was reading a book to her kids to help pass the time. Children twice the age of hers generally read the book, but she was able to borrow it from a neighbor. Besides, it was the only book in the house that the kids hadn't heard 10 times already. Even though she was reading aloud, she realized she wasn't paying attention to the story when Sam asked her a question about what was happening. Her lips were speaking the words, but her mind was on a million different topics, so she answered the question by rereading the last couple of pages.

Her mind kept wandering to their situation.

We've got food now, but if we don't go to the neighborhood meal, everyone will know about it, and know we have food at home. People are begging and bartering for any food they can get their hands on, and I'm sure a few of the people around here wouldn't feel bad at all just taking it from me if they knew.

Some of the things I heard at the meeting earlier: it was all "I ... I ... I and Me ... Me ... Me." No one is thinking about the bigger picture. No one is thinking about anything but their own immediate needs.

After hearing the news that had trickled in, she not only knew that the trials were far from over but realized that they were going to get worse, and probably much worse, over the next few weeks. She had spent the day hanging a few more noisemakers from fishing lines. These were becoming common sights around the neighborhood, so much so that spare cans were becoming hard to find.

Done in the yard, she found some wooden garden stakes. She had used them to hold up tomato plants but she had recently replaced them with metal cages. She cut the stakes to fit inside the window frames of the house. Then she lodged them between the top of the windows and the frames to prevent the windows from opening easily.

Realizing that these wooden blocks weren't enough to stop someone from getting into the house, she applied masking tape in a square tracing the outside of the windowpanes and then made an X across the window panes. On top of that, she put a few strips of clear packing tape, covering over half the window with tape. She didn't like having the packing tape on there, and hoped that she would be scraping it off in the future, but the masking tape would help section off the packing tape and make it easier to clean up.

It would be nice if a tape mess was actually my worst concern right now, she thought.

Next, she went to the master bedroom and opened the corner safe where John kept his gun collection. It wasn't much of a collection, but he did have a handful of guns. She never had an issue with him having them, even though she didn't understand why he wanted them. He had taken her shooting a few times, and even paid for her to take a class as *his* birthday present. That way she couldn't refuse. The class covered the basics, but it did help her learn how to handle a gun. Margaret never really got into shooting and was not good at it. She looked through the safe and picked out the gun she was looking for, took it out, and slid it into her purse that was sitting on the bed.

She shut the safe's door but reopened it when she realized something was wrong. The only gun she had ever been upset about John buying was missing. Any other gun could have been missing and she wouldn't have noticed, but this one had caused a few heated discussions when she found out how much it cost.

No one else has been in here, and there is no way anyone got into that safe, so it's definitely not stolen. That man, what is he doing? It would serve him right if he lost it.

Feeling somewhat safer, she proceeded to walk through the house, and double- checked the doors and windows to make sure they were secure. She tried to think of any additional precautions she could take.

Next, she repositioned the kitchen table and chairs in front of the sliding glass door that lead to the porch and made several extra blocking bars to help keep it shut. She also applied extra layers of tape to the outside of glass to give it additional resistance if anyone tried to break it.

Then, she went to her bedroom and slid the vanity so that it was next to the door. In an emergency she could then use it as a barricade to slow anyone already inside. She knew that every little thing she could do to slow someone down or deter someone could mean the difference between life and death.

A little later, she took the kids to the neighborhood cookout where there was a crowd of hungry and irritable people. The dinner for the night was a simple canned chicken with gravy over white rice. Many people complained about the food and the small portions. The cooks apologized and promised a better meal tomorrow. They said they didn't have enough time to prepare anything else since they didn't know what was available and didn't have an efficient way to cook. They promised to have a better setup for cooking and distribution tomorrow.

After dinner, everyone stayed for the nightly meeting, which was now held at the hybrid HQ and soup kitchen instead of the playground. The first topic was a "thank you" to those who had helped make the meal happen, and then a request for extra food, especially condiments and spices. The next topic was about increasing the security of the neighborhood. Problems were increasing, and if they didn't do something to address the break-ins, the situation was going to get worse. They decided to ask for more volunteers and to start a rotation where everyone, not just volunteers, would have to help with certain duties for at least a few hours every couple of days. Garret's suggestion was to use this house as the headquarters for all security related activities, and that too was readily agreed to.

Chapter 20

Radio Broadcast: This is Linda Esteban reporting from inside the DHS headquarters in Washington where we have gotten estimates that up to half the National Guards who have been called up for duty either have not shown up or are currently AWOL, or absent without leave. That means they either haven't shown up or have left after showing up. The Department of Defense defends these numbers, stating that under the circumstances, these numbers are good and a majority of those unaccounted for are not absent without leave, but merely in-between communication channels.

Seeing the figures milling about the street corner ahead of him, John turned to cross the street. The three figures nonchalantly crossed ahead of him.

They are waiting for me. They just gave themselves away.

Glancing around to see if anything else was happening, John re-crossed the street. He let out a small sigh of relief when he noticed that the three men had not noticed that he had crossed the street again, and they remained standing on the opposite side of the street. They were acting as if they weren't interested in him. John ducked between two houses, walked down a driveway, crossed an alley, cut between two other houses, and headed to a street that ran parallel to the street he had been on.

Before he made it halfway down the second driveway, he saw two men standing at the end of it. On his right side was a chain link fence, which conveniently had three strands of barbed wire running above it. And on his left side was a wooden fence. The only option was to turn back.

"Hey, where you going? Hey man! HEY! I'm talking to you! Don't you walk away!" one of the men shouted at him.

Ignoring the man, John spun around and started walking back toward the alley. As soon as he hit the divide, he bolted down the alley, but had to stop short. The three guys he was originally trying to duck away from were at the end, waiting for him, with wicked smiles on their faces. Turning around again, he saw the yelling man and his partner waiting.

***

John woke up, sore all over, shaking the sleep out of his head. Realizing he'd been dreaming, he ran his hand down and touched the scar on his side. It was left from an incident years ago when he was a teen. Growing up in a rough neighborhood, he was relentlessly hounded to "join up" and to be part of local crew. That incident left him with a broken arm, two broken ribs, and 74 stitches in his side.

And that wasn't the first time he had been attacked while growing up, and it wasn't the last, but at least it was the last time he had to make a trip to the hospital. After that incident, he had started developing habits to have eyes in the back of his head and to be hypersensitive to his surroundings. He'd learned how to read people's movements, stance, gait, and other physical descriptors to see what they were up to. He'd learned where not to go and what not to do—not just in his neighborhood, but everywhere. All the bad elements seemed to have the same habits, and he had them pegged.

Even though he despised violence, he had learned how to fight and how to be aggressive and ruthless when he needed to be. For others around him, who also tried to stay clean, it didn't work out as well. If you fought back and lost, they would come at you again with more people. If you fought back and won, they would come after you with more people and weapons.

They had come after him, and he'd won. They'd come back. And this time, as he'd stared down the barrel of a gun, he didn't hesitate, but the armed thug did. The thug paid the price by swallowing half the teeth in his mouth.

I don't like these memories. John sighed heavily. *I've tried for years to distance myself from that, but right now, today, I'm in more danger than I ever was. Stupid little kids are all they were, trying to be tough. And there were only a few of them. Now, it's everyone, and they are going to be fighting for food, water, and survival. Not just street cred and a small wad of cash.*

Standing up, stretching, and getting ready for another day's long walk, John couldn't stop his mind from racing. His body was tense, but he couldn't tell if it was fear or excitement.

No, not excitement. I don't want to do this I have to do this.

He realized it was adrenaline pumping through his veins for a completely different reason—resolve.

I will make it home, no matter what it takes.

Gathering his gear and situating everything for a quick pace, John set out to cover a couple of miles before having to cross the interstate. It was earlier than he had planned, but that was a good thing, giving him more time before the world would come to life around him.

Half an hour later, his path south reached a dead-end and emptied into a frontage road that ran parallel to the interstate. From where he stood, he could see the highway and a couple dozen parked cars, but the darkness shielded everything else. There were no lights from any fires that would indicate nearby inhabitants, and he couldn't hear the sound of anyone nearby. He didn't hear much of anything.

Too quiet. This place is too quiet. No bugs, frogs, anything.

He sprinted forward, crossed the frontage road, and crouched down in the drainage ditch on the far side of it. He spent a few minutes sitting and waiting, but nothing changed. Everything stayed dark and silent. Not wanting to just sit and wait there all morning, he started crawling slowly toward the interstate.

Crawl to the fence. Get over that. Then run across the highway, and take cover on the other side.

He spent a couple of minutes going slowly and quietly until he felt the woven wire fence in front of him. He pushed his roller-board over first then climbed over and picked it. He held it tight to his chest in preparation for the run.

No use dragging it here, it's time to move!

He broke into a run, not going as fast as he could, but still going much faster than he felt comfortable with, given the darkness.

He made it to the near side of the highway when he felt a slight tug at his right leg, light enough that he had barely noticed it—at least not until he heard the sound of something heavy crashing down, piercing the silence.

Trip wire?

He kept running. By the time he made it across the median to the other set of lanes, he could hear voices talking loudly and hurriedly. The voices weren't loud enough for John to make out what was being said, but he wasn't sticking around to find out.

He was on the other side of the paved lanes when he hit another trip wire, setting off another loud crash. He kept running and didn't slow down until he was far enough out that he had to watch for the fence on the far side. Hitting that while running wouldn't make for a good day. He found the fence, tossed the suitcase across, and jumped over. He then continued to run until he hit another drainage ditch. He ducked down and caught his breath for a few minutes.

"We know you're there. We've got guns, and we'll shoot you if you come close," a voice was saying from the dark.

The voice continued, "We don't want any trouble, just leave us alone and you'll be fine."

John couldn't help but think about the person's loud pronouncement.

Poor bastard, I didn't want to wake you up. It would be best if you just shut up. Who knows who else you're announcing yourself to now.

With his breathing under control, John got up and started down the frontage road until he came to a road running away from the interstate. From here, he turned and followed the road until he was almost in the middle of a small town. The sky just starting to brighten, so he picked up his pace. Even though he didn't see signs of life anywhere, he knew that in a few minutes the early risers would be up, and he didn't want to be there when they were.

Making his way down a few different streets, John saw that the majority of houses had massive damage. Clumps of makeshift shelters and tents had been setup here and there. The smell was overwhelming. There was no way that this kind of smell could have built up over the past few days; it must be what's left of a nearby sewage plant.

A few minutes later, he found the first bridge crossing the river. Not knowing what to expect, he was pleasantly surprised when he saw it. It might as well have been perfectly intact—at least to someone who never seen a bridge before. The old iron bridge had collapsed, but when it did, it fell in one almost-intact piece. The heavy iron beams that held the structure together were now sitting a few feet lower than the original roadway, and what was originally the overhead support was now a strong and stable walking bridge. The next bit of luck was that someone had already secured ladders to the bridge, which served as jump on and off points.

He scurried down the ladder as fast as he thought was safe and began crossing the bridge. It wasn't until he was half way across the bridge that he first heard voices behind him. He couldn't make out what they were saying, but his instincts told him what it was about.

Am I worth going after and hunting down? Maybe I have food? Maybe I have a gun? You guys argue it out. I'm outta here!

He quickened his pace, once again pushing a little faster than he would have liked. At least now, a bit of light allowed him to see where he was walking.

Finally at the other side, he climbed up the ladder, and sprinted as fast as he could for a few hundred feet and through a small group of trees along the road. He kept up a hybrid between a fast walk and a jog for a couple of miles until he was well away from the town and in the middle of farm country again.

He found a downed tree to sit on, and after seeing no signs of human life around him, he stopped for breakfast and a bathroom break.

"I've got to get rid of the roller-board. It's slowing me down too much," John said, talking to himself as he walked down the road.

He had been dragging the roller-board behind him for the past few days. And now that he could fit most of his belongings into the backpack and range bag, he was contemplating leaving the roller-board behind.

"I'm just like all the other refugees, fleeing and carrying what I can, and now I'm going to ditch what isn't helping me."

His stomach tightened up as he recalled the countless abandoned cars, with contents strewn about where the owners had picked out the most useful items they could carry and then left the rest. He thought of the piles of luggage and bags he had seen, where those people had done exactly what he was thinking of doing now—culling their meager load again.

For a while, he debated what to do and finally decided to keep the suitcase for now.

"I'll at least keep it another day or two, and then I can change into the clean clothes and leave the dirty ones behind. By then, all the food and water will fit into the backpack easily."

Realizing that he was talking to himself out loud, he shook his head.

"Time for a break, I guess."

Deep down, he knew he should ditch the suitcase right now, especially since doing so would allow him to walk off road more easily. But he wasn't ready to do that yet. Somehow, he felt that leaving it behind was just another sign of despair—that he was succumbing to the situation at hand, a sign of defeat, and he couldn't allow himself to be defeated.

While taking a small break, John pulled out the atlas and reviewed his planned path and looked for any details he may have missed. He was going to start on a south-east path toward the Indiana border. This path would take him just north of the major cities and set him up for an almost straight eastward path to home.

After today, two more days until Indiana, about five days until Ohio, and then another three days to home. I can do this. No problem.

He laid out his provisions. With the purification tablets, water wouldn't be a problem. Food, too, shouldn't be a problem. He had the gas station leftovers and the box of protein bars that he'd traded the gas for. He rifled through his clean clothes, socks, work boots, and workout gear, and picked through the backpack and range bag.

They didn't know where they are going, they didn't know what they were leaving behind, and they didn't know what was out there. But I do.

With a sudden change of mind, he pulled all the clean socks and underwear from the roller-board and stuffed them in the backpack. He then stripped down and put on a fresh set of clothes. Next, he laced his work boots together and threaded them to his backpack. After a few stretches he walked back to the road, leaving the roller-board behind. This time, despite being sore and tired from the previous days of walking, he had a little extra spring in his step.

Chapter 21

Radio Broadcast: This is a breaking BBC report. Officials have just put London under martial law in response to protests that escalated from a simmer to full blown violence today. Thousands had gathered in two separate factions—those protesting the cut in welfare and social assistance checks and those protesting against these same government handouts. Most of those against the handouts blame foreigners who many claim are draining the coffers of their country.

These actions come on the heels of a series of failed bond auctions, leaving the country unable to fund the monthly payouts to its citizens.

Garret walked around the kitchen, smiling. He couldn't believe how well everything was going. He didn't care about the welfare of the people. He cared for his own power, prestige, and wealth only, all of which were growing rapidly. The food he'd delivered a few days ago was being put to good use. He was feeding the hungry residents and building his little empire. Walking out back to the porch and patio area, he smiled and greeted many of the people who were out there eating in the sunshine. This is where he found Rick with his family near the end of the patio eating their lunch.

Rick, that little stooge, he's my favorite of them of all. Let him think he is in charge. People look to him to organize stuff, but they know who is taking care of them.

"Rick, I think we need to talk again about stepping up security, and we need to start working on the re-supply plans," Garret said, as he approached the family.

He grabbed an empty chair and positioned it so that he was close enough to talk, but not close enough to intrude on the meal. In reality, he was trying to get a good vantage point to stare at Rick's young wife without it being too obvious.

"Well, according to the radio broadcast, there is going to be another relief shipment coming in tomorrow. We are going to get everyone together again to go," Rick replied in between bites.

"Well, that didn't work out for us too well last time, did it?"

"No, it didn't, which is probably why they openly broadcast that looters or anyone causing a disturbance would be shot. Seriously, that is what they said, plain as day for everyone to hear."

"Would serve them right," Garret said, with a sneer in his voice.

"Would it? Would it really? They are just trying to get food for themselves, for their families. Does that warrant being shot?"

Garret thought. *As long as it's them and not me, yes it does. Or if they have what I want, then yes it does. But I better play along. He is in the dark, and he is going to stay that way.*

Garret replied, "No, it doesn't, but if people keep breaking order like that, nothing is ever going to get better. I hope no one gets hurt, but we need order. Anyway, what's the plan?"

"Well, the broadcast said that every adult will be given an equal share, so we need to try to bring as many people as possible. That isn't going to be easy, because almost everyone is out of gas. We are going to need to load everyone up into as few cars as possible. They said they're working toward bi-weekly re-supplies, so I doubt they will be handing out large quantities of stuff."

"All right, sounds good. Send as many people as we can. This leads to my other topic."

"Security? You think we need to increase again? We just drafted everyone to spend time on the watch."

"I know, but last night, how many people did the people on patrol scare off?"

"Only four, two separate guys and then a pair of guys trying to sneak around."

"And we still had a house broken into? So we missed at least one group. And so far, just a show of presence has scared them off."

"Yeah, yeah, but what else should we do?"

"First, we need to make sure we have plenty of security visible while you and everyone goes to the relief drop. That would be the perfect time for someone to waltz right in. Next, I want to put together a set of patrol groups, an extra set of three or four men to beef up the security at night. If we can get three of these groups going, I think it would be a great addition."

"And how do we field these teams?" Rick said, unconvinced of the idea on any level.

"Well, I want to go door to door and help perform security checks, and see who needs help securing their houses. A lot of people still have no way to tell that someone is breaking in until the intruder is already in the house. Part of the check will be to help secure windows and doors and put up protection or warning systems. We'll find out who has guns and knows how to use them. We'll ask who wants to help secure the neighborhood by patrolling at night."

Rick paused to think it over, not wanting to say the wrong thing to the hero of the day, "Well, I think you are right. We need to be doing more. Let's talk about it tonight at the meeting. Maybe we can put together a set of steps everyone should be taking and share them tonight. We can also ask for more help again. But we have to be careful of pushing everyone too hard."

"All right, I like that. I think that might work. I will get the guys together, and we'll put some details together to share tonight," Garret replied, as he stood up and waved to the kids before making an exit.

Perfect. I'll get the guys together all right. I've got plenty of plans for what is needed.

Garret walked over to Rob's house and sent him out to get the two teenagers. Garrett called them Tweedle-Dee and Tweedle-Dum behind their backs. Rob asked about Thomas, the other man who had volunteered to help, but Garret just scoffed at the question. He hated that man, always meddling in stuff Garret didn't want him meddling in.

"Actually, why don't you have Thomas start gathering up any cans, string, and tape he can find? And we should have him find a couple copies of the neighborhood directory," Garret said, as he shooed Rob out to execute his tasks.

If he is going to be in my business, he can at least do the most menial crap that I don't want to do myself. Plus, it will be good to have someone to pick on with Dee and Dum. It builds camaraderie.

Later that night, Garret brought up the need to increase security and to have more volunteers for watch and patrol. He also addressed the need for volunteers to help setup alarms and secure houses with fences and tangle foot and secure windows and doors. He didn't expect to get much traction yet, but he was surprised by how quickly it was dismissed. The only response he got was a question about what a tangle foot was. The neighborhood's inhabitants were starting to be bothered by the meetings and were becoming more apathetic by the day.

It had been six days since the power had gone out and had never come back on. The temperatures were hovering around 80, people had stopped being upset and had begun becoming outright hostile toward each other. Even with the burned down and looted buildings just outside the neighborhood and the frequent transients sneaking in, no one seemed to care about the need to increase security. Garret knew it was going to get worse since everyday more refugees fled the city with no goals or plans other than to look for food and any resemblance of normalcy. The refugees thought that something good must be beyond the horizon.

On the way out of the meeting, Garret grabbed Tweedle-Dee and Tweedle-Dum and asked them for a favor—just a small one that required the help of a couple of their acquaintances. He would offer them food, booze, or other booty in exchange for their help to scare the neighborhood.

I'll scare the living daylights out of them and also finally get back at that jerk who tried to call me out.

Later that night, the boys snuck out of the neighborhood and rendezvoused with a few of their even less savory friends.

The rest of the afternoon, Garret worked up his plans for tomorrow. He was going to be the head of security and after his plan had been carried out, people were going to be begging for his help.

***

The next morning as always, Margaret woke up before the sun rose and started getting ready for the day. Her first activity was preparing breakfast, oatmeal for the kids, which took longer than it used to, now that she had to soak the oats in water in order to speed up the cooking time. While the oats were soaking, she made the ritual trip out to the garden to gather the ripest produce for the day's meal.

Stepping into the backyard, she had only taken a handful of steps toward the garden when she stopped. There was no need to keep going. The garden was gone. Not just picked over. The plants, all of them, were gone. Instead of fumbling around in the dark, trying to find the good produce, the thieves had packed up everything to rummage through later when they had light.

***

"Now, Thomas, I know I can trust you with this. This is going to be a very important task, but we can't let everyone know about it," Garret said in a calm even tone.

"What? What is it? Why would we need to keep anything a secret?" Thomas said, dumbfounded at the entire idea of secrecy.

"Thomas, of all the volunteers, I think you are the only one trustworthy enough to do this. If you don't think it's right, let me know. But I'm sure you will agree that we need to do it, and then you will understand that it needs to be secret."

"OK, well, what is it that you think we need to do?" Thomas said, with a tremble in his voice.

"Relax, it's nothing bad, just information. We need to record details about how many people are in each house, how much food they have, whether they want to help with security or food, how secure their house is, whether they need any help with stuff, whether they have any guns, and how many children and adults live there. We should get as much detail as possible about these questions." Garret slipped through the guns topic as nonchalantly as he could.

"Why would we need all of that? I mean, it would be nice to know some of that, but what would it help with?"

"What wouldn't it help with? It will help with planning. It will let us know how many people are in our neighborhood and how many of them are kids. It would be helpful to know how many single moms with kids live in our neighborhood because we need to look after them."

Thomas bought it, hook, line, and sinker.

"Yeah, I guess you're right, that will all be helpful. But why do you want it to be so secretive? I mean, what—"

Garret interrupted him, "If you know how helpful it could be, how hard would it be to use it for bad? What if we found out that someone had plenty of food and then wanted to keep them from eating with everyone else? Or worse, what if someone wanted to break in and take it?"

Thomas looked at him blankly, realizing the gravity of the situation.

Garret continued, "And now you understand why I can only trust you, and why it needs to be kept secret, for now. OK?"

Thomas nodded his head, and then headed out the door to execute his task.

***

"All right, everyone aboard!" Rick said, loudly for everyone to hear.

All forty passengers climbed into the assigned vehicles. There were two pickups, three minivans, two SUVs, and a dirt bike, which was going to lead the way. Many thought it was overkill to have a "scout bike." They didn't feel comfortable with nearly everyone being armed. Most had not been out of the neighborhood for a week and had no idea what the outside world was like. A few minutes later, the convoy pulled through the roadblocks that prevented easy access by road and headed toward the relief drop.

Going down the road, the occupants stared wide-eyed at the destruction around them; most businesses and several houses they passed had either been smashed in and looted or burned to the ground. Cars had broken down and been looted, some had been burned out, and two had been riddled with bullet holes. For the past week, people had been angry and upset that they were dissuaded from leaving the neighborhood for their own safety. Most people didn't believe the stories of those who did brave trips, and there were no stories from the few who didn't make it back at all.

Pulling up to the relief station, they saw thousands and thousands of people already waiting. Luckily, this time, there seemed to be at least a sense of order. Four Humvees were positioned around the parking lot as well as about a dozen police cars, all with uniformed officers. Near the center of the parking lot was a black and grey APC, a military style armored personnel carrier, flanking a steel "riot tower" that had been recently purchased for the local police department. Alongside the APC were several rows of men who were handcuffed and their heads were bent down.

The convoy learned the story of the day. Early fights and shoving matches had been put down by liberal use of pepper and OC spray. A few of the more violent confrontations had been squashed by lethal force. The details of the killed and wounded weren't readily available, but several of each had occurred before the crowds calmed down and order was restored.

***

Back at the subdivision, Garret looked at his watch and said to himself, "12:15, and show time any second."

He and his posse were walking rounds through the streets, checking in on the manned post at the western most entrance when the first shot was heard clear across the other side of the neighborhood.

"Crap, what was that?" Rob said at the sound of the shot, which was quickly followed by at least a dozen more.

Pointing at Thomas, Garret said "You stay here to provide backup."

Then he pointed to Tweedle-Dee and Tweedle-Dum, "You two cut across that way. Rob and I will circle around, taking the road."

The two teens nodded, trying hard to keep smiles off of their faces, and then took off, running between houses and toward the sound of the gunfire.

The sound of gunfire continued intermittently for the next few minutes when Garret and Rob came to the checkpoint nearest the fighting. Only one man was there still, hiding inside the open door of one of the parked cars. The other was nowhere to be seen.

"They are over that way. There are a few of them. Matt was here with me and ran over to chase them off," the man said.

"You know where he is?" Garret asked.

"No, just that way, somewhere."

"All right, this way we go," Garret said, as he ran off toward the firefight.

By the time they were outside the house, smoke was billowing out of the shot-out windows on both the first and second floors, and fire could be seen clearly from the outside. The hoodlums whom he had recruited for the job were nowhere to be seen after executing his plan perfectly.

Garret kicked in the front door and yelled "Anybody in here? We need to get you out of here!"

He waited a few seconds; then, yelled loudly, "HELLO, ANYONE STILL IN HERE?" This time, a few unintelligible replies could be heard coming from the upstairs.

Just like it should be. For punk kids, they sure did execute well.

Running upstairs, Garrett pulled a wet shemagh from the small pack he was carrying and tied it over his face to filter out the hot air and smoke.

Good thing I packed this before heading out.

He kept yelling and popping doors open until he finally made it to the master bedroom where he found the inhabitants tied up and huddling in the corner. He stepped over and quickly cut the duct tape that was wrapped around the woman's legs and helped her to her feet. Then he picked up her daughter and led them down the stairs and to the outside.

"Is there anyone else in there?" Garret asked, tersely trying to get the attention of the hysterical woman.

Of course not, your jerk of a husband is off waiting in line for food, but I've got to make this look good.

"Uhhh, no, no, it's just us," She said, in a barely coherent voice, with tears streaming down her face.

Rob was helping her remove duct tape from a young girl, and Garret gathered up the teens and all the other onlookers to start trying to put out the fire. A bucket brigade was started to carry water up from a nearby retention pond. To everyone's surprise, except Garret's, it didn't take long to get the fire under control because it had been started in two metal trash cans and hadn't spread beyond those rooms. Garret's plan called for a scary fire, not a destructive one.

There was no power or fire department to help, so he didn't want the whole neighborhood to go up in flames. After he'd dumped a bucket of water inside each can and to make the fire look worse than it really was, Garret kicked the cans across the room, spreading the contents. After getting the fires under control, they saturated the house with water to get rid of any potential "hot spots" that might flair up.

By this time, dozens of people were doing what they could to help. And a few dozen people stood there staring, not knowing what else to do.

Plenty of people here now. And lo and behold, look who was here to save the day again. ME. Sometimes I can't believe how easy this is. They all see me as a hero, and I get to shut up this stupid lady's husband. I just saved your wife's and daughter's life. You want to disagree with me now?

Garret walked back inside one last time. This time he was by himself. He checked through each room, slipping a few items into his pack as he went. He then walked out the back door and went home to enjoy his handiwork.

***

A few hours later, the relief convoy arrived at the drop point. By this time, the crowd had tripled in size. There were so many cars and people packed in that small area, that it reminded Rick of tailgating at OSU football games. He estimated that there had to be close to as many people there as at the games. Even though the convoy was supposed to be for local residents only, the turn out included thousands, or more likely tens of thousands, of additional bodies.

Someone was overheard gossiping about how people had fled downtown and the more densely populated areas surrounding it. The story described how people were walking, since those who had gas were already long gone. People were grouping together–the smallest groups containing 50 to100 people —but most were several hundred people large. No one really knew why they were forming these groups, but most speculated it was for safety from robbers or gangs. Others said it was for safety from retaliation for the looting and robbery they were committing along the way.

Before the convoy even stopped, people were swarming over each other, pushing, shoving, punching and kicking their way toward the trucks. A few seconds later, the loud sound of flash bang grenades going off could be heard. That was followed by the hiss of OC grenades, which fogged the area with pepper spray and quickly broke up the hoard.

Someone came over the PA system and gave directions on the process, assuring people that there would be enough for everyone. Rick and his crew weren't so sure about how honest they were after seeing the size of the crowd.

Everyone was to get an aid package and would have the right hand stamped with a UV dye after receiving the package. Anyone found with an aid package but not stamped would be immediately arrested. Also, as soon as someone received a package, the individual was to vacate the premises for safety. Anyone who caused any sort of disruption would be arrested and would not receive any aid today.

After the first round of mace grenades was released to break up a brawl, there weren't any more fights, and people slowly made their way to the trucks where they were given a brown box containing various food items. Wherever the boxes were packed, there obviously wasn't any plan other than fill a box with stuff, tape it shut, and then fill another one. It took almost two hours for the group to make it to the front of the line and get their packages. Other than a few offers from people to buy their boxes, they didn't have any problems getting out and driving back home.

Another two hours later, about two thirds of the gathered crowd had received their packages when the last truck was emptied. No one had really noticed the disappearance of the police and soldiers—who had pulled out in anticipation of what would happen when the food ran out. And they knew stopping it would be impossible. Those who had received the last few packages were quickly attacked by anyone who was still hanging around and hadn't received anything. If the victims were lucky, they were relieved only of their food. A few unlucky ones lost their lives.

Chapter 22

Radio Broadcast: In local news, we are updating the citizens of New York City that until further notice all passage between New York City and New Jersey has been shutoff. This action was taken after protesters started walking to the city in response to the managed power shutdowns that have left the state of New Jersey without power in order to keep New York supplied with power.

The Governor of New Jersey is calling for the arrest of the Governor of New York for giving the orders to shut down the power to New Jersey. New Jersey's governor has said that he and his state will not soon forget this.

Without a cloud in the sky, the sun came up brighter than it had in the past few days. It was so bright that John pulled out his hat to shield some of the light. But because of the low angle of the sun, it didn't really help. John had already been walking for several hours so he decided to take a short stop to rest and eat. He let the sun rise a little more so he can avoid it directly in his eyes when he resumed walking.

After the break, he continued down the desolate country road. It had been a day since he last saw a live human being. He knew that there were still plenty of people around, but they were being cautious, hiding and staying well out of sight when he walked by. Even though he was also being caution without slowing down too much, he knew that on several occasions, eyes and very likely guns were on him as he passed by collapsed buildings or seemingly abandoned campsites.

He kept up a decent pace for a few hours before he decided to take another break shortly after noon. Having been up and walking for about seven hours, he sorely needed rest. The first few days of walking weren't too bad since he had still felt fresh. But after a couple of days, he'd became very tired and worn out. Now, a few more days later, he could feel his body getting used to the long hours of walking. Overall, however, he was still on the verge of exhaustion since he never had a chance to catch up on sleep.

He kept walking for a few minutes until he found an abandoned SUV that was pulled off to the side of the road. The back seat made a great place to stretch out and relax for a few minutes. It wasn't his intention to fall asleep, but he did. He wasn't sure how long he had been asleep for when he snapped awake because of sound nearby.

Crap. What was that? How did I fall asleep?

He scanned the area outside the car, looking for whatever woke him, and not finding the source. He kept peering and studying for the next few minutes as his heart continued beating at a rapid and heavy pace. Eventually, he saw the bottle of water that fell out of his backpack to the floor. It was the cause of the sound that woke him from his impromptu nap.

Serves me right, I was just supposed to rest my legs not fall asleep.

He picked up the bottle of water and took a long drink from it before putting it back in the backpack. This time, he zipped it completely shut.

Back on the road, he pushed through a long morning and longer afternoon until the sun started to set at his back. Trying to find a decent place to hide for the night, he'd walked a little further than he'd intended, as he tried to find a decent place to hide out for the night. The extra distance took him down a side street, where he found some trees and shrubs that he could hide between.

Using his knife, he sliced free a few large leafy branches from some of the bushes and brushed clear a small area that he turned into a den to sleep in for the night. After a quick dinner, he spent about half an hour stretching his overly sore and worn out muscles. After that much-needed stretch, John burrowed into his den and covered himself with the leafy branches and fell asleep.

When something awoke him, it was still pitch black out, and John guessed it was somewhere around midnight or one. He wasn't sure if it was a sound that woke him because his motion of sitting up caused a lot of rustling of leaves and branches. He stopped moving and tried to listen, but if there was anything there, he couldn't see or hear it. Unfortunately, the sky was overcast, and there was no star or moonlight available to provide visibility.

There! What was that?

A small light flashed somewhere a few dozen yards away.

A firefly? Too late at night for that, but what else could it be? It wasn't bright enough to be a flashlight, and it looked to be too close to be anything else.

He spent a few more minutes scanning the area and didn't see or hear anything so he slowly lay back down.

It had to have been a firefly, he told himself. *But why was it green?*

He fell back into an uneasy sleep.

He awoke again, this time to something brushing against his face. Reaching up with his hand, he tried brushing it away. He was startled when his hand struck something hard and cold. He started to sit up, and the offending sensation turned into a sharp pain as it pushed him back down.

"Hold it right there, don't move," said a voice with a thick southern drawl.

John couldn't see anything and was still having trouble getting his wits about him when a bright flashlight clicked on, pointed directly in his eyes, and completely blinded him.

"You just hold real still now. Don't want you to get yourself hurt," The voice continued.

Bright, damn bright. I can't see anything.

"My deputy is going to take your side arm. Don't move and everything will be OK."

His deputy? And is this guy for real. He sounds as if he is straight out of some old western, or that movie Deliverance.

A second man started pulling gear away from John's body, starting with his pistol.

What the heck is going on here?

John didn't move a muscle and still couldn't see anything except for the blinding white light shining directly into his eyes. The voice continued.

"OK, so now. That's a nice piece. I don't suppose this is your home, is it?" the voice said, laughing at its own question.

"No, no, why? What's going on?" John stammered to the voice behind the light.

"Well son, you are still in Illinois, you know what that means?"

John didn't know what to say to this, and the voice didn't give him a chance to think when it said, "It means you are breaking the law by having this out here. Not to mention we are under marshal law. Out here, this gun makes you liable to be executed on sight."

What the heck, John's mind was screaming at the man's last words.

It took a few seconds, but John finally was able to get something out, "I'm just passing through—." But he was cut off as the barrel pressed hard into the side of his face.

"That's all right. We'll check your story. Don't worry. You'll get a real bed and a meal tonight."

This brought a laugh from the man who was now rolling him over and placing handcuffs on him.

With the barrel of a gun still pressed firmly against his face, he figured it wasn't a good idea to try to resist. A few seconds later, John was on his knees, facing the ground as he was thoroughly searched from head to toe. After that search was completed, he was searched again.

"Don't worry. We've still got a cell set up for any lawbreakers. It's not too bad. You'll get along pretty well there." This time, both the men laughed together.

They directed him roughly, shoving him down the road in complete darkness. The two men each had night vision goggles, NVGs, which let them clearly see where they were going. But John was still blind from the darkness, often tripping or bumping into things in the dark.

I think they are doing this on purpose. How much can they rough me up before they lock me up? This has to be some sick game.

***

About ten minutes later, they arrived at a paved road where a golf cart was parked. John was put on the back seat, and his handcuffs repositioned around one of the bars that made up the frame of the cart. A set of cuffs was also placed on his legs; it was looped through the frame of the base board where his feet rested. After that a rope was slipped over his head and rested right around his neck like a noose. He could see the end of it wasn't tied to the frame, but was held slightly taut in the hands of the man not driving.

"Hold on. We wouldn't want you to fall off and hurt yourself," The man said, with a sinister laugh.

They zipped down the road for about fifteen minutes before they pulled to a stop in front of a brick building that was in surprisingly good shape. They lead him through the front doors, which were heavy metal with wire reinforced glass. The sign on the front door showed that it was the local Sherriff's office.

Well, at least this is just the second worst thing that could happen at this point. Being in the hands of law enforcement has to be better than being in the hands of random criminals.

They walked him down the hallway and into a cell, where they uncuffed him only to re-cuff him again with his hands in front.

"Without power, we want to take some extra precautions," the man said, slamming the heavy steal door shut.

"Toilet doesn't work, but use it if you have to. Just know we are going to make you clean it out tomorrow. No talking, period. Talk and we'll taze you … if you're lucky. Try to run. We shoot you. No questions asked," the man said, and then paused for a few seconds as if he wanted a response.

John didn't give him the gratification, knowing that any response would probably draw a physically painful reply. It was something he could tell the jailor wanted.

"Don't cause a problem, and you won't have a problem. Just shut up and go to sleep. Got it?" the man said, disappointed he didn't get to abuse his ward.

"Yes sir." was John's only response.

The cell was deathly quiet. It was so quiet he could hear several other people's heavy breathing as they slept—or at least pretended to sleep. He found the bed protruding from the wall and lay down and tried to get some sleep. His mind was racing too fast for any real rest. He knew it was a bad idea to make any noise or disturbance, so he just thought through the possibilities of what could happen when the sun rose.

Chapter 23

Radio Broadcast: In international news today, world leaders were shocked as the President of Mexico stepped down and was soon followed by almost a third of the other federally elected and appointed officials. This comes after a ceasefire was reportedly agreed to by the three largest drug cartels in the country. Through various sources, they leaked messages to the media giving gruesome details of what will happen to any and all who stand in their way.

Along with this news come reports that units of relief workers from Mexico in southern California are now taking on the role of an occupying force. The reports included the disarmament of local police forces and any remaining military and National Guard personnel.

"What the heck are we going to do?" screamed one man.

It was a sentiment shared by almost everyone in attendance at the meeting. Tensions were higher than ever after two skirmishes earlier in the day left a house badly damaged from fire and smoke, two residents badly beaten, and three people dead. Although not many people in attendance seemed to care about the people who were killed since they assailants who had tried to infiltrate the neighborhood and had caused the damages.

Even Garret had been taken by surprise by the second firefight, which had started shortly before the convoy returned from the relief drop. A group of over fifty people had walked up the road and quickly become violent when the crew at the roadblock told them to turn back. The mob had quickly overtaken and beaten the two men stationed at the roadblock. Luckily for them, Garret and his two teen lackeys had been nearby and quickly opened up a rapid barrage of gunfire, driving the crowd back. They weren't sure how many they'd hit. Some had limped away or been dragged off, but three had been left behind after the crowd had disappeared. Two of the victims were dead within minutes; the third took several hours to die.

"What do we do if they come back?" asked one person in attendance.

"What if they just start shooting next time? We were lucky this time!" asked another.

No one was able to calm the crowd or commotion. The entire meeting continued to gather more steam as everyone vented their frustrations. The neighborhood was acting like a mob instead of an organized community. Garret leaned back against one of the trees lining the backyard and used willpower to keep from cracking a smile.

Speak louder, Rick. Yell! What's wrong? No one is listening to you? I wonder why? Don't you know it's Garret who is the hero around here?

"We are so lucky that Garret was there to save the day!" One lady said in response to something he couldn't hear.

Garret smiled, *Yep, you are all very lucky to have me here, aren't you?*

A few more minutes of arguments and bickering continued before Garret stepped up and got everybody's attention.

"Ladies! Gentlemen! Please! Let's calm down for a minute," Garret said, practically yelling overtop of the rabble.

"I know everyone is scared, but we have to discuss a few things!"

He waited a few seconds for the talking to die off before he continued. He recapped the events of the day, most notably the two firefights in the neighborhood. He was the hero of the day, and everyone knew it. He was going to milk it for all it was worth. He spent a few minutes cultivating the legend of Garret before passing the discussion back to Rick to share the news about the food aid they'd picked up, and the riot that had ensued shortly after their departure.

I'll let him have a small win, especially since he gets to be associated with news of the riot.

Rick went on to explain what they'd seen and heard at the relief drop, and gave everyone all the information they had gathered. The news about how "herds" of people—just like the one that had attacked them that day—were fleeing the city toward the suburbs. Such herds were becoming increasingly frequent, and that news didn't sit well with anyone. He asked for people to brainstorm ways to deter the mobs from entering their protected space without shooting them.

A few minutes later, the meeting had broken down again, allowing Garret his chance to push his agenda on a more one-on-one basis.

"We need to have more people ready to respond, and in order to do that, we need to make sure we are utilizing our resources as a neighborhood as well as we can," He said to a small group of people.

This comment drew nods and words of agreement from everyone he talked to.

If only that asshole wouldn't have pushed me so hard about not wanting to work together, he even called me a commie, I wouldn't have picked his house to set on fire. But now, all the little sheep see that I'm the only one who can save them.

He laid out a plan to get a list of all weapons, food and other useful materials that everyone in the neighborhood had. During the next couple of days, Thomas would go by each house and perform an inspection to make sure everyone was squared away and to list all items the community might need.

Garret also worked up support and gathered commitments, to upgrade the watch. He even started talking about training and scouting missions to patrol outside the neighborhood.

Keep everyone we don't want out and bring all their loot and what we want in. This part is turning out to be easier than I ever thought possible. Everyone is just eating out of my hands.

Slowly the crowd broke into cliques, and people started wandering home. Thomas was busy going over some of his notes with Rick who was very diligently reviewing them and asking a lot of questions. Garret took this opportunity to talk to the woman who he'd eyed all evening.

Your husband is neglecting you. What a dumbass. I would never leave you alone around these people; I better come over and protect you.

"Hi, Sarah, how are you doing?" Garret said, in the sweetest voice he could muster.

"I'm fine," was her short, but polite response.

Garret walked in uncomfortably close; then, stretched his arm, propping himself up against a nearby tree and bringing him still closer to the woman.

"You holding up OK? It must be tough on you, especially with your husband being so busy helping out all the time."

"Yeah, it's hard. But it's hard for everyone. You'll have to excuse me. I've got to get the kids home, almost bedtime," she said, stepping back from the cramped space.

She walked to where her children were playing, gave a quick update to Rick, who was still deep in discussion, and started home.

***

A few minutes later, Sarah shut and locked the front door behind her. Almost immediately, she heard a knock coming from the other side.

"Hello?" she said, cautiously walking back toward the door. She could see a figure through the frosted glass, but she couldn't make out who it was.

"Rick?"

"No, it's me. Garret."

"Garret? What do you want?"

"I've got a quick question for you. Do you have a second?"

She hesitatingly unlocked the door and opened it just a crack, "Yes?"

"I just want to make sure you're OK. Is there *anything* you need?"

"No. Thank you, though, but we are OK."

"I mean it. Anything," Garret said, as he pushed the door open and stepped inside.

"No, no, uhhh, no. Really, we are fine," she replied, her voice starting to become panicky.

Her heart started to race. Afraid, wondering what the man's intentions might be.

"It's OK. I just want to make sure you are taken care of. It's OK," he said, smiling.

"We're fine, but ... but I've got to put the kids to bed."

"Good. Go ahead, and send them upstairs."

She did, trying to get the children out of possible harm's way and to buy as much time as she could. The situation just didn't feel right. As a matter of fact, it felt very wrong.

"Now, they will be OK for a little while. Where were we?" Garret started closing in on her again.

Before he could get too close, the front door opened, revealing Rick in the doorway.

"Oh, hey! Rick! I was wondering when you were going to be back."

"Why? What do you need?" Rick replied, surprised to see the man in his house. He quickly followed up with "What are you doing here?"

"Just walked your precious ones home. Can't be too safe. Just helping out since you were busy," Garret said, with a smile and small chuckle.

Rick didn't laugh, "Well ... Thanks ... I guess I'll see you tomorrow?"

"Yeah, I'll swing by. We have a lot to discuss. See you tomorrow."

***

After leaving Rick's house, Garret went on his nightly rounds, checking each of the blockades. He stopped to visit a few key friends in the neighborhood before heading home, where his wife was waiting for him.

"I know she is pretty, but she is married with kids, and you just creep up on her like that?"

"Woman, you better watch your mouth. You don't know what the heck you are talking about anyway."

"Garret, I know you. I know what you're thinking."

"If you know me, you know you better shut your mouth, too, don't you?"

She stopped talking and just hung her head, staring at the floor.

"Yeah, you know I'm right," Garret said as he walked over close to her.

It took a while for his adrenaline to wear off before he could fall asleep. He had worked up a sweat and rush from the violent workout.

Serves her right. She got what she deserved. She'll learn not to talk back to me.

It wasn't until several hours later that Garret's wife regained consciousness and was able to slowly crawl—her body badly damaged—out of the closet where Garret had left her.

Chapter 24

Radio Broadcast: We go now to our senior war correspondent. Good evening, this is Doug Horton coming to you from New York. With the temporary withdrawal of US forces from the Middle East, Israel is coming under attack from three directions by a coalition of different countries. Currently, Israeli forces using superior technology and firepower have driven each attacking line back easily. But the number of assailants begs the question of how long can they hold out.

That morning, John didn't really wake up since he never really fell asleep, but at some point, as the sun started lighting up the sky, the cell area he was in came to life. A pair of men started escorting the other prisoners, one by one, out. At last three men came to the cell for John.

"All right, here. As I'm sure you are aware, we are under martial law right now. That makes your offense of the possession of an illegal handgun all the worse," the man standing behind the other two officers said.

He paused for a few minutes, looking for John's reaction and sizing him up before he continued.

"In some parts of the state, they are shooting people for such violations. Count yourself lucky. As I said, we are under martial law and that makes me the ranking sheriff of the county, the one stop shop. Police, judge, and jury."

You left out executioner, John added silently.

The Sheriff paused for a few seconds more, hoping to get a rise out of John but it didn't come.

"You're sentenced to two months of hard labor. We need strong backs to help dig ourselves out of this situation, and who better to help us than those who ignore the law? After that, you will be free to go on your way, minus your paraphernalia, of course."

The man let out a small chuckle, and a big grin crossed his face.

"But let me warn you. If you cause a problem, try to escape, heck, even look at me or my men funny, we will have no problem shortening your stay ... If you get what I mean."

Right on cue, the men in front of him both motioned suggestively to the black carbines hanging from slings in front of them and then smiled wickedly. They unlocked the door and led John out to the hallway where they checked his handcuffs, ensuring they were still secure. Then they pulled out two extra sets of cuffs and reset them so that now, he had three sets of handcuffs chained across his hands.

"This will give you just enough room to work," the man said in response to the quizzical look on John's face.

The man directed John down the hallway and out the front doors where the other officer and four other law-breakers stood. The three men each had tools like shovels and pick axes in their hands, and another had a bucket of hammers, screwdrivers, and other miscellaneous tools. The crew walked down the road, sandwiched between the two officers, heading toward the remains of the small downtown.

The reinforced concrete and cinder block sheriff's office was the only building in sight that hadn't collapsed in on itself. Even other traditional brick buildings were completely uninhabitable. As they passed, each building, John noticed that propped up on the front of the remains was a door or large board that had been flagged with different colors or symbols. The only consistent one was a large black "X" sometimes followed by a number in red. A few others had a green slash or green "X" behind the other symbols.

Those mean something, a standard code, but they don't look anything like what I remember DHS and FEMA using in past disasters. If these guys were in charge, you would think they would be using the national standards.

A few minutes later, they came to a stop in front of the remains of a house.

One of the guards first pointed to one of the prisoners, then back to John, "You, teach him the ropes. Food, guns, cash, jewelry, electronics, yadda yadda yadda. You know the drill."

Then the officer set out a folding chair he had been carrying and sat down, keeping an icy cold glare on John and the other prisoners. The other officer walked halfway across the yard to the side of the house and did the same. This gave them both relaxed seats with a view of all sides of the heap.

The prisoner sheepishly walked over and waved for John to follow him toward the building.

"First, shut up, and don't say anything," The man said. He barely glanced up long enough to see John's response and then sneaked a quick look over to the seated officer.

"We pretty much are looking for anything useful or valuable. If you think it might be worth something or be useful go ahead and bring it out. Worst thing that happens then is we toss it back. If you miss something, don't. Don't talk. Don't ask questions. If we don't find food and plenty of other good stuff, we don't eat."

He looked back up for a split second to make sure that John was still paying attention, and then glanced back at the officer who was starting to lose interest.

"Just play it safe, and we'll all go home at night." The man said. And with one last glance back at the guard, he very quietly said, "Give them a reason, any reason, and they will shoot you."

With that, the man led John up to what was once the front door and started pushing debris out of the way, working his way inside the collapsed structure.

"Oh, and keep your eyes out for a pair of gloves, you'll need them."

A last look around before heading in, John saw the other men digging through what was left of the garage and the two officers casually leaning back in their chairs.

The next few hours were quickly consumed as John and his mentor dug through the remains of the house. They first worked their way through to the kitchen, searching for any food or food products available. Inside, a smashed pantry and in a few crushed cabinets, they found several cans of food, noodles, and other dry goods. The smell of rotting food leaking from the refrigerator made it hard to breathe, but they spent nearly an hour scouring the room. The other man kept stuffing everything into a canvas bag until it was full; then, he sent John outside to empty it and return. There were four of these trips to drop off food, some high-end kitchen knives, lots of spices and seasonings, garbage and reseal able plastic bags, and a handful of other odds and ends.

Next, they worked through the other rooms, not finding much of anything until they found a box full of formal silverware. "Might be real silver," the man said as he slid it into a canvas bag.

Working through a few other rooms, they found a first aid kit, rubbing alcohol, and tooth paste, all went in the bag. The real find happened in the master bedroom: a collection of nice watches and the contents of a jewelry box.

By the time they had finished scouring the remains of the house, it was a few hours past noon. The other men were already finished in the garage. They'd found a couple small gas cans, drained the car's gas tank, and pulled out a small pile of tools and hardware. While they were waiting, they had been salvaging lumber and other building supplies that weren't too damaged and making a pile in the front yard.

One of the officers guarding them culled out a few pieces of food and tossed it at the prisoners, "Eat up! Quick! We still want to get through three more houses today, so you better be quick about everything!" he said.

The prisoners roughly jockeyed for position over the food and quickly devoured the little that was provided. John wasn't ready for this game and ended up getting almost nothing to eat as the other men jumped and shoved, grabbing at what they could.

In the next house, while wriggling through the remains of the kitchen, John pulled out a large box of breakfast bars sealed in foil-lined wrappers.

"You want one?" John asked. "I'm starving!"

"Don't even think about it. Sure, you might get away with it, but if they catch you eating something or sneaking something, they will ..." the man slowly fell silent, looking around.

"What, shoot me? Really?"

The man nodded the affirmative.

"Really? And how would they know?"

"Maybe I tell them? I won't, but you don't know that for sure. One of the other guys might tell. They send us in regularly to check on each other, and they even try to have us set each other up."

He sighed heavily and then continued, "We shouldn't even be talking. If someone hears us, we'd be lucky if they just beat us."

John started to ask another question, but before he could get it out, the man cut him off, "SHHHH! Let's just get back to work."

Not more than ten seconds after the short conversation, almost as if on cue, one of the men from the other group came in to check up on them. He sent John's mentor outside to perform some other duties.

The next house went more quickly with results similar to the first two, and they finished with just over an hour's worth of daylight left. Once again, a guard peeled off some of the least appetizing food and tossed it to the crew of prisoners to fight over. Once again, John didn't get a decent amount of food before the others had wolfed it down.

For some reason, I don't expect I'll be able to hold out like this for two months, not that I was planning on doing so anyway. I just need to figure out how to get out of here.

They didn't full search the last house before it became too dark to finish and they headed back to the sheriff's office. By the time they made it back, it was dark outside and only a few dim lights shined through the darkness inside the building. The officers replaced the single set of handcuffs on the prisoners before walking them into the building. Inside, a handful of other deputies were sitting around, talking and playing cards, all smiling and laughing up a storm.

When they made it back to the cells, John was surprised to see that there were a number of other prisoners already there. All handcuffed, looking forlorn and dejected; all were dirty from head to toe and smelled worse than a high school locker room. John was roughly shoved into a cell different from last night. This time, he was with two other men.

"Why don't you introduce yourself, get to know one another," the officer said with a wicked little cackle as he shut the steel bar door.

He reached down to his belt and pulled a black cylinder from a pouch. Flicking his wrist the cylinder extended into a steel baton about two feet long.

"Go ahead, say 'Hi!' Please!" he egged on.

None of the men inside the cell acknowledged him. A few seconds later, he sighed while walking away, "Nobody wants me to have any fun, do they?"

That night John was able to get a little sleep, but only after playing through every bit of information he could put together.

Something isn't right, and I know if I stay here, I won't make it out alive. None of us will. First, we are looting, and it makes a little sense the way we are doing it. These guys just want to get rich. Second, everyone is afraid. Sounds as if the M.O. is to push, aggravate, and instigate. If anything happens, shoot the prisoners. I haven't seen it, but these men are scared, and these cops seem to like it that way. But for some reason, I don't think they are just bluffing. Next, I know I'm in the middle of nowhere Illinois, but these are some good ol' boys, sounding as if they came straight out of Dixie.

He replayed more of the day, trying to remember every detail he could. He stopped when he realized a few items that seemed to play together. For some reason, even though it was a hot day in the 80s, each officer was wearing long sleeves. It made sense. He thought he remembered seeing spots of ink showing from under the sleeve of one of the officers.

These aren't even cops! How haven't I put that together already? If they aren't cops, who are they, and what is really going on here?

His sleep was uneasy. He tossed and dreamed about his predicament and how he was going to get out of it. Even if he overcame this obstacle, he still had a long ways to go before making it home.

Chapter 25

Radio Broadcast: We bring you a report that the newly appointed President of Mexico has declared a large portion of the southwest United States as a part of Mexico. This follows the aggressive moves of the Mexican army throughout major cities, dislocating inhabitants at the behest of the drug king pins that control the puppet government.

The response to this aggression continues to be mounted, but the current inability to contact and transport troops and machinery leaves the United States at a distinct disadvantage.

The morning came without fanfare and the same process was performed again. Each man was led out one by one at gunpoint, in preparation for their work duty. John was loaded into the back of a truck with three other men whom he hadn't yet met and two guards, one of whom was different from yesterday. The other prisoners were divided into two groups that headed in different directions.

A few minutes later, John's crew arrived at the house they'd left off the night before, and he was sent directly in with a simple command of "Pick up where you left off, and make it quick."

The uniformed man sent the other men into a neighboring house to scavenge it.

Digging through the debris, John made quick work of what was left of the house. He found a few valuables to bring out. The next house was larger and took a while longer, but he found very little of interest. It seemed as if the house was likely uninhabited at the time of the quake. When coming out nearly empty-handed, John was quickly derided by the guard.

"What the heck is the problem, you better get back in there and find me something good!"

John didn't reply, but looked at the man and shrugged his shoulders a very slight motion. The guard quickly closed the ground between them while pulling out his metal baton and extending it full length. John readied himself for a fight, ready to pound the man into the ground when he noticed the other guard now only a few feet away, gun pointed, finger on the trigger, straight at him.

Now might not be the best time.

The first few strikes didn't seem to do much damage, coming down on his back and the back of his legs, but the next few made good work of his head and shoulders. The beating only lasted a few seconds, but John was sprawled out on the ground, barely able to move by the time it was over. Blood flowed freely from multiple gashes and lacerations.

"Now, get back in there and find me something good!" the guard said.

"I think we just toss him back and find a new mule to carry our goods." said the other with an evil look on his face, still pointing his gun at John.

"Wish we could, but we are starting to run out of fresh recruits. Let's give him one more shot."

The second guard was obviously disappointed by this and walked up to John and pressed the barrel of his gun to John's temple.

"Give me a reason, please. Pretty please, I'll make it quick and painless. You worthless piece of trash."

It took close to half an hour for John to gather himself enough to get back into the house and research the wreckage. He didn't find anything else in the second pass and reluctantly came back out completely empty handed. Luckily, the guards didn't seem to care this time. They must have realized that there really must not have been much in the house. Deciding to take more revenge, they denied him lunch.

The rest of the day went on uneventfully as he scoured three more houses top to bottom. Luckily, these houses had plenty to keep the men happy. One even had a basement with a full pantry of canned goods, cleaning supplies, and other useable goods. The guards were very happy with this find, and it took over a dozen trips to bring it all out. Unfortunately, each trip was harrowing since the main floor was half collapsed into the basement, and John knew it wasn't a safe exercise to crawl through this wreckage.

If I keep this up, it won't matter what else happens. I'll end up dead in one of these heaps, working to make these guys the feudal lords they envision themselves to be.

The next day, it was the same story until mid-afternoon when another officer showed up with a new prisoner. This man was full of fight and kept shrugging off any hand that was laid on him, often receiving a punch or kick in response. Nonetheless, he kept it up. He was put to work with the men tearing through a garage. This house had a three-car garage that was full of goodies and fancy cars. John didn't pay him much attention and went back to scavenging the ruins.

John also found plenty of loot in the house: jewelry, cash, food, and even a shiny nickel revolver sandwiched between crushed boxes in the back of a damaged closet. His spirits lifted as he pulled it out of its plastic case and inspected it. Perfect condition.

This might just be my ticket out of here!

Unfortunately, it was unloaded. But John couldn't find any ammo. He did find two boxes of .357 magnum brass shell casings that had been shot and then meticulously replaced in the boxes, but not a single loaded round. He put the brass in his bag, too. For some reason he thought that if he didn't have them as proof, they would, at best, send him back in to search, but more likely, he would be on the receiving end of another beating.

With the heavy gun and boxes of casings added to his bag, he headed out of the house to make a deposit and free up room in his bag. It was past time for him to drink water anyway. At least, the prisoners were allowed to have plenty of water.

One of the guards noticed the pistol as soon as John pulled the plastic case from the bag. He was impressed with the gun and started waving in around like a child with a new toy. Seeing his buddy playing with a shiny new toy, the other guard came running over. They started arguing over who was going to get it. Each said that if he didn't get to keep the gun, he was going to tell the boss. Then, neither would get it.

While all of this was going on, the newest addition to the chain gang took his opportunity and made a run for it. The two guards didn't realize until he was already a dozen yards away running in a sprint. They immediately took position and sent several chunks of hot lead screaming after him, but all their shots missed. After the initial volley of a handful of rounds, the men both stopped firing and just stood there.

Is it really that easy? They are just going to let him run from here?

Just then, a red cloud appeared in front of the man and he crumpled forward on the ground. A little less than two seconds later, the sound from the shot reached John's ears and the guards standing next to him. Both of the guards laughed at the sight.

"He is a show off sometimes!"

"What? You think he hit him there on purpose? I'll bet it was luck."

"Nah, he always takes out their legs if he can, and leaves more for us to play with!"

"You!" said the closest guard as he pointed at John, "Go drag his sorry ass over here. And be quick about it. We don't want him to die before he's properly taken care of."

John walked to the man, who was convulsing and rolling around on the ground, covered in blood. The bullet had entered the back of his leg a few inches above the knee, or at least where his knee used to be. Now, there was a gaping hole that a softball would easily fit into.

"They sent me over here to bring you back," John said apologetically, but the man didn't even seem to notice.

John grabbed the man's arm and hoisted him up, trying his best to not get doused in red liquid while doing so. He was somewhat successful.

"That will teach him to run," said the nearest guard, laughing at the wounded man, as John laid him down in front of them.

The man's right leg wobbled freely where the bone had been shattered and the mass of his thigh had been shredded into a mushy mass. Blood was pumping out at a rapid rate.

The other guard noticed the blood loss and realized the escapee wouldn't be alive much longer, "Well I better go get the truck so we can take care of him."

He left and returned a few minutes later with a small truck and directed John to load the man into the truck and then hop in back. An additional chain was wrapped around John's handcuffs and looped through a tie down in the trucks bed.

A ten minute, five-mile ride brought them to a small field that was surrounded by trees and an old fence. Driving through the open gate, the guards parked the truck alongside a row of fresh piles of dirt. John ran a quick estimate of the number of mounds and knew there were easily over 100 piles, more likely somewhere close to 150.

150 graves? And how many people are buried in each one?

The driver hopped out and removed the chain from the truck's tie down. John felt his body tighten reflexively as he realized the opportunity he had now in the middle of nowhere with only a single guard.

Have to time it right, like as soon as I get that shovel or pickaxe in my hands. One clean swing and I'm gone.

He directed John to pull the man out of the truck. The man's breathing had stopped being noticeable sometime on the trip there. He probably had only a few more minutes of life in him. Then, the guard made a short description of the hole John was to dig: at least five feet deep and big enough to fit three people.

Three people? I hope it's just for reference.

He pointed to the spot where he wanted it dug and then grabbed a small folding chair from the truck bed. He set it up a few feet away from the side of the truck.

John walked to the back of the truck and pulled the tools out: a pickaxe and a shovel. His first thought was that the pickaxe would make a great weapon. But as soon as he hefted it in his hands, he realized it would be too slow because of its weight. The shovel with its fiberglass handle was much lighter. Watching the guard, who was still positioning his chair, John drew up the shovel and made his way toward to guard.

Ten feet. Eight feet. Six feet. I could probably reach him. And now!

John drew the shovel over his shoulder, winding up to swing it like a bat. He would use the guard's head as the baseball. Just as his muscles pulled as tight as they could, he was interrupted by a shout behind.

"Hey stupid, what are you doing?"

John froze; the voice had come from a little distance behind him, but still close enough that the person yelling didn't have to yell too loud to be heard.

He sees me; he has to know what I'm doing.

The guard stopped messing with the chair and looked up at John, who was now only five feet away and easily within striking distance with the shovel in his hands. The guard then looked over to whoever was yelling at him. His gaze returned to John for a few seconds, trying to discern what was going on.

"You have any gloves, or anything?" John popped out quickly, hoping that would explain his situation.

It seemed to work as the guard's face almost looked embarrassed for a second, and he walked over to the truck and pulled out a pair of leather gloves from the truck's cab. He tossed them to John with a short "sorry" and then went back to sit in his chair, waiting for the other man, now only a couple of yards away.

"I thought we weren't doing any work out here today?" said the new arrival.

"We weren't, but we had a runner. Need to take care of him," the guard replied, pointing to the body on the ground and then added as a deadpan joke, "Safety first!"

"Yeah, well I'm glad you're out here. It's boring sitting out here all day by myself. Can't wait until we are done around here and can leave this Podunk town."

"Shouldn't be too long now. We have already hit all the jewelry stores, banks, electronics, pharmacies, and gun stores. Don't know what else we would want to grab around here. We keep finding less and less."

"You guys already make it through all the houses on the lists?"

"Yep, we picked up a lot of nice stuff, too. Some of those guys on the FOID list had a ton of guns and ammo, and most of them left it when they bugged out. We had to go through the papers at all the gun stores by hand, but we were able to find a few more choice pieces."

His face broke into an evil grin, "And from our favorite lists, we found a couple of kilos of grass and about half a pound of coke plus tons of pills. Awfully nice of those pigs to do all our homework for us!"

"That will last us a while. I'm surprised there was anyone carrying that weight this far out in the boonies. Those were some high end drug stashes!"

The pair continued to banter back and forth for the hours it took John to dig the hole. By the time the sun had set, it wasn't nearly as deep as the guard had instructed, but he tossed in a few broken boards and then told John to throw the body in. The guard dumped a milk jug full of gas on the body and then threw the jug in the hole. After John got back into the truck, he chained him down and shared a cigarette with the other man. When they were almost done, they flicked the butts into the hole, which was quickly engulfed in flames.

Back at the prison that night, John tossed and turned.

I'm glad I didn't take my chance today. Would have ended up shot in the back. But I need to find a way out; 150 graves against a handful or two of us doesn't sound like good odds. And it sounds as if they are almost done here, whatever that means. Looters and scavengers going from town to town? I highly doubt they will just leave us or set us free when they move on.

Chapter 26

Radio Broadcast: Reports in today say that several western states are restricting travel following a rash of refugees fleeing the coastal states. They hope to stem the tide of travelers and to help protect the property and resources of the current state residents as more people are arriving and demanding help. Comments from legislators in these states frequently compare these people to looters, scavengers, and even locusts. Legislators cite events where residents of the state have been robbed, beaten, or murdered by the roving gangs of refugees.

These comments and actions are drawing heated criticism and calls for arrest, and sometimes even calls for assassination, from the remaining officials in California.

CRACK! The sound of shattering glass rang through the house. It was quickly followed by more noise as pane after pane of glass was blown inward, showering the living room with shards. Jane began crying almost immediately, and Sam jumped out of his booster seat and ran toward his mother who was sitting across the table from him. Margaret grabbed both her kids and pulled them into the small hallway across from the table. They huddled together, hopefully out of the path of danger.

A few seconds later, the noise stopped, only to be replaced with laughter and childish taunts of who was going to tell on whom and who was going to get in trouble. As the laughter and jokes subsided, Margaret told her children to stay down while she went around the corner to see what was happening. She saw the two Rogers boys standing only a few feet outside the windows. As soon as they saw her, they turned and ran as fast as they could. The two boys ran back to the safety of their house.

After calming the children and telling them everything was all right, Margaret spent the next hour cleaning up broken glass and the dozen baseball-size rocks that had broken the windows. Even after having taped the windows to prevent them from breaking into large chunks, she had to get down on her hands and knees to clean up the mess. She wished she could use the vacuum since she knew there was no way she was going to be able to get everything out of the carpet by hand.

The next, she put the kids upstairs to play with toys. Then she marched over to her neighbors' house. Banging on the front door as hard as she could, she drew both parents to the door quickly.

"Margaret, is everything OK?" asked the boys' mother, genuinely concerned.

"No, everything is NOT OK. Do you have any idea what your boys did this morning?" she snapped back.

"What? What did they do? They've been upstairs in their rooms all morning," the boys' father said, not realizing the truth.

"No. No they haven't. About half an hour ago, they threw these through my windows!" she said, shoving a bucket full of stones into his hands. "I was sitting down having breakfast with my children, and all the sudden, it's World War Three going on in my living room. I thought we were under attack."

The boys' parents were staring at the woman dumbfounded, and unable to comprehend or believe what they just heard. They gave her a few short apologies and promises to straighten it out later. With nothing else to offer, Margaret walked back to her house unfulfilled. She wanted to press harder for a real resolution, but she couldn't figure one out that didn't entail her giving Mr. Rogers, at minimum, a black eye.

"They think there aren't consequences for anything, do they?" Margaret said aloud to herself, even angrier now because of the parent's reaction.

Half an hour later, the two boys showed up with their dad and knocked on the door. The boys gave very forced and unapologetic sounding apologies that just increased Margaret's level of anger. As soon as they said their spiel, their father dismissed them so he could talk to Margaret alone. He apologized again, making excuses about how bored they were and there wasn't anything to do to entertain them without electricity.

Margaret tried not to roll her eyes at the man, and at some points, it took even more restraint to keep from slapping him in the face.

It looked as if he was about to turn and go when he chimed in with one last point, "You said you were having breakfast with your kids? What were you having? I thought everyone was out of food except for over at the kitchen?"

Seeing the look of surprise on Margaret's face, he got an evil grin on his face, "you know, I've seen you and your kids there, too, and if you are going there, you are supposed to share what you have at home. You're not breaking those rules, are you?"

Margaret was beside herself with anger at this point.

This man is going to threaten me? After what his little hoodlums did?

She didn't know what her next move should be. If she wasn't ratted out in the next hour or so for having extra food, then she knew her neighbor was going to hold it over her head. Little did she know, both acts were imminent. Less than an hour after their meeting, Mr. Rogers came back to the door and threatened to turn her in unless she gave him half of the remaining provisions, to which she complied. Luckily, she had only minimal amounts of food in the pantry since most of it was still cached upstairs in the closet.

Not happy with his haul, a couple of hours later Mr. Rogers told Thomas, the neighborhood bookkeeper, about the food Margaret had and about the guns he knew her husband owned. Not getting a positive response from Thomas, he kept laying more information out for Thomas to record; they have a generator, a stocked wine rack, lots of bullets for his guns, and gasoline. Thomas finally perked up a bit at the last item and asked how much they might have, but wasn't able to get a clear answer.

"What? No reward or nothing?" Mr. Rogers asked.

"What? Why would you get a reward for doing what you did?" Thomas replied.

"Because I'm giving you information about people breaking the rules and hiding stuff that other people need!"

Thomas shook his head "Sorry, that's not how it works. We will ask her about what she has. If she does have the food, she can give it to the kitchen or she can stop coming. We aren't fining people or arresting them or anything."

Mr. Rogers snuffed loudly and stomped his way home.

That's the third time today! What is happening here? Whatever it is, I don't like it, Thomas thought.

Thomas, being good-natured through and through, was blind to the motives of the people coming to see him. He knew what a shakedown was, but thought it existed in the movies, not in his quiet little suburban neighborhood. Nonetheless, he continued to make notes of all information he was given.

You never know when this might really be useful information, and Garrett likes to always know as much as he can about the situation.

He did note that on his sheet, when he asked Margaret previously about having food or guns, she said "no" to both.

***

Garret looked at the information in front of him and decided it was time to branch out and secure more territory. He had a set of aerial photos pasted together covering up half of one wall. The map showed his neighborhood and the other houses, fields, and subdivisions within a two-mile radius. There were two smaller subdivisions that were a little more than half a mile away and a third that was a mile away. Between them were small farms and farm houses that were sometimes clumped together a handful at a time.

"We need to reach out to these two neighborhoods and see what's going on, and we need to start knocking on the doors of all these houses. But we'll have to figure out how to do it without getting shot," Garret said to the attendees of the meeting.

Rick nodded his agreement, not knowing Garret's true intentions, "We need to get communication up and going and have a way to warn us or others about trouble. What happens if another group of people, larger than the last, come walking up our road? I think it's a good idea." He was trying to kill Garret with kindness and agree with him whenever he could.

"Good, I'm glad you think so. Anyone else?" Garret said, looking at the handful of other members. No one said anything.

"All right, well then, I'll put together a few more details, and we can meet again in two hours to go over them?"

The crowd started to leave, and only Rick and Garret were left in the room after a few minutes.

"I'm guessing you want to talk about something?" said Garret in a flat tone.

"I do," Rick said. He didn't want to say too much or push too hard, afraid of what might happen if he did.

"Well?"

"I just wanted to thank you for all the work you've done for me, and for all of our neighbors. We all owe you a debt of gratitude."

"No problem. It's what anyone would do, right?"

"Right. But there is another thing."

"I figured. There is always a but," Garret said, interrupting Rick.

"Right, sorry. But do you think it's going a little too far, cataloging what everyone has? Asking about guns, food, and gas? And then shunning people if they don't let you inspect their house?"

"No, actually, I don't. We need to know about all of our available resources."

Rick didn't reply, trying to think of what other angle he could take. He knew that Garret was going off the deep end, if he hadn't already. And that it very well could end up bad for many people.

Garret continued, "You know what happened at the last relief drop. You know how many roving hordes of hungry people are out there. And you've heard the radio broadcasts about how bad everywhere else is. For Pete's sake, a quarter of our country is being claimed by Mexico right now! Do you think that they are going to keep trying to supply us when we are at war on our own soil?"

"I know, Garret, but it's up to us, up to you, to help these people through this the right way."

"The right way?" Garret said, facetiously.

Rick looked him straight in the eye. He didn't think there was any use trying to be kind about it. "Yes, the right way. With the freedom and dignity each person has by the right of being alive. Not to be used as pawns or extorted or anything like that. This isn't a game, and it isn't a way for someone to make a quick buck on others misfortune! The way people are turning on and exploiting each other needs remedied."

Garret's face started getting flush as his anger rose. *Hmm, what exactly does he know? I doubt he knows much. He's probably guessing. Either way, he knows too much. THAT is something that needs remedied.*

"I'm sorry. I'm sorry, Rick. I don't mean to be mean-spirited. I'm just trying to do the best I can, and I think

I'm doing a pretty damn good job of it, too. Better than YOU. But I'm sorry if I'm stepping on your toes or anyone else's. I'm just trying to do the best I can for everyone," Garret said in the most sympathetic tone he could muster.

He continued, "I'll work on it, but I'll need your help. I'm sorry. How about after our next meeting this afternoon, we have a little more discussion about what we can do to make things better?"

"That sounds great, Garret, thank you for being so understanding." Rick said, but what he really wanted to say was, "I think you are a liar and are dangerous to everyone around here."

***

After Rick left, Garret found his Tweedle-Dee and Tweedle-Dum and sent them out to scout some of the farm houses around the neighborhood. He had been to— or sent them and others to—these houses before, to collect supplies if the houses were unoccupied, and to send not so subtle messages to leave to the houses that were occupied. After making sure the houses were still empty, they were going to gather their friends again for a little surprise on the scouting party that night.

***

The meeting went quickly; all the men agreed that they should start reaching out as soon as possible. They all agreed that meant heading out that afternoon or early evening, before the sun went down. They broke into two groups of three to keep from looking scary and to provide backup and cover if need be. The first group was Garret, Tweedle-Dee and Tweedle-Dum. The other group was Rick, Rob, and another man who still had to be found. The remaining men present at the meeting were going to be busy with guard or other duties.

As everyone was preparing to roll out within an hour, Garret found Rick and apologized.

"I'm sorry. Sorry that you felt you even needed to bring that up to me!" Garret said.

Rick didn't reply so Garret continued, "As a matter of fact, I want to step aside from working with Thomas on the inventory and want you to take care of it with him. You do as you see fit."

This caught Rick by surprise, "I didn't mean you shouldn't do it; just maybe do it a little differently."

"No, I get that, but I think you will do it better regardless," Garret said with a feigned smile. "We'll get everything transitioned over tomorrow morning, sound good? For now, let's just see who else is out there."

Rick nodded, "Sounds good."

Unfortunately, Rick had too much belief in the good in people. Otherwise, alarm bells would have sounded, telling him to be careful.

***

The two groups walked out of the neighborhood. Garret's group took what he said was the more dangerous route, walking right down the center of the road. The other three men walked about 75 yards behind, and to the side of the first group, to try to keep from being noticed. The first few houses were all empty and obviously had been looted and picked over. It wasn't until the fifth house, about three quarters of a mile away from their neighborhood that they ran into anyone.

Garret and the other members of the first group had finished searching the outside of a house, which they'd found to be empty, and were walking toward their next destination. The second group was right in front of the house, when the first shot rang out. Everyone in both groups immediately ducked and tried to find cover.

Rob, knowing the shot came from inside the nearby barn, split from his group and jumped in the drainage ditch on the far side of the road. Rick and the other man ran forward into the near side ditch right in front of them. But this ditch gently sloped away from the road, giving very little cover for the men.

A second loud shot rang out and hit the road a few feet away from Rick. Then, a string of quieter shots broke the air in rapid succession. They fell all around Rick, and his unlucky companion got hit in the shoulder by one of the bullets, causing him to fall to the side and begin panicking.

Garret stood up and started shooting wildly and barked orders to fire on the house, purposely adding to the confusion.

By this time, Garret's group had started shooting at the house indiscriminately, adding to the chaos around them. Then getting the message, but unable to see a target, Rick's group started firing at the house also.

Garret started shouting orders for Rick to try to flank the dwelling by running around the side.

Instead of thinking, Rick innately reacted to the orders. He figured that Garret knew best, since he was the only man there with military training. Rick rose up out of the ditch in preparation to run a slant across the yard.

I could have sworn the shots are coming from the barn!

That was the last thought that went through Rick's mind before the next round from the scoped bolt action rifle, which Garret had neatly setup in the barn for the hired lackey to use, pierced his chest, right below the collar bone. The bullet entered his chest on the right side, severing many major arteries, and the force turned his lung inside out and threw his body backward. Blood filled his lungs, and in a few seconds, the wound became fatal.

As Rick's body, not realizing it was dead, stumbled back, another string of rapid fire erupted from an accompanying .22lr caliber rifle. This time is was more effective this time with three of the 25 rounds struck targets, twice on Rick and again on his partner.

From his vantage point across the street, Rob could see that Rick had been shot. A huge bloody circle showed halfway down his back. Rob waited a few seconds, pulled a small cylinder from the bag he was carrying, then stood up and tossed it into the house's yard. A few seconds later, smoke started billowing out of the can, the signal for the assassins to break and run.

Seeing the smoke, the attackers fled out the back of the barn while Garret took his cue to play superman. He ran toward the house, firing his rifle the whole time, and up to the front door. He kicked the door in and went inside where he fired a dozen rounds indiscriminately.

Next, he retrieved three bodies that he had stashed in the kitchen's pantry. All were previous victims of his exploits as a raider. He positioned the bodies next to the windows and doors, and placed spent brass and a few old rusty guns next to them. He tried to make it look as if they had been the shooters.

A few minutes later, the men gathered around the dead and injured men. Rick was obviously dead. The other man acted as if he were also, even though both of his wounds were only half an inch into the muscle of his shoulder and leg. He was able to walk back on his own, using one of the teens to lean on, before he realized he wasn't too badly hurt.

Garret went back inside the house and gathered up some sheets and used them to wrap Rick's body. Rob and the other teen carried the body back to the neighborhood.

Since the bodies Garret planted inside had already been dead for several days, he knew anyone with minimal forensic knowledge would know that these people had been placed there, not killed there.

I'm sure no one will come looking, but you can never be too careful.

After the other men were on their way back to the neighborhood, he used a bottle of lighter fluid and two matches to take care of any traces of foul play.

***

By the time Rick's body was back in the neighborhood, a large crowd had gathered. From the arrival of the injured man moments earlier, word had spread like wildfire about the shootout. The man, now oblivious to his injuries, was frantically telling the story of how they were ambushed from behind by a group of men with machine guns. He described the shootout in vivid detail, especially how heroic Garret had been in his charge, saving everyone's lives. The teen who had carried him back noted to himself that most of the details must have come from movies the man had seen and not the actual incident.

The crowd parted slightly as Rick's body was carried in, and it took only a few seconds for Sarah, the new widow, to find her way to the body. She almost tackled the men carrying his body as she fell, crying into them. Landing on top of the body, she clawed at the sheets to unwrap the body. All hope that he was still alive disintegrated as she uncovered his lifeless face, staring up at her with motionless, empty eyes.

She clung to Rick's body, crying for almost an hour before she went home where her kids were waiting with a neighbor to find out if their daddy was OK. She lied and said they wouldn't know until tomorrow, but that daddy said that he loves them and that they are the best kids he could ever have hoped for.

Garret was eager to start the next steps of his plan, but knew he had to wait at least a few days to put them in motion. He walked home without talking to anyone, and even though he was a major part of the story being told, he knew plenty of others would tell it.

"I heard what happened. I was going to come down to meet you but was told you were OK, so I didn't want to bother you," his wife said, when he came through the front door.

"Then why are you bothering me now?" He shot back, not happy to be broken from his thoughts of his plans with Sarah.

"Sorry, I just want to make sure you are OK. I was afraid you would get hurt, and I don't know what I'd do if that happened."

Garret took this in and laughed, "You're stupider than you look. You think I'd get hurt out there?"

"Two people got shot today, and one of them is dead. Are you telling me that couldn't have just as easily been you?"

Garret laughed again and an evil grin came over his face.

This stupid woman. Where does she get off? She ought to just leave. That would suit me very well, but for some stupid reason, she just likes to hang around.

Seeing the look on his face, she realized what must have happened, "You didn't ... Did you?"

Garret just laughed and walked out of the room shaking his head.

She knows. Who cares? Well I better care, at least for now!

Garret walked into the kitchen and grabbed one of the largest knives he could find and then stomped over to his wife. She didn't even have time to turn around before he had a handful of her hair wrapped in his knuckles and the knife pressed up against her neck.

"You might think you know what's going on here, but you know what will happen if you mess up my plans, don't you?" he said, pulling hard on the hair and pressing the knife into her skin hard.

I almost wish it would break the skin and just end her now, but now isn't the time.

He held the tension for a few seconds until his wife was crying and shuddering in his grasp. He pulled back the knife and let go of her hair, causing her to drop hard to the floor in a bawling heap. Being married to Garret for a decade, she had been frightened many times before, but she'd never been more frightened than she was right now.

Chapter 27

Radio Broadcast: These are new developments in and around us here in New York. We have new details to share. Because of gas shortages and lack of food, there has been a wave of Executive Orders from the Governors of several northeastern states and backed up by empowering orders from the President. These orders are to effectively seize any commercially-owned food products and gasoline and make it illegal to sell or transport food, gas, and a list of other goods to anyone outside of your state.

This is the latest in the clash between states as they struggle to keep order in these trying times.

There has been extensive outcry over these tactics. Many are pointing to this as pure theft by the government and they are delaying and complicating the ability of the country to get back on its feet.

John wiped the sweat from his brow with the muddy back of his hand and tried to squint out the tears and dirt that were blurring his vision. He would have loved to have had a bandana or a towel around his forehead, but he knew that wasn't going to happen, especially not now that his shirt had worn to the point of shredding. He wasn't allowed to replace the shirt with anything salvaged from the looted houses. That suggestion was rewarded with a few cynical laughs followed by thrown rocks that left bruises on his back.

He paused, just long enough to reposition the remains of his gloves, which also were in tatters from hard use. Since he and another young captive were lucky enough to be in better shape than many of the others, they had been back at the burial site for almost a week, digging a single long trench. They had been there from sun up to sun down, working on the trench. Their only breaks came when they switched to digging separate holes for the dead bodies, which seemed to be showing up more frequently.

Looks like they are tying up loose ends. I won't be a loose end.

Over the past few days, John had been diligent, looking for any weakness or gap that he could exploit to escape. But he couldn't find any. His captors were not individually very smart. However, the leader of the group was, and any weakness John had perceived ended up being a ruse. The bodies of the people they had killed and John had buried, over the past few days were a testament to that observation. His captors were crude, rude, and most seemed completely uneducated, but when it came to their new profession of slave-driving looters, they were all superstars.

He was beginning to wonder if his only option was to try to take them out before they could bring him down. But even that didn't seem promising, as the consequences of fleeing or combative prisoners were both quick and deadly.

Just then, one of the guards came over and told John and the other digger to get in the back of the truck. He chained them down tightly. After a fifteen-minute drive, they pulled up to a group of about two dozen refugees who were loaded into the truck with John and the other digger. The rest were loaded into another truck. Before letting the refugees get into the truck, the guards roughly filtered through the refugees' belongings, expertly getting rid of any items they wanted for themselves but said were now worthless, like jewelry or guns. The guards would come back later to pick up the discarded items. Within twenty minutes, they had been successfully transported far from the gang's area of operation.

This was the third trip John had been on in the past few days. He found out that they had been performing this goodly service all along. They kept up the ruse and pretended to be helpful law enforcement and transported everyone out of their turf. These trips were the hard for John to bear. In front of him were many people who might be able to help him escape, but there wasn't an effective way to recruit their help. Especially since they all had been conveniently disarmed before boarding the trucks.

He knew that if he tried to escape and failed that the consequences would be dire. He learned this from the guard who was driving. A couple of guys had previously tried to clue in the riders, prompting one of the riders to question the guards. Before letting anyone out of the truck, the guard answered their questions with fast and coordinated gunfire that killed the two prisoners and the nine riders, including six women and children. John's initiation to his new position of full-time gravedigger included hearing this story and burying all the bodies.

After dropping off the passengers, they returned directly to the clearing to keep digging the ditch. John wiped sweat from his brow and then drank heavily from the gallon jug of water he was provided while digging.

At least they give me plenty of water; otherwise, I'd already be lying in the bottom of one of these holes. Besides, today is a good day. I haven't had to bury anyone.

***

The next few days went by in similar fashion. Each day, John felt more desperate than the last. There were only five captives left alive now. Some had tried fleeing or fighting back with zero success. Most were killed indiscriminately for little or no infraction.

For some reason today, they brought all the inmates out to the cemetery, and they were put to digging the large trench. It was quickly apparent that they were digging their own graves, but there wasn't any chance to do anything about it without meeting an even quicker death than what was planned.

It's now or never. None of us is going to make it out alive today if something doesn't change.

John peered about, counting the guards. He could see five, plus the invisible guard you never could see sitting off in the trees somewhere.

Five of us, chained up, holding shovels against six of them with rifles and shotguns.

He was racking his brain, trying to think of a way out when two guards walked over to a man digging across from him. Without warning, one of the guards raised his shotgun to the man's back and pulled the trigger. The man's body contorted as the blast penetrated his skin. In a fraction of a second, his stomach bubbled out and his lungs collapsed from the pressure exerted by the hot gas from the shotgun blast. Another fraction of a second later, his chest ripped open as the lead shot ripped through. His lungs and heart were completely destroyed by the shot, and he was dead before his body even began to fall down.

"You idiots! What are you doing!?" yelled one of the other guards in response to the gunshot.

"Just testing something we had a bet on, man! I won too!" the shooter responded, with a laugh.

The first guard stomped over and dragged the shooter away with him. He was talking much quieter now, but John could still make out what he was saying.

"Screw you and your bets. You get to play secretary for that stunt."

The shooter started to respond, but was cut off, "You and Mr. Idiot here go on back and get that stack of paperwork. We need to fill all that crap out to help cover our tracks, and you get to do it!"

Not happy with the new task he had been given, the shooter sulked over to one of the trucks, and waved his conspirator over and directed him into the truck. After spinning the truck's tires, kicking dirt and grass up all around, they sped off to complete the task. He had to update the tracking documents they had stolen from FEMA and the local emergency manager. They were meticulous with adding names, usually fake, and details for all the people they killed. With paperwork from the Federal Government covering their tracks, they anticipated being free and clear of prosecution, if anyone ever investigated.

Four of us, four of them, but at this rate we're all goners.

A few minutes later, John noticed another man clad in the typical sheriff's getup walking from the woods where the sniper would hide.

"Must be lunch time," one of the guards said, noticing the other man, over a hundred yards away, walking toward them.

"I'm hungry. Let's finish this up, and then eat. That way, we can relax until the two dumbasses get back."

The first guard nodded and started walking around the back of the trench preparing to carry out his grisly task.

Knowing what was coming next, John felt a cold chill travel through his body, adrenaline suddenly coursing through his veins.

This is it. It's now or never.

He rolled the shovel over in his hands and firmed his grip on the handle about a third of the way from the top to give him the best leverage.

Turning his head, he noted the position of the guards, *two in front of me, one coming around the back and one more coming in quick.*

John took two small stutter steps toward the guard behind him just as the barrel of the guard's gun leveled with the first prisoner's head. The prisoner was staring up at the guard, knowing exactly what was about to happen, but couldn't do anything about it. The prisoner likely didn't feel a thing as the bullet entered his forehead and exited the back of his head right above the neck.

The shooter wasn't as lucky. Before he brought the gun down from the recoil, John's first shovel swing— with an almost superhuman strength—sliced through the man's stomach and down through his groin. As he stood in shock, John's second swing finished the job by making a jagged arc of blood explode from the man's neck as he fell forward into the trench.

Three on three.

John glanced at the two nearest guards, both had seen exactly what happened and were readying to open fire. John dove low into the trench. He started crawling with shovel in hand, as quickly as he could toward the guards. He crawled over the dead guard and prisoner, giving only a momentary glance at the rifle. It was just out of reach where the guard had slung it when he was first hit with the shovel.

Shoot! If only that bastard's gun had fallen in with him.

The dirt around him began to pop and break as the guards began peppering it with bullets. Luckily for John, the trench was deep enough to protect him. They were firing where he was a second before and in the opposite direction from his travel.

They think I'm running away. I'll show them!

John popped up all at once from the near side of the trench, ready to swing. He was still about 10 feet from the armed men who had been moving toward where they had last seen John. Even though the two guards were surprised by John's appearance, by the time John had covered half the distance, the farthest guard had him in his sights. Still running forward, John couldn't help but look down the dark barrel pointed directly at his face. In that instant, everything slowed to a crawl. There was no stopping now or running. No hiding. Just staring down the dark tunnel of the gun's barrel.

To John's surprise, the guard suddenly lurched forward and spun around, never getting the shot off. A fraction of a second later, the edge of John's shovel slammed into the closest guard's ear. He went down fast, taking the shovel with him.

Looking up, John saw the third guard still closing. His rifle was pointed toward the guard he had just shot. It didn't make sense to John, but it did save his life.

A few moments passed in silence as John watched the guard, gun still pointed toward his fallen comrades, close in on the ditch. The silence was broken by the sound of the approaching truck with two men in the front. Returning from their paperwork excursion, the two men saw the uniformed man pointing the rifle in John's general direction and gunned the gas hard to speed toward the prisoner.

The man quickly ran at an angle toward the truck, putting himself in a path so they were driving directly away from him and then opened fire. The automatic gun emptied the magazine in just a couple of seconds, shattering glass and puncturing steel. Not happy with the results, the man emptied two more magazines into the truck in quick succession. He stopped firing only after the truck came to a disastrous stop after nearly flipping over when it hit the trench.

The shooter cautiously approached the truck, watching for any movement or sign of life. Finding none, the man turned back toward John and the young man who had been his workmate. They were the only prisoners left alive.

The shooter kept the rifle, which had been reloaded as soon as it was emptied, and pointed in John's general direction.

As he approached and no one made any move to attack or run, he slowly let the muzzle dip a little below his waist. He turned toward John, "Thanks for the help there."

John just looked at the man, not knowing how to respond.

"I'm Deputy Sheriff Johnson," the man said, and then paused letting out a big sigh. "I'm the only deputy left alive after these animals came to town, and I've been hunting them down ever since. But they were too coordinated for me to ever get a chance to take them out."

John believed the man's story, no reason not to, and if he wanted John dead, he would have already killed him.

John finally replied, "Thank you! I've been their slave for the past few weeks. They've killed dozens of people ... and today they were going to finish us off ..."

"Yeah, I think you are right. Most of them have packed up and have been hauling all their loot somewhere pretty far away. But I don't want to stick around here for too long. There are still a lot more of them than there are of me, and I don't want to get taken by surprise."

The three men then started to pick up the guns and gear of the dead men, tossing it into the back of the still intact truck.

"You drive. We'll go over to where I parked, unload this, and get you guys out of here." Johnson said, pointing to the truck then toward the woods.

***

After quick stop to grab the sniper's gear—the sheriff had killed him earlier when he saw his chance—they pulled up to the sheriff's SUV, which had been painted multiple shades of flat brown and hidden under surplus military camouflage webbing. They loaded the guns and gear into the back on top of an already impressive collection.

"Yeah, lots of toys that these guys have been picking up," the sheriff said when he noticed John's expression. He continued, addressing the other young prisoner, "Where are you from? Around here? Where y'all heading?"

The young man let out a heavy sigh, "From Chicago … nowhere to go."

"No family? Friends?"

"Not that I'd want to see. I just want to get out of here, and I don't care where."

"All right, well, I'll be more than happy to get you on your way. How about you?"

"I'm heading east," John replied, seeing that the man wasn't satisfied, he continued, "to Ohio."

The man nodded, "I can take you a little way, not far, maybe 20 to 30 miles. That will at least get you into Indiana, but I don't want to risk going too far."

He looked at the young man, hoping he had come up with some place to go, but there was no reply.

"All right, how about you just take that truck and go? Wherever you want," the sheriff said to the other man. As if on cue, the young man nodded and jumped into the truck and drove off without saying a word.

"Not one for many words, I guess. And that leaves us. Hop in, I'll take you for a little ride."

For most of the ride, the deputy recounted what had happened in the town. After the majority of civilians had been evacuated and most of the bodies from the immediate casualties had been buried, most workers had moved on to another city that was two counties away.

Almost as soon as the crews had left, this group of criminals ambushed the remaining law enforcement personnel, killed them, and buried them in the FEMA mass casualty site—the one that John and the sheriff had just left. The sheriff pointed out how he was "the lucky one." He had been getting lunch for everyone.

"If I hadn't been out scrounging together food for everyone, I'd be just as dead as the rest of them," he said in a very matter of fact kind of way.

He went on to detail how they had stolen government records and used those to help target businesses and homes for loot, ranging from cash and jewelry to guns and ammo to a variety of illicit drugs.

An hour later, they pulled to a stop on a small county road that was running parallel to the Wabash River that was now in front of them.

"Sorry, can't go any farther, and I should definitely be getting back soon. I've got a lot of work ahead of me now that I've made a crack in their armor I can work with," said the Sherriff.

"Thank you! You know you saved our lives today. I won't forget it!" John replied. He felt himself getting teary eyed as the realization of today's happenings started to set in.

The sheriff jumped out of the SUV before John could continue, popped open the trunk, and started pulling stuff out.

"Here, take some of this. Put it to good use," he said as he pulled out a backpack and started stuffing it with food and clothes that were in the pile. "Try these on," he said as he tossed a pair of shirts and pants at John.

While John was trying the clothes on, the sheriff pulled aside a rifle, several magazines, and stuffed the bag to the brim with food and water bottles.

"Looks like they fit well enough," John said happily at his new clothes. He was now wearing something that wasn't in shreds.

"Good, take this stuff," the man said.

He then paused for a second and grinned.

He reached into the truck and pulled out a small black plastic case, "and this. This will get you home, and I don't need it because now I've probably got three extras." His face and tone turned sour on the last statement. The extras came from his fallen comrades, as he extended the case to John.

John started to open it, but was interrupted by the once again eager sheriff, "Night vision. Sleep by day, walk by night. Without any lights to give you away, you should be able to walk all night without ever running into a problem. Just make sure to find a good place to hide during the day!"

John took the sheriff's advice, and as soon as he drove away, John was curled up under a tree about a hundred feet from the riverbank.

Thank the Lord I made it through this. Now let's see. Just got into Indiana, that puts about 250 miles ahead of me. If I can keep a good pace at night with the NVGs, I should be able to be home in seven to ten days.

He dozed off to sleep, completely exhausted, but content that at least he was free and on his way home again. For the first time in weeks, he had good dreams, dreams of being at home and being reunited with his wife and kids.

Chapter 28

Radio Broadcast: Today on the BBC, we bring updates on the aid we are providing to the United States. Parliament has agreed to throw in the towel in its attempt to aid the United States in bringing home troops deployed in foreign lands. With the widespread violence and food riots at home, they say they no longer have the capacity, at this time, to aid their longtime ally. They must focus on bringing home their own soldiers for the time being.

The President responded saying he is dismayed at the actions of one of his country's closest allies. This is a crippling blow to the relief efforts inside of the United States as it tries desperately to bring home several hundred thousand troops still stationed throughout the world.

"Are you sure you are OK?" Margaret asked, looking sadly at Sarah.

Sarah nodded in response, "Yes, thank you for your help. Will we see you again tomorrow?"

Margaret smiled and then gave the woman a warm embrace, "Absolutely, we'll be here for you as long as you need."

It had been three days since her husband was killed in a firefight, and life wasn't getting any easier. She had to not only deal with the loss of her husband, but console her two young daughters. The entire world had been tipped on end the past few weeks, and in the past few days, everything had been accelerating at a break neck pace.

She let Margaret and her kids out the front door to return home. She was grateful for the help and support she had been receiving and hoped there was some way she would be able to repay Margaret in the future. As she locked the door behind her guest, she decided that tomorrow she would ask Margaret about moving in temporarily. Since they were both currently single mother households, combining homes would help provide better coverage and security.

It would be safer for both of us, and easier on me. Even if my idea is selfish, it is still a better option for both of us. Besides, she can always say no.

Down the road, Thomas was making one last stop before calling it quits for the day. He had spent the past two days going door to door again, this time with help, to collect spare supplies. He didn't really know why Garret and the other men wanted to collect as many guns and ammo as they could, but since they were just asking and not confiscating, he thought it was OK. He didn't realize how much influence his new assistant exerted on making people be generous. He thought that since Garret insisted on taking a detailed record of what was stored communally and giving everyone a receipt for everything that things were on the up and up. A carbon copy "'receipt of sale'" pad was used for this task and made it pretty easy.

They already had details on what most people had but Thomas was shocked to find that, at many houses, the number of guns had probably doubled since he last collected the data a few weeks ago. He knew they hadn't gone out and bought these guns, so he guessed they'd forgotten about them. Percentagewise the number of households that had guns was rising even faster than the total number of guns. Initially, more than half the houses didn't have any guns, but now the total number of gun owning households had doubled.

Garret talked to Thomas and the teenage boy assigned to work with Thomas about how this probably had happened. His reasoning was that people hadn't given more information before because they were afraid of being targets of theft. Now, their fears had changed.

They were afraid that others would think they're defenseless. That made a little sense to Thomas, but didn't seem to tell the whole story. He didn't let it bother him, though. He was happy to be helping any way he could.

***

Garrett watched as Margaret and her kids left Sarah's house and headed home.

All alone now. I'll let her sit for a while. Then pay her a visit.

He turned his attention to the papers on the table before him. He had amassed details on all the houses and subdivisions surrounding them for several miles. Arial maps that he had liberated from a county road truck were taped together, giving a very detailed view of the land. From the maps, he counted houses, roads, businesses, and any other landmark that might be useful.

He was devising a plan he liked to call "the protective donut," where he and others started reaching out to those around them to coordinate and build a structure for support and defense. His idea was to help align the people in a group of mutually supportive communities that would help protect each other and get everything back to normal. He led with the idea of communication and support to get back to a sense of normalcy. Most people wanted things to just "get back to normal." His main goal was to build a buffer between the outside world and his own little kingdom. He also wanted to build safe passage ways back to his kingdom for when he sent out parties looking for goods.

A discussion about the best way to organize one of the larger nearby neighborhoods kept going in circles. The inhabitants had already broken into several different factions and were distrustful of their neighbors. So, they distrusted anyone from outside the community.

Garrett knew what he wanted to do, but he liked to let the men around him think they had a hand in the plan—it made it much easier to get them to agree. Garrett's plan was to provide the nearby neighborhood with enough food to get them through a few days without anyone going hungry, but just enough to keep them dependent on his generosity.

No one else in the room knew it yet, but he had been using stolen radios from the local police department to monitor movements of food and fuel for weeks now. He also monitored the movement of the authorities, so he knew a convoy would be coming nearby tomorrow. Since it was going to be a small delivery—only three semi-loads—there was going to be very little security guarding it.

A couple of moveable roadblocks and about a dozen men, and we will be able to take care of it easily.

"All right guys, I need to step out for a little while and check on a few things. If I'm not here before you leave, make sure to be back here at 6:00 a.m. We are going to make a very important trip outside. Don't be late," Garrett said as he walked out of the room and down the stairs.

He stepped outside and started walking toward Sarah's house with an excited jump in his step.

She's alone now that the lady from up the road finally left. Let's just see how the beautiful young widow is doing.

He knocked lightly on the door and waited a few seconds before knocking again.

Kids are probably asleep, don't want to wake them.

He waited a few more seconds, and there was still no answer. Then he tried the door, but it was locked. Starting to get angry, he knocked louder. No answer. He started yanking on the door knob and shoving on the door.

His face flushed with anger that was about to tip over, he stepped back and was just about to kick the door in, when the door opened a crack, just enough for Sarah to peer out.

"Is everything OK?" Sarah said, trying to keep calm, but she was visibly panicked.

"Oh, yeah, yeah. I just wanted to check on you. Make sure you were OK."

"By beating on the door like that? You scared me half to death."

"Sorry, I ... I guess I just got worried that something was wrong."

Sarah just stared at the man, waiting for his next move. Behind the door, her trembling hand slowly brought up a pistol to be in line with the man's body.

Garret continued, "Is everything OK? The kids OK?"

She waited a few seconds, and replied, "Yes, we are fine, thank you. Thank you for checking in, but I've got a few things to do before I turn in ... thank you again. Goodbye."

She started to shut the door, but Garret shoved his shoe in the doorway, keeping it open.

Sarah's finger moved down from the side of the gun and rested on the trigger. Her heart was racing, and she was unsure of what to do. She didn't know this man very well, but what she did know, she didn't like. Even though she knew that many people around the neighborhood looked up to him, she knew that he was just using them for his own gain. She also knew that look in his eyes—he wanted in and he wanted her.

As he started slowing forcing the door open, she slowly started to put pressure on the trigger, trying to keep her shaking hand steady and the gun pointing toward the man. In her extreme concentration, she closed her eyes shut for a second, an act that Garret saw, allowing him to spring into action and taking this opportunity to get inside. In the split second she shut her eyes, Garret leapt forward, blasting the door open and knocking Sarah to the floor. As she fell, she lost control of the gun, and it skittered across the floor.

"What the hell!" Garret said loudly, standing above her. "You were just going to shoot me? For what?" he continued.

She tried to stammer a reply, but before she had time to, Garrett bent down and lifted her to her feet in one rough and jerking motion. He then turned and shut the door, locking it in the process.

I don't want to scare her too bad. Let's see how we can dial this back. I want it to be fun.

"There, stand up. It's all OK. Don't cry. I'm sorry. I can't say that I overreacted since you were going to SHOOT ME, but I'm sorry about the way I reacted," Garret said in a new friendly tone.

Guilt her into complacency, that might work.

"I, I, I, I'm sorry. I'm, I was afraid," She replied, now starting to sob and seeing no other way out.

"It's OK. Here, sit down. Relax for a second," Garret said, as he walked her through the darkness to a couch nearby and away from her gun.

"I just want to make sure you are OK. OK? How are the kids? Are they asleep?"

"Yeah, yes. I just put them down about 30 minutes ago," she replied through her tears.

"Good. Are they OK? You know, how are they taking things?" Garret's voice tried to be soft and comforting.

"As well as can be expected, I guess."

"Is there anything you need? Anything we can help with?"

Sarah's heart was still beating rapidly, so hard she was almost choked by the thumping in her throat. She knew she had to get him out of there and fast and that nothing good could be coming from this man.

"Just time, and sleep. It's that time for me, so thank you for stopping by, but I must get to bed."

She started to stand up, but Garret grabbed her arm and pulled her back down.

"No, don't go yet. I want to talk to you about a few things," he said as he stood up and walked across the room.

He pulled out a lighter and fired it up, looking around the room until he found a few candles that he lit. He turned back to look at Sarah, still sitting on the couch, fighting back tears, face red, and eyes puffed.

Still damn hot. Still better than I've ever had. Besides, next time she won't look like this. I'll make her get all dolled up. This is just the warm up.

He took his holster and gun off, setting it on the desk across the room from the couch Sarah was on. Next to it, he placed the large knife he carried.

A show of restrained force. She knows what I can do.

Next, he slid his belt off and laid it on top of the knife and gun.

He walked back across the room and sat down next to Sarah who was quietly blubbering with her eyes closed tight.

What is that smell?

He looked at the woman sitting and shaking, and grabbed her by the arm and stood her up.

What the hell? She just crapped herself. She thinks this is going to save her?

He laughed to himself, remembering the time he helped give a very different seminar to a bunch of women. His part was to wear a large padded suit and play the part of the attacker. In this class, he taught women how to gouge eyes, punch and kick the groin, bite or claw sensitive areas, and any other tactic that could be employed to really hurt their attacker. He also made fun of the mainstream rape prevention classes, where the main focus was on yelling loudly and other not very effective tactics like soiling yourself.

In a fit of rage at the mess he had to put up with, Garret reached into his pocket and pulled out a folding knife that he flicked open with his wrist.

"All right, let's go get you cleaned up," he said. Then, he leaned in close, wrapping his right arm around her, putting the knife's blade on her jaw line.

He pulled her head close to his and whispered in her ear, "Don't you ever do anything like that again. We wouldn't want to have to scare the kids or anything, would we?"

***

A little after midnight, Garret stepped back out into the fresh night air, fully satisfied for the first time he could remember.

Like a dead fish, but she will learn to warm up. I'll make sure of that.

He hefted a backpack he took from one of her closets over his shoulders, newly weighted down with a guns, knives, and anything else he could find that Sarah might try to use as a weapon next time he came over.

I'll come back tomorrow afternoon when it's light and make sure she is thoroughly disarmed, and of course, check her temperature again. Maybe she will have warmed up by then.

***

"Hey boss, what are you smiling so big about?" Rob asked Garret as he walked into the room, beaming brightly.

"I, uh, just got some great news," he replied.

Garret didn't respond, but couldn't help but congratulate himself.

And I got some great action last night and can't wait to get back from playing hero to get some more!

Garret noticed the other men in the room were now staring at him, waiting for more information on why they were all there so early.

"Guys, we have an opportunity here in front of us to do something great for our families." He looked around the room, catching each man's stare for a second, and then continued, "But we might have to break a rule or two to do it."

He paused, looking from man to man again, judging their responses. He knew he had over half of them in the bag already, having enlisted their help before. But he was still unsure about a few new additions from the nearby neighborhoods. His worries were placated by the resolve he saw in their faces. It showed that they had had enough and were willing to do whatever they could to help make things better.

"All right, so what we have are details of a relief convoy that is coming down this highway in about two hours." He pointed to a road several miles away on a map. "What we are going to do is stop them and commandeer the supplies we need to keep going."

No one in the room said anything; a few nodded their heads in agreement.

"It's a small convoy, only supposed to be three trucks, so there won't be any escort security. There will probably be armed guards in the cab with the driver, but I don't expect much more than that. We are going to put out a road block here, and then move another block in behind them when they stop. Unload the drivers and security, and drive the trucks to this building here, where we will unload and disperse the goods."

"Any questions?" Garret said, and then waited a painfully long time to see if anyone wanted to try and weasel their way out, "No. OK, let's get packing."

***

An hour later, they had the ambush set, a garbage truck parked parallel to the flow, and a pair of pickup trucks parked a little way down the road.

As the semis rolled down the highway, the garbage truck was quickly turned, blocking the road. Next, the two pickup trucks came up from behind and blocked the path behind the trucks. Thinking that he would be able to bust through the blockade and not wanting to stop or lose momentum, the first semi smashed into the garbage truck, pushing it aside. This tactic drew fire from the men manning the ambush. Reacting immediately, the driver cut the wheel hard in response to the gunfire, almost flipped the rig, and jack-knifed the truck in the middle of the road, making an even more effective barricade than the garbage truck.

Seeing their options dwindle, the other two truck drivers slammed on the brakes and the trucks skidded to a halt almost simultaneously. The drivers and guards jumped out and ran. The little training that the freshly uniformed guards had and the complete lack of training on the driver's part made this an ill-fated exercise.

Having anticipated this, Garret barked orders to "stop them" to the new recruits he wanted to initiate. They acted just as he hoped, opening fire and gunning down the four men in a matter of seconds. The fleeing men even attempted to get a shot off in return.

Not great shots, but they got the job done, Garret thought to himself in response to the men's marksmanship.

They spent a few minutes at the site. Designated teams immediately jumped into the two drivable rigs and started toward the rendezvous point.

A second team pulled the four bodies and two prisoners into a SUV, stripped them of their gear, and handcuffed the prisoners. A single driver took the SUV a few miles down the road and parked the car under a bridge. Leaving the prisoners and bodies, the driver started running back to catch a ride so he didn't have to walk to the rendezvous point.

He didn't notice as the SUV burst into flames, a long fuse fed into a few bottles of gasoline that Garret positioned strategically throughout the SUV worked as he had hoped.

The remaining men started loading as much as they could from the jack-knifed trailer into the beds of the two pickup trucks, gathered the guards' gear, and drained the truck's tank into portable containers.

Looking at his watch, Garret noted that it had been 15 minutes since first contact. He started moving everyone along, even though there still were large quantities of food in the trailer. He had been vigilant in monitoring the radio and didn't pick up any distress call leaving the truck. Still, he didn't want to stick around for too long. Hopping into the back of the last pickup, he fondled two of the new guns collected today: select fire M4s.

It's been a while since I played with one of these. Can't wait to do it again.

***

The rest of the day was spent unloading and cataloging the haul. They disposed of the two semis by driving them miles away and abandoning them along the road where they set them ablaze to help destroy any evidence.

Great day! I couldn't have hoped to pull this off any better, and it's really going to give me a ton of pull with the neighbors. Now, let's see if that cold fish has warmed up any.

Garret smiled as he walked down the street to pay his lonely widow neighbor another visit.

Chapter 29

Radio Broadcast: In international affairs, we bring you updates about the escalating violence in and around Russia. After losing control of the puppet government, Russia is citing recent aggression as the reason it has re-annexed several former states and has begun a full mobilization of all branches of the military.

With the military on full alert, the secret police have been rounding up dissidents and taking them to undisclosed locations.

The international community is questioning the validity of the claims of aggression, especially considering the recent thefts of resources from these disputed areas by Russia.

John woke up several times that day, but kept forcing himself back to sleep until it was well past sunset. There was a small portion of the waning moon above in the partly cloudy sky, providing barely enough light to see rough shapes more than a few feet ahead.

Perfect for a guy decked out like me.

He fished through the backpack until he pulled up the NVG and worked the gear onto his head. He pushed the power button and suddenly his world went from dark black to an eerie, glowing green.

He stuffed everything back into the backpack and fished out some food, which he munched on while he did a few stretches to get ready for a long night of walking. After a small meal, he drank a small portion of a bottle of water and started on his way. The first few hundred feet were problematic: walking with the NVG was more awkward than he had anticipated, and it seemed that his hand-eye and foot-eye coordination were off just enough to make him mis-step time and time again.

He quickly figured out that the best way to move was to trace a path with the NVG, pick a point, and then walk to it from memory while identifying the next path. This, he realized, helped take the lack of coordination out of the equation and sped up his pace to a normal walking speed.

After getting his feet moving, he fell into thoughts about his predicament. He hadn't had much of a chance to assess the situation since being freed earlier that day; he was too excited about being free to fully comprehend the implications. Now, he had food and water, but didn't really know how long it would last. His fear was of running out of water along the way. Food wouldn't be as much of a problem, but clean water would be.

He felt an itch on his side and reached up to scratch it.

Or, food might be a bigger problem than I thought, he thought, as he felt his ribs.

Where just a few weeks ago, there had been a little padding of muscle and fat, now there was now tight skin over his bones.

Probably dropped more weight than I realized. I need to try and make that back up.

John had always kept himself in great physical shape and never had too much spare weight on his body. But now, he was on the very low end of what would be considered healthy for a man his size.

His first test in his new role as nighttime walker came as he approached a small town up the road. There were no signs of life—no lights and no sounds—that he could discern, but he knew people were around. Luckily, they couldn't see him in the darkness. He walked quietly down the road, uncontested until he saw the turn he was looking for: the road leading to the bridge across the river.

Walking toward the bridge, he saw that it was blocked on both ends by parked cars and it looked like there was at least one person standing guard. He was still too far away to make him out for certain. As he got closer, he could make out two people sitting in the dark, holding long guns in their laps as they leaned back against the cars comprising the makeshift road blocks. As he got even closer, he could hear one of them snoring.

Quietly, he squeezed through the back of the blockade without disturbing them and walked across the bridge, taking extra cautious steps when he started to see different noise makers and alarms. Even with the NVG, he couldn't see the strings that ran in crisscross patterns, but he could see the cans and other objects, giving him enough information to evade them without drawing any attention.

On the other side of the bridge, he made his way through the second blockade. This time, it was unmanned. He picked up his pace a bit until he cleared the majority of houses and buildings, and then started due east. He kept up a decent pace through the night, stopping for a few minutes every couple of miles to take a break, stretch, eat, and drink a little.

He realized that his physical condition had deteriorated more than he had anticipated. He didn't want to overdo it the first night back on the road.

When the sun started to lend pink and orange hues to the sky, John stopped and started scouting for a good place to camp. Being in the middle of nowhere made it easy for him to find a group of trees in the middle of a few bean fields. On his way through the field, he grabbed as many bean pods as he could and stuffed them into his pockets until they were overflowing.

Might not be the tastiest, but they will have plenty of protein.

He leaned back against a large tree and scanned his surroundings. He could see two farmhouses in the distance, but other than that, he was secluded.

Can't take any chances. Better grab some cover.

After a short rest, he gathered a bunch of leaves and small branches, and piled them into a small blind to hide under.

Not the best, but should keep anyone from seeing me.

He dug through the backpack and confirmed what he was afraid of, lots of food, but not a lot of water. Most of the food he had was packaged, processed food that he normally wouldn't have eaten because they were full of refined sugars and trans fats—the stuff that comprised of a large portion of most Americans' diets. In his current situation, he knew these could be great for the same reason, easy to digest and full of calories. He figured that he had enough to last him, sparingly, for a week.

I should eat now, supplementing the packaged stuff with as many of these beans as I can eat, and then pack as many as I can before I go.

Water, however, was another thing. He had started out yesterday with five 20 ounce bottles of spring water. He had already finished one of them and was just finishing the second one.

Can't skimp on it, especially if I'm going to eat a lot. Just need to make it a priority.

As expected, he didn't find any form of purification or filtration in the bag.

In the bottom of the pack, he found the extra magazines for the rifle, extra batteries for the NVG, and a knife. He pulled out the knife and smiled, recognizing it as the one that was given to him by the old man he met several weeks ago. He pulled out his belt and looped the sheath so it hung on his right side. He smiled and leaned back, taking a rest and feeling good about his last find.

Next, he inspected the rifle—a high-end AR rifle chambered in 5.56 NATO. He broke it down and inspected it. It was clean, looked almost new, and had a matching high-end optic on top.

Great gun. Wish I would be able to keep it.

He shrugged his shoulders.

I guess we'll have to see how everything plays out.

For the rifle, he had the magazine loaded in the rifle plus three more fully loaded. One hundred twenty rounds. *That should be more than enough to get me home. If it isn't, I don't know what will happen.*

Happy with his inventory, he started thinking about what he needed to continue on.

Water. Water is critical items one, two, and three. Next, a map or atlas. Heading willy-nilly westward works, but I want to be able to skirt around any towns or cities. I'm OK on food, great on protection ... hmm, actually I'm not great on protection. I'm not sure, but it should be about the first or second week of October by now, and it's going to start getting cold at night, especially when it rains. Need to get some sort of rain gear—maybe a blanket or sleeping bag. Oh, and a notepad so I can write all of this down and stop thinking about it.

He thought some more, but didn't come up with any more needed items. He wanted tons of things but shook most of them off as nice-to-haves or even as a pure fantasy that he could even find them.

Water, map, rain and cold protection, notepad. I'll bet I can find most of that in abandoned cars along the way.

He pulled his makeshift blind over himself, pulled his hat down low, and fell asleep.

***

He woke up several times throughout the day. Each time, he ate more food and beans, and then forced himself to sleep longer. By the time the sun had set, he was unable to sleep any more and started getting ready for his nightly walk. Stretches and warms ups didn't take long enough, so he sat idly in the copse of trees until the last shades of pink were seen in the sky. He started out without the NVG, walking cautiously beside the road, but as darkness overtook him, he turned them on to light the way as he walked down the side of the road.

The small county roads took several hard turns and he knew he wasn't traveling nearly as fast as he would like, but without knowing exactly where he was, he didn't know which roads to take. He walked a little way south because he thought there was an interstate highway a few miles in that direction. If so, he would have more opportunities to pick up what he needed, but also more opportunities for things to go wrong. He felt confident that a careful and stealthy approach would keep him out of trouble.

Much sooner than he anticipated, he found a road that crossed over the interstate, but before he got too close, he saw a light coming from under the overpass. He turned off the road and gave it a wide berth, walking almost half a mile through another unharvested bean field.

Looks like most fields' bounty are still out here, and if all of this spoils, it is going to make it much harder to eat next year.

With the lighted overpass well behind him, he crossed onto the shoulder of the highway and started walking and looking for any abandoned cars. In a few minutes, he came upon the first car. It had been ransacked, but he found a few key items first; a map of Indiana that had about a third of Ohio on it, too.

This will be good almost all the way home.

A few pairs of clean socks that looked like they would fit and two large garbage bags of clothes. He dumped the clothes into the back seat and stuffed the bags into his backpack.

A couple of miles more on the highway and a dozen more cars later, he found a box with ten cans of soda, a couple of partially opened but drinkable bottles of water, and a cheap rolled-up sleeping bag tucked in the trunk of a car. He kept walking along the highway until he saw what he thought was another camp up ahead. He checked his new map, but couldn't really figure out where he was in the green light. He went off road, giving the camp a wide berth until he found another road heading east.

A few miles later, the sun started peeking up, and John found a nice place to hide in the middle of a large forest. After using his knife to put together a bit of cover, he laid back, opened a soda, and dreamed about being home with his wife and kids.

Chapter 30

Radio Broadcast: For possibly the most shocking news of the year, we go to our Middle East correspondent to cover the events that unfolded there today.

Israel ended its military campaign today and is bringing its troops home from the neighboring countries where it has been at war.

All hostilities came to an end with the unconditional surrender of Iran, Egypt, and the Palestinian leadership after Tehran and Cairo were devastated by nuclear strikes from Israel.

"All right guys, let's get this show on the road!" Garret said, slapping the side of the box truck, urging it into motion.

He and his crew had spent the morning divvying up the loot from the convoy raid. They were now getting ready to take a box truck loaded with three full pallets of various foods to the neighboring community. After expertly dividing off a large portion to keep in his secret reserve, Garret paid off each man with enough food to keep them and their families fed for the next few weeks. After that, he went to each man individually and gave him an extra bonus from the stash, indicating that it was between them and should remain a secret. Even though each man on the raid was given this confidence, Garret knew how to play people for his own good.

After portions of the loot were distributed to Garret and his men, there was still more than two thirds of the food left. This was broken into piles, half for the neighborhood and the remaining half was broken into piles to be distributed to the neighboring communities to buy their assistance. The food reserved for the neighboring communities would be given out in small portions at a time. This way, these communities would continually be dependent on Garret and his team for food. Only this first delivery was going to be this large, which is an attempt to shock and awe them into fealty.

When they arrived at the neighboring community, a small crowd waited to see if what they had been promised would actually pan out. They were all pleasantly surprised at the amount of food that was provided, and as news spread, almost the entire neighborhood of several hundred people showed up, thanked and praised the men they saw as the providers.

Soon Garret commandeered control of the populace and got them to work, cooking and preparing a community cookout in celebration. He stayed in front of the crowd, glowing in their praise. He got the pair of local henchmen to be in front of the crowd, too. His plan was to enshrine himself as the leader and to designate these men as his right and left hands in this neighborhood when he wasn't around. He knew he still needed many more "recruits" from this and the other communities. He figured, though, he would slowly solidify his position as leader. He would also carefully cover his tracks for all the crimes he had committed.

He laughed a little as his internal dialog went down a forked path.

Crimes. Ha. The only people who would ever be able to implicate me in anything are those who are as guilty or more so than me. I know this won't last forever, but my guess is, we won't see any normalcy until at least spring, probably not even that early. Between now and then, I'll make enough to retire comfortably in the sun somewhere down south.

His smile grew big when he pictured himself sitting on the beach, drinking a beer as he watched Sarah stepping out of the water wearing a bikini.

Yeah, that will be the life. Too bad she won't really be a part of it. I guess there is one person who could implicate me, but I don't want to get rid of her just yet.

Hours later, Garret returned back home to check on the progress in their endeavors. The consolidation of all remaining weapons and food was under way, and thanks to the loose lips of neighbors, it was going better than anticipated. Thomas was supplying him with the details of who said what about hidden guns and food. Then Garret would send a second team over to search the house. They didn't force themselves in, but if the residents refused, they were no longer welcome at the communal meals. When they found what they were looking for, a secret gift was delivered to the snitch, along with a promise of more for more information, and a promise of pain if the snitch told anyone about the bribe.

Snitching played out quickly over several days as more people turned on their neighbors. It had become common, but unspoken, knowledge that a person could benefit for turning someone else in. Those who initially refused to "rat out" others started changing their tune after they were turned in, sometimes by multiple people. This scheme had gone so well that it almost became a problem when people started creating fictitious stories to try to get other people in trouble or garner additional rewards.

"The more they distrust each other, the more they will trust us," Garret said to his crew whenever they asked if snitching was causing problems.

He reasoned that it's better for neighbors to hate each other, the actual snitches, than to hate those doing the consolidation. A few talks with a handful of men— who spoke out and called the consolidation a form of theft—quieted any dissent from the populace. This was partially disappointing to Garret. He had hoped to hammer down on someone as an example, but after the house fire a few weeks ago, anyone who was suspicious knew to keep their mouths' shut or else there could be consequences.

The success was easily seen as he stepped into the master bedroom of the house they were using as headquarters. Piles of guns, ammunition, knives, and other gear were spread throughout the room, almost filling up. The catalog they were keeping listed over 500 guns from 200 households. They did let each house keep one for defense. Sometimes more were allowed if there were multiple shooters willing to help with guard duty or other communal activities. They left enough ammo for a few reloads, if any. The couple of houses that didn't have any ammo were left wanting, even when there were plenty cartridges in that caliber to spare back at the HQ.

Margaret was left with her husband's first gun, an old and worn .22lr revolver, which his grandfather gave him, and enough ammo to fully load it only once. She hadn't shot that gun in years and wondered if it was even safe to shoot. She argued to keep one of the semiautomatic pistols that she was used to, but according to the confiscators, those were "too much gun" for a little lady. In reality, those guns were too prized a possession to the confiscating crew who argued over who was going to carry them.

The arguments grew when they emptied the long guns from the safe. The pile of ammo they carried away was the second largest they'd found so far, almost 5,000 rounds at first estimate, though half of that was .22lr.

***

Happy with the progress he was seeing, Garret headed down the street to visit his new friend and was unhappy to find her with company. Sarah had invited Margaret and her kids to spend their time together since they were both currently alone.

"Well ... hello. Didn't expect to see you here," Garret said, nodding toward Margaret.

"Oh, well. I think we will be here for a while. Yesterday, Sarah asked us to move in, temporarily of course," Margaret replied with a smile.

She didn't know what had transpired between Sarah and Garret.

"Oh really. When did she ask you?" He said, staring coldly at Sarah.

She thinks having a friend around will protect her? I guess she needs another lesson.

"I asked her yesterday before they left," Sarah said flatly, try to deflect the anger she could see rising in him.

"I see. Well, we need to make sure this all gets updated in the books. For safety, we need to be sure where everyone is. Are you planning on spending the nights here?"

"Well, we don't know about that yet. I guess that's something we need to discuss. I know my kids feel better sleeping in their own beds, but it's nice to have more people around." Margaret said, starting to notice the tension between the two.

"I see. Well, just let me or someone at HQ know of your decision. I'll send someone over to check on each of you every night from now on," Garret said with a smile as he waved, turned, and left.

Every part of Sarah's body was screaming to tell Margaret what had happened, but guilt and shame kept her from saying anything. Then, fear of getting Margaret hurt too solidified her resolve to keep quiet.

Chapter 31

Radio Broadcast: In today's news we bring updates about a new wave of mass desertion of cities that is getting underway as millions of people prepare to flee the coming winter and are heading south.

Several cities in the earthquake-affected zones are already estimated to be at population levels of less than 10% their normal. Many of the cities, especially in the Northeast, still have population levels of 50% to 75%, but experts predict that more than half the remaining population will attempt to make a trip south in the next few weeks.

After two days of walking John was halfway through Indiana, and he figured another three would get him across the Indiana-Ohio border.

It will be amazing to be in the Ohio again, at least! Then, only a few more days, and I'll be home with my family, easy sailing at night.

He had stopped in the middle of a field on the west side of a divided highway that ran north to south straight down the middle of the state. He had walked a little further than he wanted to in the morning light, but his goal was to make it to this point so he could setup camp and then leave the area the next night.

Leaving the area was his number one priority. He was currently directly north of Indianapolis. Even though he was at least a dozen of miles north of the highway circling the city, there were still a lot of houses and activity.

By this time, most of the houses and buildings he had seen were still standing, if they hadn't been burned, but most still showed some damage from the quake. Even though there wasn't a lot of damage to the buildings, downed power lines were commonly seen and the vast number of burned houses, abandoned cars, and other numerous signs showed how chaotic everything still was.

After doing a few stretches, John lay down in his sleeping bag, ate a hearty meal of dry soybeans and packaged junk food, and washed it down with a soda. He fell asleep, exhausted, dreaming of home and hugging his children tight.

"Noooooo!"

John stirred from his sleep.

I could have sworn I just heard something.

He sat up and looked around. There wasn't much to see except for beans all around him. He listened closely for a few seconds and was rewarded when he heard another sound.

"Nooooooo! Stop!"

He could barely hear the sound and he probably heard it only because the wind was carrying sound his direction. A second or two later, he heard a blood curdling and shrill scream.

OK, I've got to do something about this, or at least try.

He checked his gear, packed up everything, and started moving toward the sound.

It's been a while since I've been out in full sunlight. He shook his head. *I have to be careful. I need to do what I can, but I need to be careful.*

A few minutes of stalking through the fields brought him to the edge that ran along the highway. From there the sounds of screaming were louder and more distinct, and he thought he could see the source of the screams. There was a group of what appeared to be five or six abandoned cars pushed into a box formation around a camp.

I guess circling the wagons didn't work the way they expected.

The cars were over half a mile away up the road.

He went a few feet back into the bean field and continued up toward the cars, walking hunched over to hide as much of his body as he could beneath the beanstalks. By the time he was within a hundred yards, he could make out several figures within the circle. It looked like two, maybe three men, and a woman. From the way she was screaming, it was not hard to guess what was going on.

No one has seen me, and it looks like they aren't really paying much attention to anything other than the evil at hand.

He crouched down low enough to keep his whole body below the plant tops and started crawling closer.

When he was only about forty yards away, he poked his head up to survey the situation. He could see one of the men and the woman, who was lying on the ground barely covered with torn clothing.

Wait, what's that?

Further up the road he saw a group of people coming down the road. He couldn't count them, but figured there were at least two or three dozen. Out in front of the main group were five men running toward the cars.

Maybe I'm late, and the cavalry is already arriving.

He crouched down and crawled over to the edge of the field. This way, he could watch from the side instead of sticking his head up and silhouetting it against the landscape. By the time he was in position, the five men were entering the circle of cars, and he could see two of the original assaulters taking cover behind the cars that lined the south side of the ring. The woman was lying motionless in the center when the five men finally got to her.

The men spread out looking for the culprits when the first shot rang out. The sound was loud, having come from a dozen or so yards away from John.

I might have just stepped in it; there are snipers right beside me.

Before he could even finish that thought, one of the five men fell to the ground, pieces of bone and brain sprayed out on the pavement. Another shot rang out and another man fell.

By this time, the three remaining men were down, taking cover, and looking for targets. The two men who were still hiding outside the ring of cars had a clear shot at one of the men. He dumped bullets into him before squatting down behind the protection of the cars. The other two trapped men started returning fire. There was swearing and cursing heard from inside the circle as they tried to regroup—only to find they were the only two left alive and were trapped.

The two opposing forces had a run-and-gun battle, each side trying to out flank the other while both trying to shoot their adversary and to stay low enough to not get shot themselves. The men inside the circle eventually were pinned down with no where to go without taking fire from either the men directly outside the ring or the others positioned in the fields.

Almost thirty seconds went by without anything happening; then, more shots were heard. This time, they came from near the larger group of people. John could see a handful of men walking out of the field and firing into the crowd. He turned his attention back to the group of cars in front of him just in time to see the woman stir. She slowly turned over, pulled a pistol from some unseen spot and fired. He couldn't see her target, but almost immediately, the two men outside the ring popped back up and entered the circle of cars.

A few more shots were fired, and the two men who had entered the ring of cars and a few others were filtering out from the field and other hiding spots. All were walking up the road to the larger group. By the time they arrived, the survivors were face down on the ground surrounded by the first group of men who came at them from the fields.

The woman walked over to one of the nearby cars, pulled out some clothes from the back seat and got dressed before searching the dead men and taking anything she deemed valuable.

She can't be out of high school yet, and here she is setting up an ambush, killing, and stealing.

Sick to his stomach, John watched, afraid to move, as two men only twenty yards away walked out of the field, met up with the woman, and walked toward the group of refugees. They were joking and laughing as they walked.

John waited until they were with their partners in crime, several hundred yards down the road, before he made a crawling dash across the road and into the field across from him. He kept going as fast as he could until he made it to a split between fields, where there was a little tractor path. He went right down the tractor path, still crawling, and went a few hundred feet before blazing into the next field.

Have to make it at least somewhat hard for anyone to track me. Hopefully no one even tries.

While crawling through the next field, he heard the sounds of screams and gunfire. Finally stopping, as he was completely out of breath, John drank from his last water bottle. He checked his gear, making sure everything was still there. When he felt the knife by his side, he remembered the old man's words:

"Most importantly, even though I know you would want to try, don't help. You see a problem, someone struggling ... DON'T HELP. Not if you really want to get home. Once you make it there, help everyone, pour your heart and soul into making everything right again. But you have to ask yourself, what is really the right thing to do? Help someone now or get home to your family?"

He thought about that advice and the scene he just witnessed.

They lured them in, playing on their good nature, and then killed them.

He caught his breath over the next few minutes; then, he started crawling away. He was careful to keep low and be as quiet as he could. He crawled for over an hour. Finally, he poked his head up to look around. He could no longer see the road or the cars, though he could see other houses in other directions.

Don't think I'm going to get much better than this.

He pulled out his sleeping bag, drank the last of his water, which left him with three cans of soda for hydration. He said a prayer, something he realized he hadn't done in weeks, and then focused his resolve on getting home and how he was going to accomplish that.

Chapter 32

Radio Broadcast: In a CDC memo released today, we have the details of Cholera, TB, and several other diseases that are running rampant and unchecked through many major US cities. This situation leaves health officials, who are already overworked and spread too thin, to try to find a way to get the word out about these dangers.

The acting head of the CDC laments that there is little they can do at this point because of their inability to communicate or travel to the majority of the cities.

The estimated number of those sick is quickly approaching a million people on the east coast alone. Without proper medical care, the chance of recovering can be low.

"Now, I'm sorry it's come to this, but you'd make yourself a target with all of this food," Garret said, as box after box of provisions was removed from Sarah's basement.

She just stared at him with hatred in her eyes as the food she and her late husband had stored away walked out of her house.

Rick had always been prepared for any catastrophe and kept this secret to himself, but Garret happened to notice a few of the empty packages in their garbage as those typically used for long term storage. This prompted him to look throughout the house until he found the hoard: enough canned and freeze-dried food to last a year for a family of four.

Now that the last of the boxes had been carried up the stairs, Garret was left alone in the basement with Sarah.

"I'm glad you understand how this works. I do what I want, and you deal with it," he said sarcastically as he stepped closer to the woman.

Fighting back the urge to scream or lash out at him, Sarah bit her tongue.

Garret grinned and said, "You know those guys are upstairs with your kids right now? You wouldn't want anything bad to happen would you?"

***

A few minutes later, Garret came to the back porch where the other men were carrying away the rest of the food just taken from inside the house.

"What took you so long, boss?" one of the teens asked with a wink.

"Oh nothing, just wanted to check the pipes, make sure everything was working right." Garret replied crudely and laughed. He continued to address the two teens and Rob, "I want each of you guys to stop by here in the next day or two and to tell her you are looking out for her. Let her know you're looking out for me, too, and that you would really hate to see anything ever happen to me. Because if something were to happen, you just might have to lock the doors and windows and burn the house down with her and her kids still inside."

All three of these men had been party to murder and theft, but they were still taken aback by his comment. Nevertheless, all three men nodded in agreement.

"Good, that settles it. Now, what can I do for you guys?" Garret said, trying to liven the mood as they carried the loot back to their hideout.

***

"What was all the commotion over here this morning?" Margaret asked Sarah.

"They took all of our food, Margaret. All of it. What am I supposed to do now?" Sarah said, her voice starting to crack.

"Don't worry, we'll be OK," Margaret hugged Sarah as Sarah broke into tears.

And she doesn't know the half of it, Sarah thought as she wept in her friend's arms.

After she regained her composure, Sarah asked Margaret to help feed the kids lunch, and they used up the last of the food in the kitchen. The men were diligent at taking everything they could, but did leave two packages of freeze-dried food that were mostly gone. The kids went outside to play in the backyard that was protected by a cedar fence on all sides while the women cleaned up the mess from lunch and from the raiders tearing apart the house searching for food or other contraband.

While carrying out these tasks, Sarah told what had happened, leaving out the last event, which she was too afraid and ashamed to share. Someone, likely one of her neighbors, saw her burning trash and got nosey. They snuck into the backyard and found scraps of a mylar bag that had contained freeze-dried food. Using that as evidence, the men came in and tore apart every room in the house, looking for any food she might be hiding. She told Margaret how before the earthquake, Rick was adamant about preparing for any sort of calamity and had purchased large quantities of food and other gear, all of which had just left the house.

She then went on to tell the story of how Rick's family owned a farm and orchard and were part of a mutual support community of people who prepared for these kinds of disasters. If there was any way to get to his parent's farm, about 45 miles away, they would be safe.

"You and your children would be welcome, I'm sure of it." Sarah said.

She was now convinced the only way to be free of this was to leave and to go as far away as possible.

Rick had wanted to bug out the morning the quake happened, but Sarah talked him out of it. By the time she realized they should have left, it was too late and driving anywhere was too dangerous. They were stuck in their house because she was too afraid of looking like a whacko. She hadn't thought things would be nearly as bad as they had become. Now, she hated herself for that decision. Her husband had been killed, and his ability to feed and protect her and the children was gone. Now she was being abused by the same man she knew in her heart was responsible for her husband's death.

"We've got to get out of here—you, me, and the kids. The farm is about 45 miles away, but we can make it in just a few days of walking. We aren't safe here," Sarah started to plead with Margaret.

"Thank you for the offer, but we can't. We need to be here when John gets back. Besides, no matter how unsafe you feel here, I know it's much more dangerous out there!" Margaret said, trying to calm and deflect, not knowing the full extent of the circumstances.

"You really think your husband is going to make it back anytime soon?" Sarah said, trying to keep her tone flat. She didn't want to upset her new friend.

"He will. He would crawl here on his knees to make it back to us. Though I am starting to fear that might be exactly what is happening. I thought he would have been back in the first few days; then the first few weeks. It is starting to get hard waiting for him, but I know in my heart he is on his way to us," Margaret said, trying to fight back tears.

"Are you sure? I really think we need to get out of here, and fast," Sarah said, thinking of what was in her future and feeling a pain in her stomach rise up, making her want to vomit.

"I know they took your food, but is everything else OK? We can make things work as a team, but unless there is something else you know that I don't, I can't even begin to think about leaving here, especially without John to help," Margaret said, trying to end the conversation about leaving.

In her mind, it was bad there, but most likely worse outside of the safety of the neighborhood.

"One last thing, Margaret. I know I don't have to tell you this, but please don't tell anyone about what happened today or about me wanting to leave. It's to the point where I can't trust anyone, even our neighbors that we've known for years. Don't trust your neighbors either," Sarah said.

***

Margaret couldn't help but feel perplexed by the way Sarah was acting.

She is really shaken up, who wouldn't be? I wouldn't even be in as good of a shape as she is if John had been killed. She needs a strong shoulder to lean on, and some hope. I'll sneak over a little food tonight before we go home. Hopefully that will help. I wish there was more I could do.

***

That evening Margaret put her kids to bed and then packed a canvas shopping bag full of various canned and dried goods from her hidden stash in the closet.

I'll just be real quick; no one will even notice I'm gone.

She stepped out the back door and walked through a few neighboring backyards until she made it to Sarah's house. Not wanting to bring attention to herself, she stuck the bag in a small plastic box on the patio that normally held barbeque tools and briquettes. It had been empty for weeks after the last of the charcoal had been used to cook.

I'll leave it here for now. We can bring it inside tomorrow.

Now that she wasn't carrying the contraband food, she walked to the front of the house to take a more direct route home. Before she made it two houses, she was stopped by a man with a rifle.

"Stop right there!" the man blurted out, trying to sound authoritative.

"I'm just heading home. It's OK, will take 20 seconds to be back inside!" Margaret pleaded.

"Sorry, no can do. You're out past curfew. I need to take you to HQ."

"I know it's past curfew, but I just stepped out for a second, nothing bad."

"Doesn't matter. Break the rules, pay the price."

"And what's the price?" Margaret said sarcastically.

The man stiffened at her tone. He thought, *I'm the one in charge here. She is in the wrong, and now she wants to belittle me and my authority? Baloney, I'll put her in her place.*

He reached forward, and violently shoved Margaret in the direction of the house used as the headquarters for the neighborhood watch and soup kitchen.

"This way!" he grunted.

Not wanting to cause more trouble, Margaret walked peacefully in front of the man.

This is stupid. What are they going to do, ground me?

A rough shove from behind forced Margaret through the front door, and she was directed to sit in the living room while she waited for someone to come talk to her. In a couple of seconds, Garret came down from the command central they had pieced together in one of the upstairs bedrooms.

"What do we have here?" Garret asked.

"She was out past curfew," the other man said, pointing at Margaret. Garret's eyes lit up, recognizing the detainee.

"Oh, I see. Thank you for bringing her in. I'll escort her home, and you can continue your patrol," Garret said. He remained silent for the next few moments until the man left and was a ways down the sidewalk.

"OK, let's get you home. Let me guess. You were down visiting your new friend?" Garret said, helping Margaret to her feet.

"No, they are asleep. I just wanted to get out for a short walk." Margaret replied, trying her best to tell a convincing lie.

"I see. OK, well, let's go," Garret said as he held the door open, and Margaret walked out.

They walked in silence until they made it to Margaret's front yard where Garret finally spoke up.

"So you just decided to take a walk, all by yourself, unarmed at night?" his voice was dripping with sarcasm.

"Yeah, that kind of sums it up," Margaret said in an annoyed tone.

Who does this guy think he is? Sure he is helping out around here, but he isn't anything special.

Her train of thought stopped abruptly as he grabbed her right arm and slapped a handcuff around her wrist. He bore into her, almost knocking her over. Stumbling, she wasn't able to react in time, and he expertly pulled both of her hands behind her back and closed the other cuff on her left wrist.

He pulled hard on the handcuffs, metal digging into her flesh, and almost lifted her off the ground to keep her from falling. In a fast and fluid motion, he pulled a knife from his belt and pressed it against her neck.

"All right, don't do anything stupid, like make a sound," Garret said, emitting a low sounding cackle. "Now listen. You're out past curfew. That's dangerous. You don't know who or what is out here. That is why we have patrols like the one you were got caught by."

Margaret stood rigid, adrenaline coursing through her body, causing her whole body to shake.

This bastard! How dare he.

"You won't get away with this. You can't treat people like this!" Margaret spat at him.

He pressed the knife hard against her neck and pulled hard on the handcuffs.

"Oh, I've already gotten away with it. What are you going to do? Nothing."

I'll kill you, that's what I'll do.

Margaret had never thought about hurting anyone before, but now, she was having clear visions of what she would do to Garret.

"Nothing, is what you are going to do. You know why?" He pointed toward the front door of her house. It was already wide open.

"You bas—," she was cut off as he threw her to the ground and started dragging her inside by the handcuffs on her wrists.

There was no source of light inside the house, but she could see figures already inside. Garret continued dragging her until he threw her on the couch in the living room.

"All right, let's get this clear," Garret said quietly.

"If you hurt my kids, I'll kill you," Margaret said, her voice full of hatred.

"Shhhhhh," Garret said, holding his finger across his lips.

He leaned in close, again placing the knife to her throat and brought his lips to a few inches from her ear.

"I won't hurt your kids. I promise. Unless you make me hurt them." He emphasized the "you" in his last statement. "As you can see, it's not just me who take this seriously. This is about the safety of the neighborhood." He paused and pointed around the room where other dark figures were standing. She couldn't see in the darkness but caught the drift anyway.

"You play nice, and follow the rules like everyone else, and we play nice. OK? That's all. Now, if you don't play nice. Say, if you go and keep walking around after curfew, or keep talking to the wrong people about the wrong things. Well, then, you might make me break my promise."

He paused as he put the knife back in its sheath on his belt.

"Understand? I hope so. I really don't want to have to come back here."

Too angry to say or do anything, she nodded her head in response. He seemed to have been able to catch the motion in the darkness as he reached around and unlocked the cuffs from her wrists.

"Now, you think about how you were wrong in this situation. OK? And we'll go ahead and leave you alone."

He leaned back in close, and ran his hand from her thigh to her neck, enjoying everything in-between and said, "Unless you want me to stay for a little while?"

He laughed out loud and walked away.

Margaret sat in the darkness as she listened to the men leaving. She could hear them talking and joking as they started down the sidewalk.

Now I think I know why Sarah was so upset. I think we might need to get out of here soon.

Chapter 33

Radio Broadcast: The latest reports we have show that the US and Mexican forces are at a stalemate in the south. Both sides are unable to advance because of a lack of fuel to move forces into position. The leaders of the Army are referring to warnings they raised months ago as the President and Congress moved to sell more of the nation's strategic oil reserves, which has now left the Army without the ability to move troops or equipment.

Reports from the occupied parts of California tell of forced relocation of millions of residents. There are fears that the rumors of ethnic cleansing might be true as the drug cartels continue to flaunt their power by burning, looting, and killing throughout the south. Right now, they are completely unchecked.

"All right, this is going to work out almost perfectly," John said to himself as he put the last pair of batteries in the NVG.

He had started with a full box of batteries, and generally only made it through one and a half nights' walk before they were too weak to power the device. After almost a week on the road, he was now out of backups.

It had been three days since he was awoken by the screams from the young woman lying in wait at the ambush. Luckily, he hadn't run into any more trouble, at least any that he saw as he snuck by under the cover of darkness. Once again he realized how lucky he was to have the NVG to help keep him out of trouble.

It wasn't even midnight yet and from his calculations, he had another five miles to go before he was safely home. He could barely contain his happiness.

I can't wait to see my kids! Margaret, you beautiful thing, I can't wait to kiss your lips! I'm sorry I haven't been here to take care of you, but I'll be there soon!

With an extra spring in his step, he almost jogged the rest of the way home. He would have run the whole way except that whenever he tried to go faster, he started having problems finding good footing. A little over an hour later, he found the first entrance to his neighborhood and was both happy and saddened to see it was blocked and manned by armed men.

Makes it a little harder to get in, but that also means that they are probably safe inside!

He veered off the road and looked for a way to walk in between houses, but dismissed that idea when he noticed the cans and other items suspended from trip wires.

Protected the sides, too. Good for them.

He smiled at the thought, glad that precautions were being taken to prevent entry. After a little poking around, he decided to find a safe place to get some rest. He'd try to walk in during daylight, figuring it would be much easier and safer than talking to armed men in the dark.

Brimming with excitement, he waited until the sun was fully up before walking to the checkpoint.

***

"Stop! Turn around. No one is allowed in here!" yelled one of the men standing at the checkpoint.

John stopped and put his hands above his head before replying, "I live here."

"I'll bet you do!" The man responded drawing a laugh from another man at the checkpoint.

"I do. I live at 9702 Walnut Street. My name is John, John Washington."

The men were silent for a few minutes. He could see them rummaging through some sort of notebook.

"So you found a phone book and got a name, so what? Now go on, turn around, and leave." The man yelled, trying to sound threatening.

"Look, man, I've been on the road, walking home for weeks now. I don't want trouble. I just want to see my wife and kids. OK? What do you want?"

The men conferred with each other for a second before asking to see his driver's license. When he told them he didn't have it or his wallet. They were at another impasse.

"Get my wife, or a neighbor. There are plenty of people around who would recognize me."

***

A few minutes later, Mr. Goldsmith was at the checkpoint and vouched for John. The guards reluctantly let him in, but only on the condition that he turn over the firearm before entering. He did so without even being bothered.

Anything to get them to let me in! Besides, I've got plenty of replacements in the safe at home.

"Thank you for that!" John said as he first shook Mr. Goldsmith's hand and then hugged him.

"But I'll catch up with you later!" John blurted out, as he broke into a full sprint toward his house.

Not wanting to scare the inhabitants, or possibly get himself shot, John stopped at the front door and knocked. He waited a few seconds; then, knocked again. After a third attempt, he walked to the side of the house and retrieved the key that was hidden for such emergencies. Slowly opening the door, he leaned in and said "hello" loudly. Still no response, so he stepped in, announcing himself again and again, but didn't find anyone.

He looked throughout the house, and it looked as if everything was as it should be, but no one was home. Seeing the destruction of the windows that were now boarded up with shattered glass still held in place, his heart sank.

What happened? Where is everyone?

He was beginning to dread what might have happened when he heard Mr. Goldsmith at the door. "John, they are probably down the street. Been spending a lot of time over at Sarah's house."

"Good! I'm glad someone has been helping her out while I've been gone!" John said, smiling.

He had talked to Rick and Sarah only a few times, but found them to be good people. He noticed a pained look across the old man's face at his last comment, but didn't give it too much thought as he started running down the street.

Knocking on the front door, he immediately heard people walking around inside. A huge smile creased his face as the door opened a crack.

"Hello?" Sarah said.

"It's John. Is Margaret here?"

Before Sarah could respond, Margaret yelled, "John!?" and started running toward the door. Soon the kids and wife were all wrapped in hugs and covered in kisses. The elation didn't subside for almost half an hour as the family celebrated being reunited.

After the fanfare died down, Margaret pulled John aside and whispered in his ear, "You should have been here."

She rubbed her wrists, both raw from the attack she suffered the night before, and continued, "I'm glad you are back, but you should have been here."

She started to cry into her husband's chest as he held her in his arms. Quickly, the kids joined in, and the family was engulfed in a group hug. There wasn't a dry eye in the bunch.

Looking up at her husband Margaret said, "We've got a lot to talk about."

If you liked this book, please leave a review and tell your friends, family, co-workers, congregation members, book club, forum members, mutual support groups, hunting buddies, mailman, classmates, strangers on the street, etc.

Signup for the monthly newsletter to be notified of future releases, giveaways, and other great information. You will never receive more than 2 emails a month from this list:
AFM Monthly Newsletter

Thank you for your support and God Bless!

Stay tuned for Part II and Part III of The Wayward Journey: *Fires at Home and Winter Without Walls*

Also soon to be released, **California Dreams**, a short story of survival. **All** royalties will be donated to charity.

Find other great information at:
www.AbundantFuture.net

Follow me on twitter: @NateHaleJeffers

www.facebook.com/NathanHaleJefferson

www.ingramcontent.com/pod-product-compliance
Lightning Source LLC
Chambersburg PA
CBHW030119180626

46812CB00002B/478